The Secret of Gällivare

By Clarine Hanson

The Secret of Gällivare is a work of fiction.

The characters, events, and places in this book are fictitious.

Any references to historical events or real places are used fictitiously.

Any similarity to real persons is coincidental and not intended by the author.

All rights are reserved, including the right to reproduce this book or portions thereof in any form whatsoever.

www.SecretOfGallivare.com

The Secret

of

Gällivare

Clarine Ione Hanson

A Message From The Author

One night, twenty-one years ago, I had a dream. Little Anna appeared out of nowhere, she was laughing and playing while her Mom was hanging clothes on the line. It was so real! I was right there in the middle of it all. The next day I told my daughter Karen about my dream. She couldn't believe it! She said, *"Mom, that has to be a book!"* Everyone who I told the story to agreed. I began to write it all down in longhand cursive but it got set aside. Karen would always tell me, *"Mom, you have to finish the book!"*

I began working on the story during a turbulent flight home from Arizona, and continued working on it during trips to the Mayo Clinic for my husband's kidney transplant. Whenever I found time I continued writing. I am not a computer person, but at the age of seventy-eight, I began to type the story into the computer. During this time I was scammed by a publisher for over five hundred dollars. They kept asking for more money and promised I would be featured on daytime talk shows; I fired them three times! My grandson Bobby stepped in and made it possible for me to complete the book. My husband helped with any tech problems I had. One day I was typing on the computer and I couldn't find the exclamation point. I had to run out to the garage and ask my husband where it is! He laughed and told me where it was. Years later, my dream of publishing this book has finally come true.

The last day I had with Karen, she said, "Promise me you will finish the book." That was the last thing that she said to me. I told her I would. That was on a Saturday, and she passed away on Tuesday. I hope that this story leaves a lasting impression, and instills the ideals of forgiveness and love. No matter how bad things may seem, there are always better days ahead!

Karen Jean Hanson

12-10-1957 - 6-15-2015

Dedication

Karen Jean Hanson

This book is dedicated to my beloved daughter, Karen Jean Hanson. She shared her caring and nurturing spirit with everyone she met. Her compassionate heart has inspired her children to live the same way. We worked together in many different jobs and spent much of our time after work together. We loved gardening, working on arts and crafts, and always treasured the holidays. While together we spent many days talking about each part of the story. Karen always encouraged me to finish the book! When I pressed the last key on the computer to finish the story, I cried and Karen smiled down from Heaven.

Tatijanna Mary Glor

I also dedicate my book to Tatijanna Mary Glor, one of God's smallest angels. She was only here for a very short time but she filled our hearts with an everlasting love. She was a beautiful little girl, perfect in every way. God called her back to heaven and gave her the title of Guardian Angel. Now she watches over her mother, father, sisters, and brother.

Translations

Fika – Daily break for coffee and pastries

Filmjölk – Fermented milk product similar to yogurt

Hallå – "Hello"

Hallongrottor – Cookies with raspberry center ('Raspberry Cave')

Kafé – Cafe

Kaffe – Coffee

Kanelbulle / Kanelbullar – Cinnamon Roll(s)

Knäckebröd – Crisp type of cracker, made mostly of rye flour

Kommunhus – City Hall

Köttsoppa – Soup with meat and vegetables

Krona – Currency of Sweden

Ljusstake – Candle stick

Mazariner – Almond tart made with shortbread

Rostad Hjortkött – Roasted Venison

Skål – Cheers

Spela – Play

Tre Kronor Blomsterhandlare – Three Crowns Florist

The Secret

of

Gällivare

1. Forgiveness

The white sheets are flapping in the wind as Anaya hangs clothes on the line. She glanced over her shoulder to make sure Anna was still playing in the yard, and paused to treasure the moment. It was a picture-perfect day in the beautiful town of Gällivare, Sweden.

Her beautiful little Anna, a small replica of her mother, is sitting on a quilt with her teddy bear, Mr. Thissel, and her dog Boulder. JP the mailman had given Boulder to Anna for her birthday. He is a big ol' mixed breed puppy with big brown eyes and shaggy black and white hair. It's hard to tell who loves who the most. Boulder obeys most of Anna's commands and he is her best friend, she talks to him just like he's human.

Anna was having a pretend tea party with water and soft bread that she pinched into little round cakes. She talked on and on, pretending that Boulder and Mr. Thissel were having a conversation with her.

Laughing as the wind blew through her lovely long blonde hair, she looked up and saw her mom looking at her.

"Hey Mommy! Don't worry, I'm here!"
"Okay honey, don't go far."
"I won't, I'm having a tea party with Boulder and Mr. Thissel."

Anna continued on playing and talking to her stuffed bear.
"You're the best teddy in the whole world! I'm so glad mommy made you for me."

Mr. Thissel was sewn together from an old denim shirt; frayed seams stuck out all over. He had a hand-stitched nose, and eyes made from buttons, one red and one black. Mr. Thissel was rough, but he was made with love in every stitch.

Anna's curls bounced as she ran over to her doll Emily.
"Emily, you're late for our tea party!"
She stood back and placed her hands on her hips.
"You know, it's not polite to be late."

Anaya noticed the time and began to hang the clothes more hurriedly. Her hands started to tremble. Everything around the house needed to be perfect before Johan got home. Thinking about what would happen if it wasn't scared her to death.

It was a day she would remember.
It was a day she would long to forget.

While she finished hanging the laundry, Anaya listened to Anna chatter with Boulder and Mr. Thissel.

"We are having a tea party, Mr. Thissel, would you like to join us? Just one cake for you today, okay? Boulder, you can have one too. Boulder you get to wear the red floppy hat today. Now, that means you have to be extra nice, and that starts right now!"

Boulder walked closer to Anna and sat down on the quilt.
"You almost sat on Mr. Thissel, say you're sorry!"
Boulder stood up and accidentally knocked over the teacups.
"Oh, Boulder, what am I going to do with you?"
Boulder began to jump around playfully.
"No, Boulder, you sit!"

He picked up Mr. Thissel, started to shake him, and ran away.
"Drop! Drop him!" Anna chased Boulder.
"You listen, Boulder! You listen to me!"

Anaya saw what was going on and shouted out to Anna.
"Anna, stop chasing after him and he will stop running away!
Just call his name and he will come over to you."
"But he's not listening..."
"Boulder still has puppy energy, they like to shake things. He
will listen. He doesn't want to hurt Thissel."

Anna stopped chasing Boulder and waited.
"Come here, Boulder ... come on," Anna called.

Boulder stopped and tilted his head; Mr. Thissel was hanging
out of his mouth.

Anna walked up slowly and then snatched her teddy bear back
from him. She started sobbing as she saw what happened to her
beloved Mr. Thissel. "Naughty!" Anna was frustrated, "Naughty
Boulder, I hate you!"

Boulder quit wagging his tail and hung his head low. He was a
sight to behold, with his floppy hat crooked to one side. He tried to
look as innocent as he could. Unfortunately, the sad look in his big
brown eyes was not working this time.

Anna ran over to her mom with tears in her eyes.
"Mom! Mr. Thissel's tummy is falling out of his leg!"
"Uh oh, it looks like he's had an accident."
"Can you please fix him?"
"Of course I can, he will be as good as new."
Anna hugged her mom's leg

3

Anaya winced in pain. *"Let go. Let go, Anna."*
"Mom, are you hurting again?"
Anaya had become accustomed to lying about being in pain.
"No, I'm just exhausted."
She brushed back Anna's long curls and gently held her face.
"Anna, you don't hate Boulder."
She looked into Anna's eyes.

"Listen to me dear, and don't ever forget what I have to say.
Hate is a terrible word, a word this world would be better off
without. It causes pain, suffering, and broken hearts. Anna, always
replace hate with forgiveness. Be kind to everyone, even if they
don't forgive you."

"But Mom, what if they're so bad that I don't want to?"
Anaya placed her hand on Anna's head and explained in a
loving voice.
"Anna, your heart will let you know, it's the right way to live."
Anna looked at her mom and let out a long sigh.
"But what if they are still bad, and hurt people again?"

Anaya replied, "My darling, my sweet, innocent angel, maybe
no one ever told them about forgiveness. Maybe they don't know
that they can change. Remember Anna, the people of this world are
like snowflakes, no two are alike. God put all of us here on earth
together. Just like it takes a million snowflakes to make a wonderful
big snowman, it takes lots of love and forgiveness to make a
wonderful world. Go and forgive Boulder. He's your best friend.
Puppies have a lot of energy, and they like to shake things, it's how
they play."

Anna took a step back, "How did you get so smart?"

Anaya smiled, "I had the best father a girl could ever ask for. He even taught me how to play the violin, just like I taught you! We often played together at the church."

Anna looked up at her with teary eyes, she looked into her mom's eyes.

"Mommy, can I go to church sometime, to play violin with Grandpa?"

With a sad heart and feeling of regret, Anaya softly touched her face.

"Please, Mom? Just like we do?"

"Anna, go and forgive Boulder, before he wanders off."

Boulder had walked away while Anna talked with her mom.

Anna ran after him, "I'm sorry, Boulder! I love you, Boulder!"

She caught up to Boulder, threw her arms around his neck, and hugged him tightly. She cried as she gave him a long hug.

"I don't hate you, Boulder, you are my very best friend. I will always love you. But no more shaking Mr. Thissel, do you hear me?"

Boulder whimpered and began to wag his tail. Anna hugged Boulder again, and whispered in his ear, "I forgive you Boulder. Now we are both forgiven."

Anaya was almost done with her chores, she had a few items left to hang on the clothesline, and was taking a short break on the porch. She was tired and rested her eyes. Anna was sitting Indian style on her bed reading a book to Boulder and her doll Emily. Soon she heard the old postbus coming down the road. Anna stopped everything and came running outside.

"Mommy, JP is here! Mommy, Mommy, I hear JP coming!"

Anna always loved to see the old postbus chugging down the road. She would get so excited when JP arrived to deliver the mail. He would always bring her books to read. Sometimes he even brought her chocolate, or candy, and treats for Boulder.

JP really got to know Anna and saw how isolated she was. He was her only contact with the outside world. He always looked forward to their visits. Anna always gets a big smile when she hears the postbus, and then runs outside to meet him. She would throw her arms around him as he knelt down to her level.

"How's my favorite little one today?"
"I'm just great!" Anna replied, like he taught her to say.

JP had a large family of his own, but Anna was a very special little girl in his life. They both enjoyed each other's company so much. Their visits were always the highlight of the day.

After JP and Anna chatted and joked around, he gave Anna a bag of peppermints and some doggie treats for Boulder.

She squealed in delight, "Oh, he's going to love this!"
JP laughed, "Let's check on your mother and deliver the mail."

He was glad that he could bring happiness into Anna's life. Today was a special day because he had a package for Anaya.

JP announced, "Special delivery for Anaya Magnusson!"
Anaya was surprised, she wasn't expecting any deliveries.
"Wow, what could this be?"
Anna encouraged her, "Mom, open it up!"
Anaya read the return address.
"Ms. Ingrid Magnusson ... This is from my mother."

It had been such a long time since they last spoke. Anaya wondered if her mother could possibly have any idea what she is going through. Anaya opened the box and inside she saw a gold heart shaped keepsake locket—no letter, just the locket.

"Look, it opens up... Anna, this is a picture of my mother, her name is Ingrid. And this is me, when I was six years old."

Anna did a double take, "You look just like your Mom!"
"That's right, and you look just like me when I was younger."

On the back of the locket an inscription read:
"I will always be with you."

Anaya decided to give the locket to Anna as a very special gift.
"I want you to have this locket. Promise me you will keep it forever. It's from your only grandma, Mrs. Ingrid Magnusson."

"I promise Mommy."
"Turn around, Anna, I'll put the necklace on you."
Anaya put the necklace on for her.
"I love it! It's the most beautiful little thing I've ever seen!"
Anna was so happy.
"I'm going to show my doll Emily and all my rock friends!"

JP was so glad, it wasn't often that he saw happiness in Anaya's eyes. He recognized the sadness she carried, and saw the bruises he saw from time to time. He knew Anaya needed help.

JP felt the tension she carried. He could see it in her face.
He asked, "How are you doing?"
He feared what the answer might be.

She lied like she always did, to avoid the truth that she did not want to accept.

"Everything is fine."

JP knew better.

Anaya reached to pick up more clothespins as she hung their clothes. The wind blew her skirt, exposing bruises and long red scratch marks on her legs.

"Anaya," JP was shocked.

"If you don't do something soon he will kill you. Maybe Anna too ... please, Anaya, let me talk to your father."

"No, JP, he won't help me ... I've disgraced him."

Tears welled up in Anaya's eyes as she recalled their argument.

"He raped you, Anaya. That is not love."

Anaya could still hear her father's voice as he tried to convince her to change her mind. She recalled the dreadful day that she argued with her father.

"Anaya, you come from a good family! You are well educated, and you have a good reputation. For God's sake, don't throw it all away! Johan doesn't love you, Anaya! Your life will be ruined if you insist on marrying him. It would be a destructive marriage. He is known as a womanizer, and is a self-centered illiterate drunk."

These are the words that she would remember in her mind.

"If you marry Johan we will totally disown you! It isn't happening!"

These words echoed in her mind. As she recalled that day, she thought to herself, "Oh, Daddy, I should have listened to you. You were trying to protect me. I was so stupid. I miss you so, so much."

Ever since that day, the memories have continued to haunt her.

"I will never forget how much I hurt you. The look on your face. I know I broke your heart. I'm so sorry, Daddy. I've suffered every day because of that decision. I was happy at the time, but in a way, I knew something was not quite right. Johan wouldn't come into the house with me, and I couldn't understand why. He knew you didn't like him. It's all so clear to me now. I can still hear your voice, Dad … I never saw you so mad. Even the Gällivare Ladies heard it all. I was so foolish, I thought I was in love with Johan. He told me he would love me forever."

The whole neighborhood could hear the commotion. Carol was waving her arms as she ran towards Maryann and Corrine; she knew something terrible was happening. She was short of breath.

"I'm glad I ran into you two! What's going on?"
"It's Mr. Mag, he's acting like a crazy man!"
"Who is he arguing with?"
Maryann looked down sadly, "It's his daughter, Anaya."
Kathleen arrived next.
"I came as soon as I heard the noise, this is bad!"
Carol explained, "Mr. Mag is screaming at Anaya, he's lost it!"

They could hear Mr. Magnusson from outside. He was carrying on about Johan, and slamming his fist on anything within reach.
Corrine started to pace back and forth. She wrung her hands nervously as she tried to put the pieces together.
"A rusty old truck is parked in front of Mr. Mag's house."

"Is there anyone inside?"

"I don't know," Kathleen shrugged.

They went into Mr. Mag's garden and moved in closer to get a good view.

"That's Johan's truck!"

They looked closely and saw a figure in the driver seat.

"See, *it is Johan!* Mr. Mag can't stand this guy!"

Maryann gasped, "There's been rumors that Anaya was sneaking around with Johan. For his entire life he's had a real hatred for women. Ever since his mother died while giving birth."

Carol told the ladies how, from a very young age, Johan's father abused him. He often left Johan alone and let him go hungry most of the time. His dad would come home drunk, late at night, and forget to give him any food at all.

Johan's father cursed the day he was born. He blamed Johan for killing his mother. She died shortly after child birth. He called him a bastard, and said he was no son of his.

"Shh! Listen, so we can hear what's going on." Kathleen hushed the other ladies.

Mr. Mag started to yell at the top of his lungs, "Anaya, you can't do this! Johan is no good for anyone, he is going to hurt you! Listen to me, Anaya!"

Anaya cried, "But Dad—"

"Don't you 'but' me Anaya!"

Mr. Mag waved his finger in front of her face.

"You had the best education, and the best of anything that money could buy. You've lived your whole life in this mansion. You have no business associating with someone like Johan. Remember when I taught you the violin? Remember the special times when we performed together at church? You are a religious woman, you have nothing in common with him."

Anaya sobbed, "He loves me! He needs someone to give him a chance."

Mr. Mag held on to her shoulders, "Don't give up your future for this low life, he is a no-good bum! He is known to be violent!"

Anaya pushed her dad aside.

"Johan wouldn't hurt me, he loves me! I'm going to marry him, he's waiting in the truck outside."

Maryann held on to Carol's arm, "Oh no, this is getting bad!"

"He's begging her not to do this…"

Carol was in disbelief, just like Mr. Mag.

"If he gets her pregnant all hell will break loose!"

Corrine shook her head, "This is not going to end well."

Carol and Kathleen crept up closer and hid behind the pillars near the door. They listened carefully.

"It's too late Dad, I am already pregnant!"

Mr. Magnusson threw his arms up in the air!

"I give up! May dear God in heaven watch over you, because you will need God!"

"I have to leave, Dad … Johan is waiting."

Mr. Mag shouted, "If you leave this house today, Anaya, you are no longer my daughter—you can never enter my house again!"

Anaya thought of the promise she made to Johan.

"Fine. I'll get a few of my things. I'll never see you again."

"Then go! Take whatever you want, you are a disgrace to our family!"

Anaya grabbed two violins and some of her clothes. She paused in the doorway, she looked back and saw her father standing there. They both felt so hurt. They knew that this was not right. Without another word she walked out of the door.

The Gällivare Ladies saw the townspeople showing up. Everyone wondered what was going on. Mr. Magnusson was blinded by his frustration and didn't notice anyone was watching.

Mr. Magnusson stomped through the flower garden and knocked down the statue of his daughter playing the violin. After one of their very special violin performances, Mr. Mag commissioned a well known sculptor to create that statue. It was such such a beautiful piece.

Kathleen was in shock, she put her hands on her head.
"Wow, I can't believe this is happening!"
Carol quietly replied, "Anaya just made her dad a broken man."

Corrine heard sirens in the distance, "The cops are coming!" By now crowd of neighbors had started to gather outside.

When the police arrived they spoke with Anaya first. They asked her to leave so they could try to talk to Mr. Mag. He was throwing things around the yard, breaking expensive vases, cursing and crying out in rage.

The police had to forcefully get Mr. Magnusson to settle down. They asked him what was going on and let him have his say. They made sure he would be safe and not harm himself. They stayed for quite a while to disperse the crowd.

When they finally left, Mr. Mag was sitting all alone on the front steps. He was so broken-hearted. His wife Ingrid was in shock, she had been watching from the window upstairs.

Maryann shook her head, "People may condemn him for this, but I'll stand up for his honor no matter what they say."

2. Not Today Anna

Anna tugged on Anaya's skirt to get her attention. She started jumping up and down with excitement.

"Mommy, is it Friday? Can we go to The Happy Place today?"
"Oh, Anna," Anaya hated to tell her no.
"Not today, Anna, it's getting late. Dad will be home soon."
Anna was used to broken promises. Her little heart just sank.
"We'll go tomorrow, I promise. We can even have a picnic!"
Anna started to get a smile back on her face.

She loved to practice her violin, especially when they went to The Happy Place. She was a very gifted child. She could play right along with her mother, who is an accomplished violinist. Her mother started to introduce her to the violin at a very young age.

Anna pouted as she started to walk away. Anaya turned her around and said, "Anna, remember, we don't want to make Daddy mad."

Anna became very frustrated and she spoke up.
"Dad scares me so much."
A tear rolled down her cheek.
"He get loud and breaks things, and he says bad words."
They both began to cry together; Anaya held Anna close.

"I'm so sorry, Anna ... I never meant for us to be in this situation. *I stayed too long.* Someday things will be better ... I promise ... I love you, Anna."

Anna stomped on the ground and got really upset.

"Daddy yells so loud at you, and he calls you bad names. I wish he wasn't my dad!"

Anaya looked down at her precious little girl and saw the sad, worried look on her face. She is so young. Anaya wished that she never had to be trapped in such an abusive way of life. She sat down next to Anna. She tried to cover up for Johan.

"Anna, Daddy just gets clumsy. It's really my fault he gets mad, I need to be more organized. He's had a hard life, and didn't have a mother to love him as he grew up. His own father was very mean and would let him go hungry. He never learned how to love, instead he gets angry. I know it's hard to understand. When your dad gets home, just go to your bedroom and pretend you are asleep."

Anna started to sob, "But Mommy, will Daddy hurt you again?"

"No Honey, I'll be OK. Just don't come out of your room. Take Boulder with you. No matter what you hear, I will be alright."

"When Daddy gets so loud he scares Boulder too."

Anna knelt down to hug Boulder.

She whispered, "We will be together. We will not be afraid."

Anaya warned Anna, "Whatever you do, do not cry. Pretend you are asleep. If he hears you, then we will both be in big trouble. Daddy hates it if anyone cries. He will call you a sissy. Go quickly now, he will be home soon. Boulder will stay by you. *Lock your door.*"

Anaya checked the time. She started to feel her heart race. She paced the floor, making sure everything was in order. Tension mounted with each passing moment. Like so many times before, she knew what she was in for. She feared the pain and humiliation.

How much longer could she take the abuse?
Anaya said aloud, *"This isn't love, it's survival."*
Anaya knew Johan would never give up control.
"Will I have to give up my life to be free?"

Anaya checked the food on the stove. She had hurried to get dinner ready. Johan would get very mad if his food was cold. He would throw it against the wall, grab Anaya by her arm and toss her to the floor, demanding that she clean it up with her hands.

Anaya heard the sound of Johan's old pickup outside. Her hands started to tremble as she looked out the window. She couldn't pull back the curtain. If Johan saw her looking at him, he would accuse her of spying on him. Her heart started to pound in fear.

As he parked, Johan almost crashed into the house. He was drunk. He usually was when he came home. The truck door opened slowly. Johan fell out onto the ground. He gazed up at the truck in stupor. He stumbled and staggered as he tried to stand up. He slammed the door in a fit of drunken rage.

Johan burst through the door, yelling and slurring his words. "I'm home, the boss is here! Where are you slut?"

His shirt tails were out, and buttons were torn off his shirt. There was a massive bump on his forehead and some blood on his face. He must have been in another fight.

Anaya had checked to make sure everything was perfect. The food was hot, the house quiet, the fireplace was lit, there was no dust anywhere. Everything was just the way he liked, but most days that made little difference.

Anaya quietly slipped into the kitchen and told herself, "Just do what you have to do, in order to make it through this night alive, for Anna's sake."

Johan's mother was the only woman that his father had ever loved. When she passed away during childbirth, he was left a broken man. He had no idea how to care for a child.

Johan fell into his favorite old chair and slumped over. He started to mumble about how miserable his life was. He used his mothers death as an excuse for everything he's done in life.

"My dad hated me, and I hated him back! That no good—"
Anaya spoke softly, "Your dinner is ready."
He staggered to the kitchen to check his food.
He slurred his words, "Not too bad for a tramp!"
She dished up his food for him.
"Pooor lil' rich girl …"
Anaya stayed near the stove and pretended to be busy.
"What makes you think yer so mussh better than me?"

He was slurring his words, and it frustrated him.
He shouted, "Gimme a drink bitch! Make it a strong one!"

"This is my chance to save myself for tonight," Anaya thought.
She poured almost a quarter of the bottle in a tall glass.

She placed it in front of Johan, "Just like you wanted."
Johan took a long, long drink.

Shortly after, his head slowly fell onto his plate. He was out.

3. The Happy Place

The next morning, the first thing Anna said was, "Mom, Mom! We're going to The Happy Place today, remember? You promised! We can practice our violins together, it's the best time we have!"

"Let's go right after chores, okay?"
"Okay Mommy, I'll help you."
Anna threw her arms around her mom.
"I love you, Anna."

Their house is a very spacious, gray, weathered and old, but exquisite home. It was very elegant in its day, and has a big porch with very large pillars. The living room had a large marble fireplace, and was lined with tall glass windows that look out upon the forest. Behind the house there is a pond that flows into a small creek.

Anaya and Anna have made a pathway that follows alongside the creek. It leads to a beautiful clearing in the forest. They call it The Happy Place. It is a place of freedom from worries and fear, where all of their cares are left behind.

They finished their chores in no time at all, and got ready to go.
"Great work, Anna, we are all done."
"That means it's time to go to The Happy Place!"
"That's right."
"Boulder and I will go get the violins."
"Okay, I will get lunch ready for our picnic!"

They always enjoyed walking together along the path to The Happy Place. They would see many animals. Some would appear alone, others were in pairs, and sometimes a whole family!

They enjoyed taking their special *'scenic route'* through the forest. Each trip to The Happy Place was a very special occasion. The smell of fresh grass and wildflowers during Spring in Gällivare is like a masterpiece from Heaven.

"Come along, Anna, we don't want to waste any time."

"I'm right here, Mom, remember I have shorter legs. Slow down so I can keep up!"

Anaya smiled, "Oh, I'll slow down for you, my little angel."

They walked together in silence for a while.

"How many times do you remember walking this path?"

Anna looked like she was thinking very carefully.

"Well, I guess a hundred million and one, counting today!"

She lifted her hand up, they both laughed.

Boulder would dart off once in a while to chase a bunny or even a butterfly. He always came back empty-handed and looking worse for wear.

Anna pointed up, "See how the trees sway back and forth? It looks like they're dancing!"

"There is an old Swedish saying, 'Words called into the forest echo back.' The trees really do talk to each other!"

"Mom, look, there's a baby bunny!"

Anna bent down and slowly walked towards the little bunny.

"Hello, bunny rabbit! Aww … Don't go!"

Anna looked so sad as the bunny hopped away.

"I only wanted to pet him."

"He must be looking for his family."

"Do you think he will find his mom?"

"I'm sure she is not far away, they stay close to their babies."

Anna still looked worried.

"Don't worry, he'll be fine. His mom will find him."

Another of Anna's favorite things to do is look for rocks. She would look for larger ones to be the boys, and smaller ones to be the girls. She would paint them and give each one a name. Each of the rocks was one of her friends. She kept them on a special bench in their front yard.

"I hope we find some nice rocks today. I told my friends at home that I would bring back a new friend for them. I think they need some new friends. Mom, can you help me find some?"

"Of course I will Anna. Let's get looking!"

"Mom, did you ever have any friends?"

"Yes, I had lots of friends in town and in college."

"Where are they now?"

Anaya didn't know how to answer, she thought for a while.

"At first, my friends came by, but Johan was not very nice to them. He called them snobs. He made me quit answering the door. They gradually wouldn't come by anymore."

Anaya wasn't sure if Anna could understand.

"That's okay, Mom. We have each other, and I'm your friend!"

After finding a few rocks by the creek they kept walking. They came upon a reindeer and her baby fawn.

"Look, Anna!"
Anna's eyes became wide in amazement.
"My goodness!"
"Don't they have such big brown eyes?"
"The little one is so cute, I just love her little tail!"
"Be very quiet or you will scare them away."
"They are just like you and me, Mom!"
Anaya loved to see her daughter so happy.
"Look, she is wagging her little white tail just like Boulder."

Boulder heard Anna say his name in this distance and he started running toward her. The deer froze and their ears perked up, they heard Boulder coming!

"Oh no, Boulder heard his name, here he comes!"
"I hope he won't scare them away."
Before Anna could turn back around, the deer both sprinted off.
"Aww ... they're gone! They run so fast."
Anaya was amused by Anna's amazement with the world.

Anna has always been very thankful for her dog Boulder. In the morning he wakes Anna up, and at night he lays next to her to watch over her when she is sleeping. They have been inseparable since they first met.

Anna called out to Boulder to get his attention.
"Here, Boulder, let's go! We have to hurry along."
They were starting to get close to The Happy Place!

Anna continued to think about the deer.

"Mom, am I wonderful, like a baby deer?"

"Anna, you are more than wonderful!"

They both slowed down.

"You are my whole world! You are beautiful, caring, intelligent, and kind. Always remember that!"

Anna smiled as she proudly tossed her hair over her shoulder.

"Well, Mom, that's because I'm just like you!"

Anaya was raising Anna to be such a wonderful daughter, she felt so proud.

"And you are my whole world too! Just you and Boulder ... and JP."

Despite the happiness she felt, Anna realized how secluded her daughter had become. She was missing out on many things that other children take for granted. Her greatest hope was that Anna would one day live a normal happy life.

"Mom, we're here! We made it to our Happy Place!"

Anna jumped for joy and shouted with delight!

"I love this place, I'm so happy we are here!"

They treasured the time they shared in The Happy Place.

"Anna, should we play our violins first?"

"Yeah, let's get the music out!"

They opened their violin cases, and took out the bow and rosin.

"Let's tune-up and make magic in this wonderful land!"

It didn't take long to tune their violins. With a nod to each other, they both looked ready.

In unison they both said, "Let's play!"

Anna began to play and tapped her foot to the music. Soon she was twirling round and round, dancing and swaying to the music as she played. Anaya could not believe how she had mastered the art of the violin at such a young age. She had natural talent and truly was a child prodigy.

Anaya sat on a large rock; her long floral dress draped over the edge and cascaded to the ground like a waterfall. The sun lit up the golden highlights in her hair. She was a vision of beauty to behold.

Anna was wearing her favorite light blue dress. It was one that her mother had made for her. It was flared out on the bottom of the skirt, and on the sleeves. Anna always felt so happy when she wore this dress.

Seeing this mother and daughter in such a beautiful setting was like a masterpiece painting in an elegant museum.

"Mom, can we play the Byssan Lull? I love that song."
Anaya smiled, "Of course we can."
"Did your dad really sing this song to you every night?"
"Yes, it's one of my fondest memories, one of many."

Anaya paused for a moment before they began.

"Before we start, I want to tell you what my father once told me. *'The violin has a soul, it can project emotions—love, happiness, and excitement! If you send your feelings into the violin, and put your soul into the strings, you can create magic!'* My dear father taught me this."

They both lifted their violins, and without another word, Anaya gave the nod to start. The mountains were filled with the beautiful, heavenly music they played. Birds in the trees chirped along as they played. A lovely breeze gently carried the beautiful music across the town of Gällivare.

Together they played folk, classical, polka, and love songs. As they played, they challenged each other with different songs and melodies. They could now play as equal violinists.

As they finished their last song, they both bowed from the waist, then raised back up with a smile—exactly how Anaya had taught her.

"Anna, you're so amazing! Now you know everything I can teach you."

After they had their picnic lunch together in their Happy Place. "It's getting late dear, I think it's time to head back home."

"Mom, I need to tell you something ... this morning Dad told me we are going to town when he gets home from work. He shook me real hard. He made me promise to show people what a perfect, loving family we are. He said, *'We have to be the perfect loving family.'* He looked real mad. He kept saying, *'Do you get it? Do you get it?'* I was so scared I cried."

Anna had a hard time explaining this to her mom, but she continued on. As Anaya heard the story she was heartbroken.

"He said he wants everyone to see what a wonderful Husband and Father he is. He held my shoulders so tight it hurt me, and he shook me. He made me promise I would not open my big mouth

24

about what he is like at home. I cried and cried, but he didn't even care. Daddy just shouted real loud and told me, 'Listen up and do what I tell you to do. I talked with your mother. She knows what to do, or she knows what she'll be in for.' "

Anaya was deeply upset by this, she did not know what to say.

"Anna, I am so sorry you had to go through that. Just do whatever he told you so we don't get in trouble when we get home. We are leaving at six o'clock. We'll make the best of it."

4. Going To Town

Anna looked so amazed! It was her first time going to town.

"Oh Mom, Storgatan street is so lovely! There are so many people, I love this town!"

Johan became frustrated listening to his daughter.

He parked the car, "Get out, and remember what I told you. I'll wait here for you."

"Gee Mom, people are watching us. Why?"

"They remember me from a long time ago, Anna."

They walked together into a department store. Right away a saleswoman approached them.

"How may I help you today, ladies?"

Anaya replied, "First we'd like to find her a pair of shoes."

Anna walked so proudly. She slightly kicked her feet out to the side as she swayed side to side. Despite her worries, Anaya had to smile. Anna sat down, kicked off her shoes, and flipped a few of her curls over her shoulder.

"Mom, can I get a pair of blue shoes? Please?"

"Sure! Your dad wants you to get whatever makes you happy."

Anaya did what she was told to do, and spoke loud so anyone close by to hear. The saleswoman came back with three pairs of blue shoes. Anna tried all of them on, the last ones slipped on easy and fit perfectly. Anna started to prance around.

"I feel just like a princess!"

"We will get this pair," Anaya told the lady, "now we'd like to see little girls' dresses."

On the way there, the lady smiled, "So you are Anna?"

Anna looked at her, "Yep, it's the only name I know!"

Some ladies in the store got quiet so they could hear what was going on.

"Mom, I see a pretty red dress over there!"

"Can we try on that red dress in size five?"

Anna slipped off her dress right then and there, and put on the red dress. She twirled around in the red dress and threw her arms in the air. Just then, Carol and Maryann came into the store.

"I will love this dress forever," Anna cheered!

Anaya told Anna, "Be nice to them, they know me."

"Okay," Anna whispered back.

The clerk returned and asked, "Do you want the red shoes to match that dress?"

Anaya shook her head 'Yes' with excitement!

"Yes, we'll take them. Anna, can you try them on?"

It was not often that Anaya had the opportunity to shop for Anna, especially to get new clothes. She picked out some things that were very special, and some that Anna really needed.

"Anna, have a look around while I finish up. We need undergarments as well."

While Anaya was still shopping, Carol and Maryann took a short walk around so they could run into Anna. Maryann bumped into Anna on purpose.

"Oops! You must be Anna? You're such a pretty little girl."

"Daddy made me promise, if anyone says I'm pretty to say, 'Thank you' and curtsy. I can't say anything about what goes on at home. I'll keep my big mouth shut, or there will be all hell to pay."

Anaya heard this and panicked, "Anna, where are you?"

"Here I am! I am talking with these two nice ladies."

"Come over here, Anna. Stick with me."

Anaya looked up and saw Victor enter the store, her old friend and lover. Their eyes locked and he started walking toward her.

"How are you, Anaya?"

Anaya looked into his eyes as she took his hand.

"I'm fine …"

She felt old feelings come flooding back.

"It's such a surprise to see you!"

"Yes, it's been a very long time …"

Victor paused and took a discerning look at Anna.

"This must be your daughter? She is so pretty."

"Thank you," Anna curtsied in her red dress and red shoes.

Anaya sat down and crossed her legs. She didn't notice that her skirt slid up, revealing the black and blue marks and scars on her legs. As his eyes glanced down, he saw the bruises and scars on her legs. He was shocked. His expression changed.

Anaya looked down, grasped her skirt and covered her legs. She looked back at Victor and saw tears welling up in his eyes. Victor looked broken-hearted. He hesitated to speak.

"Anaya ... I still love you ... I've always loved you, and I always will."

"I still love you too, Victor ..."

"I have to go—"

Victor left without another word.

Anna stopped twirling, "Mom, who is that?"

Carol and Maryann were nearby, Anaya knew they heard it all.

In an emotional voice, she sadly replied, "He is just a friend from my past."

Anaya saw Johan pacing by the door.

"Anna, come on, we have to go."

She quickly asked the clerk to ring up her items.

"Anna, we have to go now."

They couldn't let word of what Anna said get back to her father.

When they reached the car, Johan opened the car door for them.

"Wow, Dad never did this before!"

"Hush now, Anna ... don't talk so loud."

Anaya was silent, she could tell that stress was building up.

As they started to drive home, Johan began complaining that Anaya hadn't prepared dinner. In a demanding voice, he announced, "We're going to stop for dinner. So remember, be on your best behavior."

Anna skipped happily as they walked into the restaurant. Johan called out to her, "Anna, behave yourself."

They were greeted by a hostess, and she led them to a table. As they walked past the other tables, Anna ran her fingers across the table cloths.

"Why are the tablecloths all white?"
"Oh, it's just so they all match honey."
Anna was talking loudly and everyone around could hear.
"It's so pretty! Look, there's flowers on each and every table."
This upset Johan. He glared at Anna and pulled her by the arm.
"No more. Remember what I told you."

The hostess brought the three of them over to a lovely table. Just then, Johan looked up and saw Carol and Val being seated at the next table. He became frustrated and pounded on the table, "Oh, just great. This is going to be a real nerve-racking ordeal …"

He asked the hostess if there was another table available.
"I'm sorry, this is the only one open."
"This will be fine. Thank you," Anaya stated.
Carol whispered to Val, "Anaya ran into Victor at the department store."

Carol and Val were having a business dinner. Val works as a lawyer at Mr. Magnusson's law firm. She is very well-spoken, and has a 'say it like it is' type personality. She has short wispy hair, and a contagious laugh, but you would not want to make her mad.

The waitress came to take their order. Johan did all the talking, "One rostad hjortkött," a Swedish venison roast, "with all of the fixings. Two house salads, two cheeseburgers, and one ice cream for the child, after the meal. Thank you."

The waitress smiled at Anna and asked, "How are you today?"
Anna shyly wiggled in her chair, and looked down, "I'm fine."

Anna started to play with the silverware, and it was making Johan nervous. He left the table.
"I need a break. I'm going to have a cigarette."
As Johan left, Anna got very scared.

"Mom, did I make Daddy mad? Don't let him shake me again!"
"Everything will be OK honey, I won't let him hurt you."

Carol heard what was going on, she leaned over and asked, "Anaya, are you okay?"
Anaya thought, *'This is my only chance to let someone know what is happening.'*
"No, we need help, Carol."
Anna spoke up, "Dad hurts Mom, he says she is just clumsy."
Carol whispered, "What can we do to help you, Anaya?"

"Johan said if I tell anyone, he will kill me, my dad, my precious little Anna, and even our dog, Boulder. He said he will make me watch."

"Anaya, Johan is spreading word around town that you are trying to kill him! He is setting you up! You need to make a plan, and soon. Meet me in the ladies room."

Val got their attention, "Johan is walking back in!"
Carol quickly came up with a plan.

"Val, take these papers and look busy. We can't let him know we talked."

Val shook her head, "This asshole is the scum of the earth."

While they ate dinner, Anna talked about how happy she was to get ice cream. She thanked Johan three times while she ate her cheeseburger and fries. After they finished dinner, Anna waited for her ice cream. She was playing with the silverware again, when all of a sudden, her fork flipped down on the floor.

Anna cried out, "I'm sorry Dad, I'll pick it up! Don't be mad Daddy, please?"

Johan grabbed Anna and firmly put her in her chair.

"You will sit like a young lady!"

He got right in front of her face, "Look what you did! No ice cream for you!"

Anna started to cry, tears fell from her eyes.

"Johan, let me take her to the ladies room. We'll be right back."

"Fine. I'm going to have another cigarette."

Carol shook her head, "I can't believe this, Val."

Val had a very sad look on her face.

"We need to help Anaya. Go now, before Johan comes back."

Carol left to go and meet Anaya in the ladies' room.

Carol could see by Anaya's face that the panic had overcome her. Her face turned pale, she looked like she was going to faint. Carol helped her take a seat on a chair in the ladies restroom.

"Anaya, you have to protect yourself and your little girl."

"I know, we are running out of time."

"Do you have a gun?"

"Johan has a hunting gun—"

"Do you know where he keeps it, and how to shoot it?"

"Yes," Anaya nodded, "he keeps the gun near the fireplace."

Carol spoke very calmly and clearly.

"Anaya, you have to be prepared to use it. Do whatever it takes to save yourself and Anna. Let JP help you. I'll go back to the table before Johan returns."

Carol knew that Anaya and Anna were in grave danger. Val watched as Carol walked back to the table. Johan was already there, and pounding on the table, with a frown on his face.

"Where in the hell is that bitch?"

Just then, he saw Anaya and Anna returning.

He called the waitress, "Bring us the bill, we are leaving."

Anna was crying and looked scared.

The waitress asked, "Do you want the ice cream now?"

Johan shook his head, "*No!*" he slammed his first on the table.

"Please, Daddy? *You promised!*" Anna asked.

"I said no! Naughty little girls do not deserve ice cream."

By now, the whole restaurant was watching what was going on. Johan had become the center of attention.

"He's had a rough day today,"Anaya tried to make light of the situation.

The waitress gave Anaya the bill, "Thank you."

She felt Anaya's hands shaking as she handed her the bill.

After they paid the bill, Johan pulled Anna in front of him.

He told everyone watching, "See? We are leaving now."

Anna was sobbing; everyone felt so sad, they could see how scared she was. Anna decided to let everyone know.

"Daddy," she shouted, "you made us promise to be perfect so they would like you! Like you told me, the perfect loving family!"

Johan shouted, "Shut up, Anna! Let's get out of here."
As they left he slammed the car door as hard as he could.
"You are just a spoiled Brat."

The ride back home was silent, Anna sobbed softly in the back seat. Anna knew if she cried too loudly that Johan would call her a sissie and say she was faking it. He would always tell her, *'I'll give you something to cry about.'* He would grab her by her shoulders and shake her until she begged him to stop.

Johan pulled into the driveway and they all got out without saying a word. Boulder was on the steps and could sense something was not right. As Johan walked by, Boulder cowered and his ears and tail went down; he whined as he followed Anna to her room.

Anna laid on her bed, covered her head with a pillow, and cried. Boulder jumped up next to her, he put his head on her back and cried with her.

Anna heard sounds of yelling and things breaking. Anna heard Johan say, "Maybe my prostitute can teach you how to be a good lover!" Anna remembered what Mama told her, "No matter what, stay in your room."

Anna stroked Boulder's head. She sobbed as she talked to Boulder.

"We will be safe here. At least I have you. I love you, Boulder."
Boulder curled up next to Anna and they fell asleep.

5. Boulder, Where's Mom?

As the sun came up, Boulder jumped out of bed and it woke up Anna. "Good morning, Boulder! You are up early, you must be hungry. Come on, let's go." Anna poured the dog food in the doggie dish. Boulder gobbled up his food very quickly. He looked up at Anna, and started checking around looking for something.

"Well, Boulder … we need to find Mom."
She started to call out to her, "Mom? Mom, where are you?"
Anna checked every room.
"She's not here. Maybe she is outside doing laundry?"

Anna looked outside, but she could not find her mom anywhere. She started to panic. Boulder kept running back and forth toward the pond behind the house. Anna shouted out as she looked for her mother.

"Mommy, where are you? Mommy, answer me!"
Anna was checking everywhere.
"Mommy! Where are you? You can't leave me!"

Boulder started barking to get Anna's attention. He pulled on her nightgown.

"Don't Boulder, we need to find Mom."
He barked a few more times and ran behind the house.
"Boulder, stop! Come back!"
Anna ran after Boulder and he led her to the pond.

Just then, Anna heard a soft moan. Boulder ran over to Anaya. "Boulder, you found her! Boulder, I think Mom is hurt."

Anaya was lying half way out of the water. She held on to the tree roots along the shore. She tried to pull herself out of the water, but she didn't have enough strength.

"Mom, how did you get here? What happened?"
Anaya tried to pull herself out but she was too weak.
"Anna ... pull me up ... help ... grab my arm ..."
Anna tried to help pull her back onto the bank by the shore.
"I can't Mommy, I can't!"

Anaya tried to push herself up, but lost her footing on the slippery rocks under the water. Anna cried out to Boulder, "Help me, Boulder! Help me get Mom out!"

Boulder grabbed Anaya's nightgown in his mouth and gave a big pull, digging his feet in. Together they pulled as hard as they could. They had to get Anaya out of the water and back onto the shore, she was very weak.

"You found me ... I am so cold ... Anna ... get some towels."
"Okay, Mommy. Boulder, you stay with Mom, keep her safe."
Anna ran to get towels to help her mom dry off and warm up.

Earlier that morning, Johan and Anaya had an argument before he left for work. When they were at the department store in town, Johan saw Victor talking with Anaya. The more she denied it, the more angry he became. There was no way to convince him otherwise. He had already made up his mind.

Anna returned with towels as fast as she could. Anaya had swallowed a lot of water when Johan held her under the water. She could hardly speak, her voice was so faint.

"I need you to push on my back," she coughed.
Anna started to pat her mother on the back.
"No ... I need you to roll me over."
"I can't, Mommy!"
"It will save me ... you have to, Anna."
Anna pushed on her side and got her turned over.
"Sit on my back ... it will," Anaya coughed, "get water out of my lungs."

Anna sat down on her back, and Anaya started to cough up water. Anna could not believe what was going on. She watched as Anaya kept coughing and gasping for breath.

"Again ... Anna ... it's working."

After a few more times, Anaya could talk better. Anna helped her mom stand up and she wrapped the towels around her. She helped her walk back to the house.

When they made it back to the house, Anaya laid on the sofa to rest. She was covered with towels and a blanket. She was in disbelief.

"Johan tried to drown me, Anna. He held me under the water."
"Why is Dad trying to hurt us?" Anna cried.
She put her arms around her mother. Anaya held Anna close.

Anna did not know how to explain what was going on to her daughter. She tried to console her as best she could, despite being in shock herself.

"Anna, your father has never known real love. He is angry; he needs help. He has resentment toward us because we can feel love and he can't. We have to get away. We have to leave here … if we don't, he will kill us. I have a plan for us to get away. As soon as I feel strong enough, we will practice the plan. For now I need to rest."

Anna walked to the front step and called Boulder.
"Come on, Boulder! Come here, come and sit with me."
She pet him; he listened closely as they sat on the step.
"Now Boulder, Mom needs a lot of rest. We need to stay busy and don't get in trouble. You saved Mommy today, Boulder. You are a real hero."
He lifted his head and licked Anna on her cheek, then laid his head in her lap.
"That's right, you are my hero! I will love you forever Boulder."

Anna saw Mr. Thissel sitting next to her rock friends.
"Oh, don't worry Mr. Thissel! I will keep you in my heart too. Mom made you for me, and I love you too."

Anna decided she would paint some of her new rocks from The Happy Place. She gathered all of her brushes and pretty colors of paint. She went to sit by the special bench that JP made where she keeps all of her rock friends.

As she painted them, she gave them each a name. She named them after the ladies that she met in town the other day. She talked with Boulder and Mr. Thissel as she painted.

"This one should be Maryann. And I think this one will be Carol. What do you think, Mr. Thissel? Maybe this one can be Mom's friend Corrine. Oh, I think Kathleen would love this one!"

Anna even decided to paint a rock for Victor.

"Mr. Thissel, I am going to paint this one for Victor. He was very cute! He was Mom's friend from a long time ago."

Even though they met just briefly, she remembered Victor and how kind he was to her mother. She couldn't understand why he was crying.

"Boulder, I love my bench JP made for me. My rock friends love it too. They have a nice place to sit to be my audience when we sing and read books."

JP's daughters had a great book collection. Anna loved to read the books that JP would bring to her, and the books they got from school.

"Now I have a pretty rock for each of the nice ladies in town. I hope that I can show them if I see them again. I think they are trying to help Mom. Guess what Mr. Thissel? I have a real friend, his name is JP! He's the one who gave me all my books."

They stayed busy painting for a long time. Anna had become accustomed to spending so much time alone

"I wish you could read Boulder."

Anna heard the old postbus chugging down the road, "JP is coming, Boulder! JP is coming!" JP drove down the long road, turned into the driveway, and parked in front of the house.

JP yelled out, "How is the little one?"
Anna jumped up and down, "I'm just great!"
"My friend in town told me you need some ice cream!"

When JP heard what happened to Anna, he felt terrible. He wanted to help make things better. He brought a cooler with ice cream for Anna.

"So, I brought ice cream and chocolates for you, and a bone for Boulder too. Remember, keep the chocolate away from Boulder."

Boulder ran up to JP, took the bone and wandered away. He laid down to gnaw on his new bone by the bench where Anna had painted her rocks.

JP told Anna, "Make sure to eat your ice cream now, before it melts. Your dad won't have to know, *you are not a naughty girl!*"

Anna walked with JP to the bench that he made for her rock friends. JP laughed as he watched Anna gobble down her ice cream. She introduced JP to her new rock friends, the ones she named after the people she met in town.

"Look JP, here's my new friends. I have five new friends!"
Anna showed him the rocks they got from The Happy Place.
"Now, everyone, I want to introduce you to JP!"

JP waved as Anna made the introduction.

"Carol, Kathleen, Maryann, Corrine, and Victor, this is my friend JP. He's my best friend! The rest of you already know him."

"They are very glad to meet you."
She got a big grin and put her hand on her hip.
"I am happy to meet all of you too."
"I just painted them just before you got here!"

Any small thing that JP could do to make Anna's life better brought him happiness. She was so happy with the bench he made for her rock friends. In the past few years, he had brought Anna so many books. When she was very young, he brought coloring books. As she grew up he started to bring story books, and school books. His daughters were just a few years older than Anna, so it worked out perfectly.

He knew the challenges they faced. He knew that Anaya and Anna had both been very secluded. They never had a social life; they never got together with other people. Johan has isolated Anaya ever since they were married.

"How is your mother today, Anna?"
"Well, I think Dad is crazy! He tried to drown Mom in the pond last night. I couldn't find Mom, but Boulder helped me find her. She is inside sleeping on the couch. I covered her with a blanket to help keep her warm."

A tear fell down Anna's cheek.
"Oh, JP, I am so afraid!"
She threw her arms around JP and started to cry.

"I need Mom, I'm just a little girl. If Dad kills Mommy, then I will have no one to take care of me."

JP held her tight and tried to comfort her.

"Anna, your mom has a plan to save you, just follow her plan and listen to whatever she tells you to do. Always remember that you are very special, and very loved by everyone."

JP realized he needed to change to a happier subject.

"You know, Anna, I've never heard you play the violin."

Anna looked up at JP, she still had tears in her eyes.

"I think we need some beautiful music to calm our soul, played by an amazing, talented, lovely little girl."

"Of course, I love you, JP! I wish you were my dad."

Anna started to perk up, she wiped the tears from her eyes.

"You know, my rock friends are my audience when I practice."

The thought of playing her violin for JP helped her stop crying.

"Stay right here, I will get my violin."

With that, Anna turned and ran toward the house.

He thought of what a sad life she's had.

"She is so intelligent. She can spell, write, read music, and she has read every book I gave her. She's way ahead of her age level."

This was the first time JP would hear Anna play her violin, it was a very special moment. He wanted to share her performance with his whole family. Fortunately, he had his camera with him. He quickly went to his postbus to get his camera and video camera.

Anna brought her violin; her curls bounced as she ran.

"Can I record your performance? I want to show my family."

"Sure you can."

Anna opened the case and slowly lifted her violin. She was so excited to play for a real person. She took a composed stance as she prepared to play.

She waited for a few seconds before starting to play the melody of an old Swedish folk song. Each note rang out so loud and clear! She began to sway and twirl as she played. JP was so impressed, he didn't realize she was such a professional!

She finished the first song and JP started to applaud.
"You are wonderful, Anna!"
Anna announced, "Now, let's get down to real violin playing!"
JP interrupted, "Wait a minute, you need one more thing."

He walked over to her and placed his Gällivare Postman hat on her head. It slid backward, she pushed it forward but it covered her eyes. She lifted up the bill of the hat and made a silly face.

JP laughed, "I can fix that."
He tucked an envelope behind the hat so it would fit.
Anna looked down, "I still have my nightgown on."
"That is okay, Anna, the music will sound just as beautiful. Always remember that you are a little angel!"

There she stood, no shoes, a light blue nightgown, and JP's Gällivare postman's hat. JP sat on the ground and started recording. Before Anna raised her violin to begin, she shared a very special message, the same one that her mother had taught her:

"My mom told me a secret! *'The violin has a soul, it can project emotions—love, happiness, and excitement! If you send your feelings into the violin, and put your soul into the strings, you can create magic!'* "

With a much more serious look on her face, she proudly lifted her violin. She took a moment to put her feelings into the violin like her mother taught her.

"Now, I will play the Swedish National Anthem."
He would hear the anthem played better than ever before.

From the first sound, JP knew this little girl was a prodigy. Each note had such crystal clarity. She commanded attention and prestige. She controlled the feeling of the music. JP felt that her music came directly from her heart.

At the end of the song, Anna placed the violin at her side and took a bow, just as her mother had taught her. She came up and smiled at JP.

He was speechless, no words could explain his feelings. He walked over to Anna with great excitement!

"Bravo! Bravo! You are a *master violinist!*" He looked into her beautiful blue eyes. "I want to get a picture of you just as you are right now. Can you hold the violin like you are still playing?"

Just then, Boulder came and sat next to Anna, he wanted to be in the picture too. JP loved to take pictures as he delivered mail throughout the day. This would become one of his most treasured photos.

"It's lovely, Anna! How about you put the hat on Boulder? I'll take another one!"
Boulder looked like he didn't like that idea. Anna bent down and gently placed the hat on his head. She put her arms around him and gave him a big hug. JP got another great picture.

Anaya came to the front door looking and was looking for Anna. She started to call out to her, "Anna, where are you?"

"I'm here Mom! I just played the National Anthem on my violin for my best friend JP!" Anna was so proud of herself, "I played a folk song too!"

It brought a smile to Anaya's face to see that Anna was happy. When she played her violin it was like she was in her own world. Anaya was still exhausted and could hardly stand.

"I'm going to put my violin case away. come on Boulder." Boulder followed Anna as she went back to her room.

Anaya was so weak that she fell down to her knees. JP carried her into the house and placed her on the sofa.

"This has gone too far. We need to make a plan, Anaya. Time is of the essence. We need to keep you alive for Anna. She needs her mother."

Anaya was still a little short of breath, "I stayed too long, JP … I stayed too long. What can I do? Johan thinks I am dead … when he gets home and finds out I am still alive, he might try to kill me again."

JP reached out to hold her trembling hand.

"Anaya, I can help you."

Anaya cried, "No, JP, no one can help me now. I should have left a long time ago. I stayed too long."

JP had never seen such a look in her eyes, she was terrified.

"You can stay with us until you make plans. I can take you both home with me right now."

Tears fell from her eyes as she tried to explain what Johan had told her so many times over.

"If anyone tries to help me escape, he will kill them. He will kill your family; your wife, your children, your dogs. He will make you watch, then he will kill you too. He would do the same to our family. He is crazy!"

"We have to make a plan, Anaya, but first you have to eat something and regain your strength."

JP took over the kitchen and prepared a healthy breakfast for all of them. They ate together quietly, until Anna broke the silence.

"I wish this is how our family always was."

JP smiled, "Anna, this is the way life is in a normal family. I pray that one day you will have a normal and happy life."

"Anna, let's clean up the kitchen so your Dad won't have anything to complain about."

JP washed the dishes; Anna dried them and put them away. When they had finished, she ran outside to play with Boulder and Mr. Thissel.

"Anaya, I hate to leave you here alone. You have to do something. You have to protect yourself. Is there a gun in the house?"

Anaya nodded her head, "Yes, he has a hunting gun."
"Find it and hide it. Put it someplace where you can get to it."

"I will try ... he always keeps it next to the fireplace, he will notice if it's not there."

JP looked around as he thought of a plan. "Place a chair in front of the fireplace, with a blanket covering the chair and the gun. You know, I could stay and shape him up. I was in the service. He is just a damn coward. Only a coward would raise his hand to a woman. I can make Johan feel the same fear in his soul that he enjoys making you feel."

JP could see the pain in her eyes as she sadly looked down. "No, if you did that, as soon as you left, we would all be dead." Anna took a deep breath over her plan to survive the night.

"I will bide my time. I know where the gun is. I will use it if I have to. I may not be able to save myself, but I will save Anna. She doesn't deserve to live like this. Thank you, JP. You've helped us so much. Anna has read all of the books you gave her. She can read at a fourth grade level now."

JP got serious, "You are the best mother in this world. You taught her how to read at three and a half years old. She is what she is because of you. You taught her to play the violin and read the music at four years old. She is a brilliant girl and a master violinist."

Even in this challenging time, a great look of pride came upon her face.

"Anna is a very gifted child, she learns so quickly. She is a musical prodigy. Songs that took me years of practice, she can play right along with me. I want her to have a good life. I have a plan for her that no one can know about. I have to save her if I can."

JP could not believe what he heard. He couldn't help but think there must be something more that he could do.

"I am glad that you have a plan in place, Anna."
He gave her a long emotional hug before preparing to leave.
"Don't be afraid to shoot if you have to."

Anaya spoke strongly—
"I have to stay strong and put him in his place."

JP stood in the doorway; as he looked back at Anaya, he had a feeling that this may be the last time he would ever see her.

"If this is the only way ... I trust you. God bless you, Anaya."
"Thank you for caring about us, JP," she softly replied.

As JP walked out of the front door, he saw Anna playing with Mr. Thissel and her new rock friends. Anaya watched as he hugged Anna and waved goodbye. Then he was gone.

"Anna, come in now. We need to have a serious talk."
"I'm going to put my new rock friends under the bench."
Anna talked to each one as she placed them under the bench.

"Okay—Maryann, Carol, Corrine, Val, Gary, Kathleen, Victor, Sue, and JP—I have to go talk to Mommy now, and I might not see you again for a while. I hope you all enjoyed my songs. I am so glad that I got to share my secrets with you. I found you in The Happy

Place, so always stay happy, and be good friends to each other. If you get lonely, share your secrets with the trees and they will dance for you. Take good care of each other, until we meet again."

Anna slowly walked toward the house, Boulder walked by her side. A feeling of sadness overcame her, she knew her dad was going to be angry. Then she got an idea, one she thought might just work! It was all she could think of at this time.

Anna walked into the kitchen and saw a desperate look on her mother's face. A look that made her feel scared and worried. A look unlike anything she had ever seen before.

"Sit down here Anna ... please listen very carefully and remember everything I say."

They sat down in the living room and Anaya began to explain the plan.

"When Dad gets home we will watch and be very quiet. The best we can hope for is that he will be so drunk that he will just pass out. Then he will go to work early tomorrow morning. I have a plan for you. If it gets dangerous and where you might get hurt, stay by the window."

Anaya pointed toward the big tall windows in the living room.
"See the big windows over there?"
"Yes," Anna nodded her head.
"You're going to stand by the last window, before the hallway."
The whole living room wall was made up of tall windows. They looked out to a great forest in the backyard, which leads to The Happy Place.

"You have to stay by the window, the last window before the hallway. When I tell you to, take the little metal stool and hit the glass as hard as you can. Do you think you can do this?"

"Yes," Anna looked puzzled.

"I will let you know when to break the window, Anna. When you hear me say *'break the window'* you have to do it right away."

Anaya leaned a little closer, she spoke very softly, but very desperately.

"Take Boulder, Mr. Thissel, your blanket, and my violin. Have Boulder go out first. Quietly throw the blanket and the violin outside. Carry Mr. Thissel with you. Always hold on to Mr. Thissel and you won't feel alone."

Anna sadly looked into her mom's eyes, "Mommy, will you jump out of the window with me?"

"I will do everything I can to be with you. I will try, Anna, but when I tell you to break the window, you have to go right away."

For a moment, Anaya was silent. She did not know how to tell Anna what was in store for them. "This is a time for us to be very brave. I need you to do whatever it takes to get out of that window and get to safety."

Anna had a blank, confused look on her face.

She whimpered, "Will you be with me, Mom?"

Anna looked directly into her eyes, "You're going to stand by the last window, right before the hallway."

Anaya looked very scared, she became very emotional.

"I may not be able to save myself, but *I have to save you*. I won't let you lose your life because I made a stupid mistake, and hesitated to change. You have a wonderful life ahead of you. But Anna … I may not be with you."

Anna threw her arms up and cried out, "Why are you saying this, Mom?"

Anaya saw how upset and distressed Anna became. She held her close and stroked her head as she let Anna know how dangerous the situation had become.

"Anna, life can bring many changes that we didn't plan on. We have to figure it out as we go along. Sometimes it can be very hard, but we can make it. In the end everything will turn out fine. Always keep the music I gave you in your heart. You will have a good life, Anna. *I will always be with you.*"

Boulder curled up next to Anna and listened too. He placed his head on her lap and she softly pet him. In their years together, Boulder always remained by Anna's side.

"If Johan is drunk and starts breaking things, you have to remember our plan. Even if you see him get his gun out, you have to follow the plan. Be as quiet as you can. Make sure you have shoes on. Wait for me to say *'break the window now!'* Please don't forget, Anna. I have to save you."

Anna started to cry, Anaya stared right into her eyes.
"Stay by the window, Anna. The last window before the hallway. When you see the gun, Anna, tell me what you have to do."

Anna sobbed as she retold the plan. "I break the window ... with the small metal chair ... and get Boulder out ... throw the violin case out ... take my blanket ... and Mr. Thissel ... and I jump out."

Anaya looked worried, "That's right. Come here, Anna."
Anna dove into her mother's arms. After a long tearful hug, Anaya instructed her what to do once she got outside.

"Take the path to The Happy Place, like we always do."
Anna looked up with a puzzled little face.
"Without you, Mom?"
Anaya softly held her hands.

"Anna, I will always be close to you. Even if you can't see me, I will be there when you need me. Take a while to rest when you get to our Happy Place, you'll be tired. Remember all the times we talked about the Ski Lodge? There are very kind, loving people that live there. Look down the hill and you will see the lodge. Go to the cabin at the end. You have to remember this. There is a nice couple who lives there, they will help you. I would go to the lodge and ski when I was a teenager, and they know my father—Anna, do you know what I am doing?"

Anna looked sad, "Yes, Mom. You want to save me."

Anna came running out to meet Johan as he was walking toward the house.

"Daddy, I saved Mom today! You wouldn't believe it, me and Boulder found her by the lake. She almost drowned, she just got clumsy again, I guess. Are you so proud of me, Dad?"

"You talk too much. Leave me alone, Anna."
That was all Johan had to say.

Anna followed him, all the while saying, "Are you happy, Dad? Boulder was so brave. It was hard to get Mom to the house, but we did it!"

Johan opened the door and walked inside. Boulder slid in behind him before the door closed and went into the hall to hide. Anaya was in the kitchen preparing dinner.

Johan looked around the house, then went to the kitchen. In a harsh and demanding voice, he started to yell at Anaya.
"What the hell have you been doing all day? This place looks like a damn junkyard!"

Anaya didn't say a word.
She could not keep her hands from shaking.

"It must be too much to ask for you to have dinner ready when I get home. Looks like a liquid dinner tonight."

He walked to the liquor cabinet and grabbed a bottle.
"Dinner will be ready in just a few minutes," she softly replied.
Anaya tried to prevent an argument.

Johan slugged down two shots in a row and pounded on the table. He started his *'feel sorry for me'* speech. "My own mother would rather die than stay and raise her son. Have you ever thought about that? I never felt the love a mother has for her son like other boys had—I hate her for that. You have no idea, you had *everything* that I didn't have."

Johan's anger was building up inside. He took a long swig off the bottle and glared at Anaya. He stood up and started shouting as he staggered toward Anaya.

"Why do you do this to me? You are the one who makes me do this, it's your fault!"

He grabbed Anaya by her arm, flipped her around, and slapped her across the face so hard that she fell backward. Anaya just laid there, she didn't try to get up. Johan turned and went to the bedroom. He yelled, "I hate women, they are all alike!"

After the door slammed shut, Anaya stayed still, tears ran down her face. She wiped away her tears to hide the pain, then walked to Anna's room and wiggled the doorknob.

"Open the door, it's Mom," she whispered.

Anna came and opened the door. Anaya could tell that Anna had been crying. She heard everything. Anaya picked her up and carried her to bed.

"Dad is out for the night," she softly explained, "we have some time. Don't be afraid, I will stay with you. We will lock the door and pray that Johan leaves for work early."

Anna sobbed, *"Mom, what are we going to do?"*
"We have to do what we planned. Let's rest while we can."

Anaya called Boulder to come on the bed with them, "Boulder, come on," she patted the bed. "Up here, Boulder, come on!"

Boulder pounced onto the bed, made a few circles, and laid down next to her. Anna was on one side, Anaya was on the other, and Boulder in the middle.

Anna whispered, "Mom, I wish we could always be like this. I am so happy we are together. We're almost safe."

Early in the morning, Johan left for work. After he left, they all peaked around the corner of the kitchen, Boulder on the bottom, Anna in the middle, and Anaya the top.

"Dad is gone," Anna announced!
Anaya gave her a hug and twirled her around.
"Let's have breakfast, I bet you and Boulder are hungry."

Anna fed Boulder and got him some fresh water. Anaya prepared breakfast for Anna; muesli with filmjölk and raisins. She made a smiley face with raisins in Anna's muesli. Then she served toasted bread and boiled eggs.

"I love it! Thank you Mommy."

As they sat together eating breakfast, they talked about how nice it would be if Dad were no longer here. "We could be happy like this all the time."

They were happy, but fear always lingered in their hearts.

Then came an unexpected knock on the door. They looked at each other wondering who could be here so early. Anaya slowly opened the door—she gasped in disbelief! A young lady stood in the doorway, she was shaking and covered with blood.

She shrieked, *"Johan attacked me! He is crazy!"*

She frantically explained, "He wanted me to come here to make you jealous. I told him no, I would never do that to another woman. He is drunk and smells of booze. He laughed about what he did to me, and bragged that he was going to *'finish you off'* today. *You need to leave, now!* If you don't, this will be your last day to live."

"My sister in New York said I could stay with her. I will be safe there, and she will help me find a job. My friend is taking me to the airport. I'm leaving right now, *you need to leave too!"*

She didn't stop to hear Anaya's reply.
"Johan will kill you and your beautiful little girl."

She turned and walked away, then got into a car and drove off. Anaya could not say a word. Her heart was racing, her emotions filled the room. She stood in silence before she closed the door.

Anna was traumatized by what she just saw. She had turned very pale. She could not believe her dad had done such a thing.

"Mommy, is Dad going to do that to *us*?"
"No, Anna. Remember what we talked about. We both have to be very brave."
Anna followed Anaya over to the window that she told her to break. As she stood by her side, Anaya could tell that she was still in shock from what she saw.

"Anna, let's get some hot cocoa and talk for a minute, OK?"

Anaya began to heat up some milk on the stove, then lit a fire in the fireplace. She came back to mix in the chocolate and got out two cups, one for her and one for Anna. They sipped hot cocoa in silence for a few minutes.

Anna cried out, "I don't know if I can do it!"
"I'll help you Anna, I'll show you what you have to do."

Anaya knew that she had to better prepared. Somehow she had to help Anna to understand.

"I love you very much Anna ... We are so close to each other. But the time has come for you to go into the world. Life is not like it is here. Put this part of your young life behind you. Let the world see what a wonderful little girl you are. Your music will take you such a long way. Every day of your new life will become a happy adventure. You will know happiness and love; no more stress and violence."

It was so hard for them to imagine life without each other.

"*I will always be close by and watching over you, Anna.* Right now, we have to do what it takes to get to that new life. Do you understand what I am saying?"

"Yes, Mommy," Anna tried her best to understand.
"Be very brave, Anna. If you feel scared, weak, or lonely, tell yourself, '*I can do this.*' Repeat it to yourself, '*I can do this!*' You will be OK, you will do this."

They finished their hot cocoa together and left the kitchen. Anaya knew it was important to continue preparing, they had to practice the plan.

"Anna, I put the violin case and Mr. Thissel here behind the chair. You will take Boulder and Mr. Thissel with you. The metal stool is right next to the window. You have to hit the window as hard as you can. I know you can do this. When I tell you to leave, Anna you have to do it right away."

Anna listened to her mother very closely. She could not believe this was happening, but at this point she knew the plan.

"I will watch you, Mommy. I will listen for you to say '*Break the window now!*' "

Anaya was very sad, but it comforted her that Anna was somehow beginning to understand.

"You have a life filled with love and a great future ahead of you. The people at the lodge will take good care of you. They knew me a long time ago, they were friends of my parents. You can trust them, Anna. My father took me skiing there many times. Just let your new life happen one day at a time."

It was difficult to prepare her for so much that was unknown.

"Anna, you must know that all men are not like your father. Think about JP, he is a very kind and loving man, and a great father. We can't judge all men just because of Johan. I'm so sorry, Anna; I am sorry for all the violence you had to see. I'm so sorry, Anna ... so very sorry. My bad decisions put you in this horrible situation. Please forgive me if you can."

Anna innocently looked up to her mother, "Mommy, you taught me everything about forgiveness. I forgive you Mommy!"

"Even if I am not there with you, Anna ... when you make it to the lodge, you will start a whole new life. It will be a life filled with more love than you have ever known before. One day, you will understand why I had to do this to save you."

6. Breaking Free

"I will lock the door. It will give us time so we know what to do. We can be where we have to be. I will stay by the fireplace, next to the gun. Remember, you have to stay as close to the window as you can. Tell Boulder to 'Stay, and be a good dog' so he doesn't wander off. No matter what, do as I say. Okay, Anna?"

"I will Mom, but I'm scared."

"It's okay to be scared, Anna. Just keep telling yourself, *'I can do this, I can do this. Mom will be proud of me.'* "

"I hear the truck … he's home." Anaya took a deep breath.

"Now it's time to follow the plan, Anna."

"We are ready."

They heard the doorknob jiggle, then Johan kicked the door in and there was a *loud crash!* He was swearing every word he knew.

Anna and Boulder ran over to the window near the hallway. Anaya went over to the fireplace near the gun. Johan stood in the doorway, with the light of the day behind him. His silhouette cast a frightening shadow. Johan stumbled over to Anaya and grabbed her, then started to shake her very hard.

Anaya started yelling, "Stop, leave me alone! I hate you!"

Johan viciously replied, *"You married me."*

Anaya screamed, *"I never loved you, I pitied you!* Pity is not love. No one would stand for the things that you put me through. You are a sorry ass woman abuser. I saw what you did to your lady friend, she was here this morning, bleeding and in pain. She apologized to me."

Johan yelled back, "Oh, go to hell! She is just like all the rest of you women, she only cares about herself. I hate all of you!"

Anaya shouted back, "Just look at what you've done to me! Look at the kind of life you have put Anna through!"

Johan grabbed Anaya by her shirt and pulled her over to him. "Let go of me," she yelled, trying to push him away.

Johan tightened his grip, as he pulled on her shirt it raised up to her neck and buttons popped off onto the floor.

"I never loved you Anaya! You were just a con job, just a pretty little rich girl. I watched you grow up; you had everything I never had. Fancy clothes, an education, and so many friends. Your mother and father worshiped the ground you walked on. I listened to you and your father play violins at church. I hid behind the bush near the door. I cried all the way home. I envied you and hated you at the same time! That is when I made up my mind, I would con you into my life. Now you know what it feels like to be me, don't you? Do you like it? Tell me, do you like my life? Say it! Say 'I like it' "

Anaya started to choke Johan, but he overpowered her and she was losing her grip. He pushed her toward the fireplace and she fell down. She looked up and saw Anna standing in the hallway—frozen in place, she had heard everything. Anna held Mr. Thissel close as tears fell from her eyes.

Anaya shouted, *"Now, Anna, break the window!"*
Anna didn't move.

Johan saw his gun near the fireplace, it was behind the chair and under the blanket Anaya used to try and hide it. He moved towards the gun before Anaya could lift herself up from the floor.

Anaya had left the fireplace poker in the fire. When she grabbed it, fiery embers were cast across the floor. She came up behind Johan as he went to get his gun.

Flames started to spread to the drapery and furniture. He laughed like a mad man.

"So you're getting brave now? You don't have the guts!" Anaya stood up to him for the very first time.

"You should have been locked up a long time ago. I should have left the first time you hit me. I can't change the past, but we have a long life ahead of us *without you!*"

Johan noticed Anna standing in the hallway near the window. As he turned to look at Anna, Anaya lifted the poker up as far as she could and hit Johan on top of his head. She used all the strength she had. He fell forward and blood spattered everywhere.

Anaya dropped the poker and it fell hard on the floor.
Anna started screaming.
"Daddy's blood is on me! Take it off! Take it off, Mommy!"
She ran over and used her dress to wipe off Anna's face.

Anaya looked back at Johan, the flames had traveled up the curtains by the fireplace and spread to the walls. Smoke began to fill the house.

Johan started to get up, he had the gun in his hands.
Anaya yelled to Anna, "Now is the time!"
Anna stood there in shock, crying and coughing.

Anaya took the metal stool and broke the window. As the wind came through the window, the flames rose up all around them.

Anna tried to get Boulder to go out of the window.
"Jump, Boulder! Jump!"
He didn't move, he didn't want to leave Anna behind.

Anna tried to pick him up, but he was too heavy. She struggled to lift him up to get his head through the window. He let out a sharp whimper as she pushed. She got scared and set him back down. She did not know how she could get Boulder out of the window.

As she tossed the violin case out of the window, she looked up and saw Johan towering above them. He pointed the gun at Anaya. He was drunk with rage; blood dripped down his face.

Anna cried *"Stop Daddy! Stop! Don't do this!"*
"Burn in hell," he said.
He lifted the gun and fired one shot.

Anaya fell next to Anna, she started bleeding very badly. Anna just stood there and screamed as she watched. Boulder was by her side and making a whining sound.

The fire started to rise up around Johan.
"All you had to do was say you were sorry," he yelled.
He stumbled backward and fell over the chair.

Anna kneeled down by Anaya, too scared to leave her behind.

"Mom, I can't leave without you!"

"Please, Anna, you have to go. Take Boulder, Anna, run!"

With her last breath, Anaya struggled to say:

"I love you. I will always be with you."

Boulder got hold of Anna's dress and pulled her away from the fire and toward the window. She stood there, frozen in fear, with blood on her dress and her face. The house was engulfed in flames.

With Boulder by her side, and Mr. Thissel still in her hand, Anna jumped out of the window. Boulder followed right behind her. They ran away from the house, and didn't look back until they reached the edge of the woods.

Completely out of breath, she finally stopped and turned toward the house. As she watched the house began to collapse. The flames of the fire sent sparks and smoke billowing high into the sky. Anna fell to the ground in tears.

Boulder whined as he sat by her side. He started to walk in circles, then nudged her and barked for her to follow him. Anna looked up at Boulder and threw her arms around him. Anna and Boulder cried together.

"It's just you and me now, Boulder, but we have each other."

Anna recalled the plan her mother had explained to her. She knew that she had to run as quickly as she could, and follow the trail to The Happy Place. She would make it through the forest and go to the lodge. Anna started to run.

Anna held on to Mr. Thissel in one hand, and the violin case in the other. With Boulder by her side, she ran faster than she had ever ran before. Now and then a tree branch would scratch against her face. She didn't feel anything. All the animals and beautiful things she had seen so many times before became a blur as she ran through the forest.

In her mind, Anna recalled the time she spent here with her mother. Together, they used to rest at the end of the trail, on the blanket that her mom had made. They would pick wildflowers and make wreaths for their hair.

They would dance in a circle and sing their song, '*This Is Our Happy Place*'; these were their best memories.

Boulder started to slow down, so Anna slowed down too. The forest became dark as the sun began to set. Anna tripped on a rock and fell into the brush and twigs in the darkness. She was tired and now in pain from her fall.

"Let's rest here, Boulder, next to this big rock. I love you Boulder. Thank you for being here with me. Always remember you are my hero. We are almost there, Boulder, but I need a break. I can't see the trail anymore, it's getting too dark!"

As they sat together in silence, Anna noticed a strange shape in the distance. She pointed toward an object in the distance on the other side of the path.

"Boulder, what's that?"

Anna stood up and took a few steps.
"Boulder, it's Mom's blanket!"

She walked toward the tree and carefully took the blanket off of the branches. Without this blanket it would have been a terribly cold night for her and Boulder.

"I thought I lost it, Boulder, last time we came to The Happy Place. I was afraid to tell Mom because it's so special. Mom told me it's a magic blanket. She told me, 'If you feel sad, you just hug this blanket, and you will feel all better'—I know it's true, because It works for me!"

Boulder started to whine, Anna hugged him and they sat down together. "Don't be afraid, Boulder, we still have each other. I will always love you forever." He placed his head on Anna's lap as she started to tell him a story.

"Did you know that when we go to Heaven, we will all be together? Mom told me animals have a special place in Heaven too, just like we do. It's called Dog Heaven. The dogs are so happy there, they jump and play all day long. They never get hurt or sick. They watch over us, just like Mom will watch over me. *Oh, Boulder, you fell asleep.*"

Anna covered them both in the magic blanket. She held on to Mr. Thissel in one hand, and put her other arm around Boulder. They fell asleep that way. When Anna fell asleep, Mr. Thissel fell out of her hand and laid down on the blanket. A ray of moonlight beamed down through the trees directly onto them.

In the morning, a bug landed on Anna's face and woke her up. She rubbed her eyes, and everything that happened came flooding back to her. She became confused and sobbed. She didn't want to stay in the forest any longer.

"Wake up, Boulder, it's time for us to get going!"
She shook Boulder but he didn't move.
"Come on, Boulder, we have to go now."

Anna pushed on Boulder's side and saw a puddle of blood. She dropped to the ground and cried, "Boulder, get up! We have to stay together, Boulder!" His body was limp, "Boulder! Can you hear me?"

"Oh no, Boulder, don't leave me! I can't do this without you!"
The fur by his neck was very red.
"You must have got hurt when we jumped out of the window."

Anna started to realize that Boulder was no longer here with her. She knelt by Boulder's side and cried for a long time. She felt so alone. Now it was just her and Mr. Thissel.

She held Boulder's face in her hands and talked to him.
"I'm going to miss you so much, Boulder. You know how much I love you. I know you are in Heaven, now ... you and Mom are together."

A sudden breeze surrounded Anna.
She heard her mother's voice, *"I will always be with you."*

As Anna looked up to the sky, the clouds rolled away and the sun started to shine down through the trees.

She felt her mother's presence.

"Mom, is that you? I heard your voice!"

She knew that she was not alone.

"Mom, I know … you'll always be with me … I am not alone."

Anna knew what she needed to do.

"I love you, Mommy, I remember our plan."

She placed her mother's magic blanket around her beloved Boulder. She hugged him for the last time.

"I will never forget you. You will always be in my heart."

She knew it was time to go.

"Now you have Mom's magic blanket, Boulder. You are in Heaven now, and you are not alone."

She picked up Mr. Thissel and her Violin case.

As she slowly walked away, she repeated to herself, *"I can do this! I can do this!"*

She was so little, she was covered in soot from the smoke, and had blood on her face and clothes. She made it this far, but knew there was a long way to go.

"Okay Mr. Thissel, it's just you and me. We'll make it out of here together. I am glad you're with me, I'll always be here for you. I hope you don't miss Boulder too much … Mom and Boulder are in Heaven watching over us now."

After a long journey, Anna arrived at the edge of the forest. She made it to The Happy Place, where she had come so many times with her mother. A smile came across her face, all of the happy memories filled her mind.

She looked out and saw the lodge down in the valley, it looked so far away. Anna yelled for help but no one could hear her. She had no one, except Mr. Thissel. She started to feel more alone than she had ever felt before.

"Mom, Mom, where are you?" Anna cried out.
She fell to the ground.
Suddenly the swirling wind encircled Anna once again.

A heavenly voice called her by name:
"Anna, I will always be with you."

Anna lifted herself up onto her knees.
She raised her arms up to God.
She cried back to the Heavens, "Mom, is that you? I love you!"
The wind carried her words up over the mountains.

Encouraged by the voice of her mother, she became determined to make it to the lodge. She repeated to herself again, *"I can do this! I can do this!"* Seeing the lodge in the distance gave her hope that she could make it. With a strong will to survive, she kept reminding herself, *"The last door on the end."*

"We better leave right now, Mr. Thissel. There is still a long way to go before we get to the lodge. I'm scared, but I'm sure glad you're here with me. You are my only best friend now, Mr. Thissel"

Without knowing what she might encounter on the way, she began to walk out into the clearing in the direction of the lodge.

"Wow, Thissel, there are so many rocks! I need you to hold on to me Thissel, so you don't fall." Anna struggled to keep her balance while holding onto her mother's violin case. "Thissel, I don't dare drop Mom's violin. She would be so sad if it was broken. Don't be scared Thissel, we will make it. You can do this!"

She carefully made her way forward, but there was no clear trail to follow. "If I fall and get hurt, nobody is here to help me."

The long journey was starting to take a toll on her. As she began to move downhill, the rocks became larger and the ground was more uneven. It was hard to keep her balance, Anna got very tired.

"This is hard Thissel, but we have to keep going. *We have to keep going.* We're getting closer."

She started to see more bushes on the way. She followed along the bushes because it helped her keep her sense of direction.

"Mr. Thissel, look—Blueberries! I'm so hungry I could eat them all! You watch over Mom's violin, Mr. Thissel. Now, don't go anywhere, just stay over by this rock."

Anna set down the violin case, and put Mr. Thissel on top of it.

"These blueberries are so big! Mmm! They taste so good! Blueberries are my favorite! I remember Mommy always put them on my oatmeal."

Anna had found a huge patch of wild blueberry bushes, and it was just at the right time.

"Let's go by those big blueberry bushes over there!"

Anna picked up Mr. Thissel and her mom's violin, and walked down toward a whole bunch of very big blueberry bushes.

"It's too bad you don't like blueberries, Mr. Thissel. Just wait here for me—and remember, be very careful with Mom's violin."

Anna walked into the giant field of blueberry bushes.
"These sure are big bushes, they're even bigger than I am!"

She was eating blueberries by the handful. For the first time since the fire, Anna didn't feel so scared. Unfortunately, that changed very quickly. Anna looked up and saw something very large moving in the distance.

"Mr. Thissel! What's that? Do you see that?"
There was something moving behind the bushes.
"What is that?"
The blueberries she was holding fell out of her hand.
"It's coming closer," she whispered, *"we have to hide!"*
She grabbed Thissel, *"Come hide in these blueberry bushes."*
Anna held Mr. Thissel very close.
"Shhh! Don't make a sound."

Anna crouched down inside of the giant cluster of blueberry bushes. She got very low to the ground and looked out from underneath the big bushes. She felt her heart start to pound.

"It's coming our way," Anna whispered.

She looked out under the bush again.
"Mr. Thissel ... it's a bear!"

Anna curled up to make herself as small as she could be. She looked to see where he was going. His big paws were just a few bushes away. The bear stood up on his hind legs and looked around. It seemed like he was looking right at her!

Anna became so silent, she was almost holding her breath. The ground shook as the bear's big paws came back down to the ground. Her heart was racing now.

"If he sees Mom's violin he might find me!"

Anna thought the bear was looking for her. He started pawing at the bushes, then began to eat the berries right off of the big blueberry bushes! As he ate the blueberries, Anna realized he was just hungry and looking for food, just like she was.

"I hope he's not mad that I ate his lunch!"

Even though she was very scared, Anna still had a hard time not talking to Mr. Thissel. She was lucky that the big bear was hungry, and that he couldn't hear her soft voice.

After he ate most of the berries off of that bush, he heard a noise and raised his head to look. It was another big brown bear! Anna was in luck, he walked over to the other bear and they wandered off together. She didn't move for quite a while, she waited until both of the bears were out of sight.

"Mr. Thissel, we have to leave right now! Let's go in case he comes back."

Anna picked up her mom's violin case and kept moving downhill. She walked in silence for some time until she was past all of the blueberry bushes. After there was some distance between her and the bear, she started to feel a little bit better.

"Thissel, if that bear saw us, you would've had to run! You would be very tired! Let's keep going this way. I can see the lodge, it's getting closer."

Her shoes were slippery on the bottom, and the terrain very rough. This made it hard for Anna to stay on her feet. She was not used to walking off of the trail. She tried to watch where she was going, but she tripped and fell down many times. Her legs and knees got many scrapes and bruises.

Anna came upon a dense forest of old trees. The ground was covered by old branches, tall grass, pinecones, and big roots from the trees. There was no way around it, she had to go through the forest.

"Mr. Thissel, we have to keep going as best we can."

Climbing under and over the branches was exhausting. The further she went downhill, the more steep it became. The ground was still wet and slippery from the morning dew.

"Look at that big tree, Thissel!"
There was a great old tree that had fallen down during a storm.
"Do you think we can walk on top of it?"
The large tree trunk made a bridge to walk across.
"We will have to be very careful."

After stumbling and falling down so many times, Anna thought it would be easier to walk on top of the great big tree trunk. She made her way over to the tree through the tall grass. It was nearly as wide as she was tall. She climbed up and tried to balance herself.

"Hold my hand Mr. Thissel, we need to keep each other balanced."

Compared to little Anna, this tree was very, very large. Anna held her arms out to the side. She had her Mom's violin case in one hand, and Mr. Thissel in the other. The sun shined down through the trees as she carefully walked to the other side.

When she reached the end, she sat down on the tree and carefully lowered the violin case to the ground. She climbed down from the tree and looked off into the distance. The lodge was closer than before, but there was still a long way to go.

"Come on, Thissel, we have to keep going."
Other than birds that flew overhead, the forest was very quiet.
"I am so tired, Thissel, my legs don't want to work anymore."
There was no one to be found anywhere.
"I don't want to be here all alone. We have to keep going."

Anna stumbled along as she continued toward the lodge. The morning dew made the leaves on the ground very slippery. The descent into the valley took every bit of strength that she had left. She was totally exhausted and hurt from tripping and falling all along the journey.

As she stepped down from a big rock, the ground slipped out from underneath her. Anna shrieked! Her mom's violin case flew out of her hands, and she went tumbling down the hill!
Anna was tossed across sharp rocks that scratched and scraped her arms and legs. She tried to grab on to something, but she

couldn't keep herself from falling—she continued to crash on down the hill. Suddenly her head hit very hard on a tree trunk and she came to a abrupt stop. She lost consciousness.

After some time passed, she came to, and began to hear the sound of birds chirping. She opened her eyes and saw them flying in the sky above her. She laid there for quite some time. Her vision was blurry, she was dizzy and disoriented. She tried to stand up, but her legs were unsteady.

Anna started to look around but she could not remember where she was. She was in excruciating pain and had very little strength. There was a large bump on her head, and she still had double vision.

Her mind went blank.

Mr. Thissel and her mom's violin case lay next to her on the ground. She sat by a large rock and tried to remember where to go. The lodge was the only place in sight, it was not too far away.

After a few moments she tried to get back on her feet. Her ankle was sprained from the fall and became very swollen. She was in so much pain she could hardly stand. She picked up Mr. Thissel and her mom's violin case then began to slowly limp along.

"I can do this … I can do this."

Her legs were so unsteady. She tried to keep going but fell again. As she laid on the ground she cried out in pain. Tears were falling from her eyes. She was lost, confused, and wanted to give up.

A strong wind suddenly began to circle around her.
She faintly heard her mother's voice in the wind.

"I will always be with you."

The wind circled around her and she felt an urge to keep going. She made it to her feet, and with the last of her strength she started to put one foot in front of the other. The door of the lodge was getting closer. She knew she just had to make it to that door. Right before she made it to the doorway, she collapsed.

She still carried Mr. Thissel, and her mother's violin case.

7. Safe At Last

The owners of the lodge, Sven and Svea, were inside having lunch. Svea is a kindhearted, middle-aged woman in her early forties with long light brown hair. A jolly soul, her big blue eyes can see the good in everyone she meets.

Sven is a typical Swedish man just a few years older than Svea. He has sandy blonde hair with just a little wave, and a mustache. He likes to sing old Swedish songs, the ones that his father taught him as a child. Sven had hoped that one day he would pass these songs on, but they were not blessed with children.

They live in a spacious cabin near the lodge. During the day, Sven works as a ski instructor and makes skis in his shop. Together, they have run the ski lodge for many years.

Sven came home for lunch, as he read the paper he hummed a tune once in a while. They sat down together and had kaffe while listening to the midday news on the radio.

"We had a frost last night, but it is going to be a very nice day. I can't wait to plant flowers, I just love spring!"

Svea had prepared köttsoppa, a soup with meat, carrots, potatoes and other vegetables. Along with their soup they had knäckebröd with cheese.

There was an interruption on the radio for a special news report. They announced that there had been a fire at a house in

Gällivare during the night. The house burned to the ground and the whole family is presumed to have perished.

Sven and Svea looked at each other in disbelief. Gällivare was such a small town. This tragic news came as a great shock to everyone.

"Let's turn on the TV so we can see what is going on."
The television broadcast gave details about the fire.

"By the time the fire was spotted, it was too late. The family home burned to the ground overnight. Today all that remains are the smoldering ashes from where the home used to stand. The cause of the fire is unknown. First responders were unable to locate any members of the family. The search for the remains of the family will start later today. This evening we will have a special report with more information."

Sven folded the paper just like he always did, and set it down on the table. They both remained silent.

"Oh Svea, my dear … what a shame. That is the family on the other side of the forest, just over the hill. They were so secluded."

"I think a woman and her child lived there. She may have played the violin, when the wind was just right, there were a few times I heard the faint sound of beautiful violin music. I wonder, could that be the family who lived there?"

No words could explain how they felt.
"Let's say a prayer for this family."
They looked into each others eyes and held hands.

"Dear Lord and Heavenly Father,
    Please bless the souls of this family.
    Welcome them to your kingdom in heaven.
    Embrace them with your loving arms.
    Send your angels to care for their loved ones.
    In Jesus' name we pray, amen."

Over the years Sven and Svea had learned that some things in life cannot be changed, and that these things should be left in God's hands. They had to go forward with the day, but Svea was still very distraught.

"I had work to do today, but now I just can't do anything. They may not have lived next door, but I feel like I knew this family."

Just then, they both heard a rustling noise outside.
"I guess it must be the wind?"
Sven and Svea both looked puzzled.

They finished lunch and kaffe without much conversation. Sven forced a smile as he put on his jacket.

"Well, I best be getting some work done now."

Sven put his arms around Svea and kissed her goodbye. He recalled when they were young. Even now, the love and deep passion they have for each other remains. With a slight pat on her butt, he turned and walked towards the door.

"I'll see you at dinner time!"

Sven was still looking back at Svea as he opened the door. Suddenly there was a strange sound from outside. He looked up and saw this small, lost little girl.

Her clothes were tattered and torn, covered in dirt and blood. Her blond hair was full of soot. She was holding a frayed and funny looking teddy bear. She was trembling and had a blank stare. She stumbled toward the door, fell, and passed out.

"Svea, come here right now!"
"Oh my!"
Svea took one look at the little girl and her heart sank.
"We will help you, little one. You are safe now, you are safe."
Sven gently wrapped his jacket around her, and picked her up.
"Everything will be okay."

As he carried her into the house, Sven noticed that her tears had made white streaks through the soot that covered her face.

Seeing the little girl in such bad shape made Svea very worried and anxious. She was crying as she paced the floor. She became very tense when she got nervous.

"Oh dear, this little girl just has to make it!"
She was flipping her apron up and down.
"What can we do? We need help."

"Call Dr. Leif, just make up a reason for him to come here. Say you have chest pain, just have him come right away! I'll stay with the little one."

Svea sat next to the little girl on the bed. She wiped the tears from her face and spoke softly to console her.

"You will be alright. You are safe here with us. Dr. Leif will be here soon. He will help you, he is a great doctor."

The little girl didn't respond, she only whimpered in pain. Sven came back with a look of relief.

"Dr. Leif is on his way."

As they waited for the doctor to arrive, they got warm water and towels to clean her up a bit. They did what they could to make her comfortable. The little girl was very pale.

"Oh, Sven, I think she's passed out."
Just then, Dr. Leif knocked on the door.
"I am so glad he's here, she needs help now!"
Svea walked to the door to let him in.

"Dr. Leif, come in quickly. You won't believe what happened!"
Svea began to explain as he walked inside.
"This poor little girl was outside our door…"
Dr. Leif set down his medicine bag and took off his coat.
"She is in such bad shape," Svea continued, "I'm so glad you're here. We're lucky we found her!"

Sven showed Dr. Leif where the little girl was resting.
"She is covered in cuts and bruises and she isn't talking."
He opened the door and there she was, so little and all alone.
"There's a huge bump on her head that had been bleeding."
"Please, Doctor, help her—"

Dr. Leif walked over to the bedside. He opened his black bag, took out his supplies, and started to check her injuries. Sven and Svea stayed at the end of the bed. Their faces had a look of great concern. Dr. Leif could see that their hearts went out to this young child.

Svea wrung her hands, "Where do you think she came from?"

Dr. Leif mentioned the fire during the night. Sven and Svea looked at each other. Their eyes met at the same time; somehow, they both knew. Svea wiped a tear from her eyes.

"I am just glad that she is here with us."

The little girl had many cuts and scrapes on her arms and legs; she had bug bites and even a few burns on her legs. By the patch of blood in her hair, Dr. Leif found a very large bump on her head. He checked her reflexes and looked for signs of a concussion. He checked her eyes and noticed her pupils were larger than normal. She was dehydrated and exhausted.

Tears filled Svea's eyes as she thought of what that little girl had witnessed.

Dr. Leif asked the child, "What is your name?"
She didn't answer, only stared into space.

Dr. Leif continued to speak to her, "You will be alright little lady. Everything will be OK. Don't be afraid. These are two great people and they will take good care of you."

Dr. Leif covered her up with a blanket to keep her warm and she gently closed her eyes. They quietly left the room to have a discussion. They went into the kitchen and Sven poured them each a cup of kaffe.

"It appears she has a severe concussion. She has many bruises and abrasions, and some first degree burns. She is in shock and needs a great deal of rest and care."

Sven and Svea assured Dr. Leif they would take care of her.
"We will do whatever it takes to help her, Doctor."
"She is so small, and all alone ... she needs help."
"Tell us what we to do and we will see that it is done."

Dr. Leif took a long pause as he stared at the floor.
"This child must've escaped from the house that burned down."

Just then an update came on the news regarding the fire. The news anchor referred to the house as *"the house on the hill."* He reported that a search has been completed and that no one survived.

Pictures of the house were shown—it had burned to the ground. The ashes were still smoldering. Firefighters were still on the scene. People from all over town showed up in disbelief of this great tragedy. The reporter spoke with one of the townspeople that arrived on the scene.

A young mother sobbed as she described, "The young lady who lived here needed help. She was kept very isolated. They couldn't get away from this evil place. This never should have happened ... they needed help."

The anchorman mentioned that the townspeople are arranging a memorial service next Saturday. Sven turned off the TV.

In a pleading voice, he asked Dr. Leif, "Will the authorities have to be notified, since both of her parents are deceased?" Before the doctor could answer, Sven continued.

"Lord knows what she has been through. Dr. Leif, no one knows she is here, and you know we have wanted a child for a long time. We can love her and take care of her. We have the patience to give her the care that she needs. She needs us."

Svea added, "Please, Doctor, if you help us, we will give her the best care and life that we can. I've always wanted to have a daughter ... I had a sister, Greta Karlsson ... she had a baby girl that died soon after she was born. My sister had cancer ... a short time later, she passed away. Her baby was born at a hospital in Uppsala, and would be about the same age as this little girl. You could switch the birth certificates—"

Dr. Leif interrupted, "Stop right there! What you want me to do is illegal. I could lose my license to practice medicine forever."

Sven stepped forward, "Doctor, no one knows she is here but us. We would do everything in our power to care for her. She is so little. Please, I beg of you ... let us give this little girl the happy life she deserves."

Dr. Leif started to become very concerned and worried. "According to law, I have to report it."

Sven asked desperately, "Please Dr. Leif, don't do anything yet. She needs lots of good care. We can help. Just tell us what we need to do. On the news, they said that everyone perished in the fire. At least give us a few days and see what happens. Please, she's going to need a family that will love her. Just a few days."

Dr. Leif took a long, sincere look at his two old friends. Their look of desperation overcame him. Their fate and the child's future depend on his decision. In his mind, he recognized the great hope they had. They so dearly wanted to help this small, and now homeless little girl.

The short moment felt like a long silence. Dr. Leif cleared his throat, and brushed his face with his hand.

"It seems God has put us in this situation for a reason. How the Lord put her on your doorstep, I will never know. We will see how it goes for a few days. Then we'll figure out what the next step will be. As a doctor, I've taken the Hippocratic oath. I must treat the ill to the best of my ability, and preserve my patient's privacy. I will fulfill my oath to keep her safe from harm."

Sven, Svea, and Dr. Leaf vowed that for now they would keep her a secret. The doctor was very serious as he explained how to care for the little girl.

"This is what you have to do. First, she needs a bath in lukewarm soda water. Use this cream to treat her burns twice a day. She needs rest and lots of fluids so her body can heal. Keep the dressings on her wounds clean so they don't become infected. This medicine will help her rest so she can recover, give it to her twice a day. Make sure one of you stays with her at all times. I will check in with you each day in case of any complications."

Svea graciously thanked Dr. Leif, "I will do everything I can to make her well again. Bless you, Dr. Leif. Thank you for this chance to have this little one in our lives."

Svea quietly opened the bedroom door. She walked softly over to the bed and looked closely at the little girl. She thought to herself, "Somehow, I feel like I know you … I've heard the faint sound of violins blowing in the wind many times. It was so beautiful. That sound left a memory in my heart. Somehow I feel like I know you, little one."

Svea gently took off the little blue gingham dress, ever so slowly not wake her. It was torn, blood-splattered, and smelled strongly of smoke.

She knew, "This is the girl from the fire."

A seamstress herself, Svea could tell that very loving hands had sewn the stitches of this beautiful dress. Svea gently washed her with the soda water. She whimpered a few times. Svea stroked her little hand and whispered, "You are a blessing. You were sent to us for a reason. We will love you, and take care of you."

Svea cleaned and dressed her burns, using the cream Dr. Leif had given her. When she finished, she wrapped her in a soft pink blanket that she made so long ago. Svea often wished she would have a little girl of her own to use it. She looked at her tiny face as she lay fast asleep. Svea saw the child in a way only a mother can see. She quietly sat on the bed and stroked her hair gently. She began to softly sing the Byssan Lull, an old Swedish lullaby that she learned as a child and loved very much.

Dr. Leif and Sven were just outside the door when they heard Svea softly singing. They stopped and opened the door just wide enough to see. This memory of Svea singing to the little girl was one they would never forget.

Sven could feel the love in his wife's soft voice. The miracle they had hoped for and dreamed of for so many years was right before his eyes. His dear Svea looked like an angel.

As the sun set over the hill, a bounding light filled the room! It illuminated his very soul. Suddenly he felt overwhelmed and big tears fell from his eyes. He knew they couldn't part with this beautiful child that had appeared from nowhere.

They took turns caring for the little girl all throughout the night. The next morning, Dr. Leif called to see how she was doing.

Sven answered the phone, "I am so glad you called!"
"How is she doing?"
"She is doing very well. Svea is taking good care of her, she got her to drink some water and juice."
"That's good news. I'll come over after my rounds at the hospital. I'll be there in just a few hours."

When Dr. Leif arrived, Sven answered the door. The doctor looked very worried.

"Sven, have you seen the news? They're searching through the ruins of the fire before making out the death certificates."

Sven looked deep into his old friends' eyes.
"I hope somehow we can keep her."
"Let's see what they come up with, we'll see where we stand."
Svea scrunched up her apron as they spoke.
"The most important thing now is getting the child well."
"We followed your instructions, she's still sleeping …"
"I'll go back and check on her, wait here."

Dr. Leif took his black bag and went to see the little girl. He checked her wounds, and the bump on her head. He checked for a fever, and listened to her lungs. He changed the cream for the burns to one that would work faster. When he was finished, he wrapped the blanket gently around her shoulders and took a long look at this innocent little girl.

He thought, "I will do my best to make this happen."
He quietly left the room.

He returned to the living room and shared his concerns with Sven and Svea.

"You've done a good job. Her lungs are clearing up, and the wounds will heal. However, I am worried about the trauma and shock the child went through. We don't know what she experienced before she arrived. She needs the exceptional care have been giving her. Let's keep her awake a little more and see what she has to say. Try to get her to eat and drink so she can regain her strength. If you need anything, call me."

The next day on the morning news, the police and the fire inspectors confirmed that the whole family had perished. The fire was so hot that the bodies became cremated. This tragic news affected the entire town.

The bench that JP made for Anna was still near the remains of the house. People continued to visit; they started to leave flowers next to Anna's rock friends. The visitors all said prayers for Anaya's father, Mr. Magnusson.

When he visited the house, he became overwhelmed with sorrow. He was taken away by a police car and no one has seen him since.

The next day, there was another update on the news. Mr. Magnusson visited the church and changed the arrangements for the memorial service. He wanted the service to be very traditional and elegant. He was very precise in explaining his wishes.

Only the ashes of his daughter and little Anna were to be in this service. They will have a beautiful ivory casket with angels on all sides. A light gray monument made of marble will be inscribed with the message '*Love is eternal*' beside their names, their dates of birth, and death. Everyone will gather in the church cemetery, where there will be a special blessing.

The sculptor, Pierre, has begun work on a statue of little Anna playing the violin. This information was shared with the news by the Gällivare Ladies. Commemoration of the statue will be scheduled once it has been completed.

Suddenly, there came an unexpected knock at the door. Sven went to see who it was. When he opened the door, he was surprised to see Dr. Leif.

"Oh, Dr. Leif, come inside!"
With a big smile, he slammed a copy of the gazette on the table. "What do you think of this?"

In the newspaper they saw the report from the fire inspector. It indicated that there were no survivors—everyone had perished in the fire. Sven and Svea began to feel that this may truly be possible. They may finally become a mother and father.

Just as Anaya wanted, little Anna had completed her journey to the lodge. Her new life was just beginning, and she wouldn't live in fear ever again.

"It will be complicated," Dr. Leif stated. "If anyone finds out, I will lose my license and my reputation. We have to be very secretive because this *is* illegal."

Svea was filled with joy, she was so excited she could hardly speak. She kept flipping her apron up and down.

"This means we can keep her!"
They both gave Dr. Leif a big hug!
"Thank you, Doctor!"
"This is the greatest blessing we could ever ask for."

After their discussion with Dr. Leif, Sven and Svea felt relieved. For many years they had always wished to have a child of their own.

Sven and Svea were close friends with all of the townspeople. They've watched as their friends started families, and saw their children grow up before their eyes. Sven had taught many of them how to ski. For the first time, Svea believed that their dream of having a daughter may finally come true.

8. Anna Will Be Remembered

Dr. Leif ran into JP while on his way to check on the little one. They talked about the family that passed away in the fire. JP mentioned that Anaya and Anna were very isolated. He was the only one to visit them, he saw them when he delivered the mail. It became clear to Dr. Leif that JP was devastated.

"Over the years, I brought Anna so many books to read. She could read at a fourth grade level. She was like a daughter to me. Since the age of three, her mother taught her how to read music and play the violin. They would go to a special place together and practice their violins, they called it The Happy Place. She could play many different types of songs right along with her mother. They would find special rocks together and little Anna would paint them. She called them her friends. She would have tea parties with them and carry on long conversations, and even read stories to them. She didn't have any real friends, only her rocks."

Recalling these memories caused JP to break down in tears. Before he walked away, he mentioned that he will be speaking at the service on Saturday.

JP's words lingered in Dr. Leif's mind all the way to the lodge. When he arrived, he told Sven and Svea how important it was that they get the little one some new books to read.

"We need to get her books to read right away. It will help keep her mind busy. Story books with pictures will bring her some happiness. JP mentioned that she can read at a fourth grade level.

She is starting to recover, but it will take a long time until she becomes a normal little girl again."

Sven promised, "We'll get new books for her right away."
"Have you heard any new news about the fire?" Dr. Leif asked.
"No, we haven't, let's check on the television."

Sven turned on the news to see if there were any updates. Many people were visiting the old house, they cried as they left flowers. Just then the reporter started to make an announcement regarding the funeral.

"Anyone who would like to help with the service, speak, or say a special prayer can sign up at the church. Mr. Magnusson asked that we send a special thank you to everyone for all the kindness that they've shown him."

"Look how many people are there visiting," Svea pointed out.
In the background, you could hear people talking, "This is such a tragedy. This never should have happened. It's so sad."

Sven walked into the kitchen and got kaffe for Svea and Dr. Leif. They had kaffe and hallongrottor cookies together. Dr. Leif felt distraught, he was still thinking about his conversation with JP.

"It looks like everything will work out well. Let your friends know that you are in the process of adopting a child, and that it will be finalized within the next few months. Remember to keep her out of sight. I have to go now, but keep me informed of any changes."

On Saturday afternoon Sven left to go to the church service. Normally they would both have gone, but Svea stayed with the little one. It was a lovely spring day, the sun was shining, and there was a slight breeze.

The church looked so beautiful. A large spray of pink roses was placed on each side of the church doors. At the front of the church, there was an arch of pink rosebuds. The altar looked very serene, it had tall flowers in the back and white spider chrysanthemums in the shape of a heart on both sides. It was so heavenly. The casket held two silver vases of ashes that were set upon large sprays of white and pink roses. Carvings of each of the seven angels flanked the sides of the casket and were lit up by candles.

Mr. Magnusson stood to the right of the casket. He looked very sad and tired, yet distinguished. JP stood on the left, he had a hard time keeping it together.

When the service started, the sound of the organ filled the entire church. Reverend Gabriel began the service with stories from Anaya's childhood. He mentioned the times that Anaya and her father played their violins together at the church. After he spoke, he led the congregation in prayer.

JP spoke next, he did his best to hold back his tears as he stood before the altar. He had life-size portraits made from the photos that he had taken of Anna.

JP pointed towards the pictures, "This is Anna ... her life ended very short of what it should have been. Her mother gave her the very best life that she could. This picture was taken only one week ago, when she played her violin for me for the very first time. I would like to share this special video of her great performance with you. You can see and hear the happiness of this beautiful child as she played two of the songs which her mother had taught her."

JP prepared to play the video of the first song. The townspeople smiled and cried as they watched her play the violin and dance. During the video, Mr. Magnusson was sobbing. He remembered when Anaya was young and he first taught her to play the violin. Anna, the grandchild he never met, reminded him so much of his beloved daughter.

"In the next video, Anna shares a very special lesson about the violin that her mother taught her. Remember this message as you watch her next performance. You will hear our national anthem played as you've never heard it before."

JP started the video, it began with Anna's special message:

"My mom told me a secret! *'The violin has a soul, it can project emotions—love, happiness, and excitement! If you send your feelings into the violin, and put your soul into the strings, you can create magic!'* "

This was the same lesson that Mr. Magnusson taught Anaya when she was young. Hearing these words from little Anna broke his heart.

Everyone stood up when Anna began to play. They were in awe of her amazing talent. By the end, they all had tears in their eyes. There was a very solemn moment of silence.

After the video, JP showed the last picture of Anna next to her dog Boulder. She was barefoot, wore her little blue nightgown, and had JP's postman hat on her head. She had her arms around Boulder, and a big smile on her face.

JP's daughters walked up to the altar. They each placed a vase of wildflowers next to the casket, and then sat back down. JP left the picture up as he started to talk about little Anna. Despite his regret, his words carried a message of love.

"This young girl was a musical prodigy. She deserved to live. By the age of five she could read at the fourth grade level. Her mother taught her to play the violin like a master violinist. She was wise beyond her years and had a great sense of humor. Just last week," his voice started to crack, "I found out how much she loves ice cream—"

He was unable to go on. Reverend Gabriel put his arm around JP to comfort him, and he stepped back. The Reverend said a prayer before they concluded the service.

"Dear Heavenly Father,
Today we gather to honor the life of Anaya and her daughter Anna. Their presence will be greatly missed. We accept that the time has come for them to take their place by your side within the gates of your kingdom in heaven.

"Although their time here was brief, we thank you for blessing us by bringing them into this world. We pray that they look down upon us with a loving heart. Amen."

9. Meeting An Old Friend

After a few weeks went by, the townspeople started to return to normal everyday life. Dr. Leif continued to visit and check on the little one almost daily. Together, they started to discuss how to make this work.

One day, while Dr. Leif was visiting, the little one walked out of the bedroom and saw them all talking. She just stood there and stared straight ahead.

"Well hello there, little one!"
Dr. Leif noticed she had a slight smile, and he smiled too.
"Come to the kitchen, have something to eat and drink."

The little girl had a glass of milk and grabbed a cookie, then went back in her new bedroom to rest. Dr. Leif turned to Sven and Svea, "She is ready for more activities, and she should take a short walk each day. But remember, don't let anyone see her yet."

Svea went into the bedroom to check on the little girl.
"We're going to take good care of you. You're safe here."

The little one nodded her head as she finished her cookie. Svea tucked her in, and after a quick hug she left the room.

In the living room, Sven and Dr. Leif were making a plan for the next day. They wanted to ensure that the little girl started to eat more food and get more activity each day. They wanted her to have a good start in her new life. Dr. Leif stressed that they had to keep her presence a secret for quite a while.

The next day, shortly after the morning news, Dr. Leif came to visit again. Sven showed Dr. Leif to the living room. He was surprised to see Svea and the little one sitting there together.

"How are you today, sweetheart?" Dr. Leif asked.
The little one didn't say a word.
"She still hasn't said anything yet," Svea replied.

Dr. Leif explained that it may take a while until she begins to speak. She had been very traumatized. Sven went to the fireplace to build a fire. When he tried to start the fire, the little girl became hysterical, she cried and screamed. They tried to calm her, but nothing worked. Dr. Leif gave her some medicine to help her calm down. Svea and the little one went back to her bedroom. She stayed with her until she fell asleep.

In the kitchen, they all sat down together around the table to have fika, the traditional Swedish coffee break. Sven prepared three cups of kaffe latte and served kanelbullar, Swedish cinnamon buns. They had many things to discuss.

"It is important that we talk about how we should proceed. We need to discuss how to make this work."

"Dr. Leif, my sister had a baby about six years ago. The baby died shortly after birth, and my sister passed away a year later from leukemia."

Svea was very sad as she shared the story.

"The baby was a girl. When my sister died, I was given a copy of her daughter's birth certificate. I have both of their birth and death certificates right here. Can we do something with this?"

With a wrinkled brow, Dr. Leif carefully put on his glasses. He slowly unfolded the papers and began to examine them. He checked over the documents very carefully.

After a few ah-ha's, he said, "I see she was not married."
He rubbed his hands together, his face lit up with a great idea.

"An old friend of mine from medical school has a practice in Uppsala—his name is Erick. With his help, we may be able to use her birth certificate. I will call him tonight."

They hoped that the plan would be successful. As they finished their kaffe, Sven and Svea expressed their gratification.

"Thank you, Dr. Leif. You know that we have always wanted to have a child. We never imagined that it would happen this way."

Dr. Leif picked up his coat and medicine bag.
"I will call you tomorrow after I speak with Erick."
Sven shook his hand, "Thank you, Dr. Leif. God bless you."

The phone rang the following morning, and it was Dr. Leif. He gave Sven all of the details.

"I called my friend Erick and set up a meeting with him. I will visit him so we can discuss the matter further. I will leave on the train this evening and reach Uppsala tomorrow night. I'll stay with Erick at his home and we'll figure out what can be done. He is a well known doctor in Uppsala and has access to the records department at the Kommunhus. I will call you as soon as I get back. Meanwhile, make sure the little girl is able to get more comfortable with her surroundings."

After the phone call Sven told Svea the good news. They both went to check on the little one and saw that she was still sleeping. They stood by her bedside; she had such peaceful look upon her face.

They glanced at each other and somehow their hearts knew this little girl would soon become their daughter.

It was very late in the evening when the train arrived in Uppsala. Dr. Leif got off the train and waited for Erick to arrive. A dense fog had formed around the station. He paced back and forth hoping that Erick would be on time. Dr. Leif noticed the silhouette of a man approaching in the fog. The man was walking toward him with a slight limp and a cane. As he came closer, he knew that it was his friend Erick.

"Erick, my dear friend, it's very nice to see you again!"
They greeted each other with a handshake.
"I am glad to see you too! Welcome to Uppsala!"
They walked together back to Erick's car.
"It's been so many years, my how time flies!"

As they drove away the car disappeared into the fog. After a short drive they arrived at his home. A long curved driveway led to the house. Pillars flanked the double doors of a very elegant entryway. Light from inside of the house shined out through large arched windows.

Leif was impressed by his friend's accomplishments. He could tell Erick had done well in his practice. A butler took their coats and they went to the living room. Their conversation quickly got to the point of Leif's visit.

"Well, Doctor, tell me what the problem is and we'll see what we can do."

"Erick, do you remember Sven and Svea? They married and settled in Gällivare. A few years later, they opened a ski lodge together. They have always wanted to have a family, but were never blessed with children. I have a plan to help them adopt a child who desperately needs a loving family—they are caring for the little girl at this time. The two of us can make this happen. Svea's sister had a child that passed away shortly after birth, and the mother passed away one year later. There was no father listed on the birth or death certificates."

Erick was surprised to hear this request. It was very out of the ordinary, and also very illegal. They spoke further about the situation as Erick looked over the two birth certificates. As Leif told him more about the situation, he began to understand the great care that Sven and Svea could provide for this child who is so greatly in need of a new beginning.

Dr. Erick paused in deep thought.

"We will go to the Kommunhus in the morning. We will make this happen, and she can begin her new life."

They stayed up until after midnight, talking and laughing about old college days. After a few drinks, they talked about Sigurd and Nels, two trouble makers they knew in medical school.

"Remember when Nels stole the dean's brand new car?"
Erick laughed, "Yeah, he sunk it in the river!"
"Only after he took it for a joy ride and dented up the fenders!"
"Did he ever get his diploma?"
"I don't know, I'd be surprised if he did!"

They laughed aloud as they recalled the good old days.
"How about that time Nels set you up on a blind date?"

"Nels told everyone you were going on a date with Viktoria, the prettiest girl on campus! You shined your shoes and put pomade in your hair."

Erick became embarrassed as Leif recalled the story.

"You wore your best suit, and even bought flowers! Nels hid across the street to watch when you went to pick her up. When she opened the door, it wasn't Viktoria, it was Nina! I don't think that shy young lady had ever been on a date, but she sure was happy to see you. You just smiled and handed her the flowers, then you took her hand and the two of you left together. Nels laughed about that for weeks."

Leif was amused by the old stories.
"Did you ever get married, Erick?"

With a sad look on his face, Erick replied, "Well, you know … I married that lovely lady. We had two beautiful daughters. Our girls are both nurses now, they work at the hospital. They're both married. Sara has a daughter, and Laura has a son and a daughter. We had a wonderful life … Nina passed away about two years ago. She was the love of my life. I sure miss her … cancer took her from us in just three months."

Erick's head hung low, he continued on with tears in his eyes.

"Life goes on, like it or not. You know, Nina had a crush on me for a long time and I never knew it. She was just a shy girl with a very beautiful heart."

The two old friends talked, cried, and laughed together until late in the night. Finally they prepared to get some rest. Before bed, Erick turned off the lamp and pledged that he would help.

"I will help you. Tomorrow morning we will get this done."

This next morning Erick and Leif began to put the plan in motion. They left together and drove to the Kommunhus.

"I have access to all the original birth and death certificates. No one works in the record department on Sunday. I can pull the records myself without putting anyone else in jeopardy."

A guard greeted them as they approached the entrance.
"Good morning, Dr. Erick!"
"Good morning, Oskar!"

All you could hear was their footsteps as they walked down the long hallway. Above the door to the records department, Leif noticed a sign indicating it is a restricted area. They went inside to retrieve the files and closed the door behind them.

"Let's find the original documents for Greta Karlsson."
They went through many files, before finding the right one.

Erick spoke with a sense of urgency, "Okay, here we go. The birth and death certificates are both here. Let's hurry up and get this done, so we can get out of here!"

Dr. Leif's eyes lit up; he lifted one eyebrow, just like the old days when he got a bright idea. They read the birth certificate for Greta's daughter, Kaya Sue Karlsson.

"Greta wasn't married, so she has the same maiden name as her sister, Svea Karlsson."

"That's in our favor. Let's change Greta to Svea on the new certificate. Then we will put Svea's married name in place of Karlsson. Since the girls would be about the same age, we will keep the birth date the same. We'll list Sven as the father, Sven J. Nilsson, and Svea as the mother, Svea L. Nilsson. We'll change the child's name, from Kaya Sue Karlsson, to Kaya Sue Nilsson. This will be her new name."

Dr. Erick made two copies of the new birth certificate, one for the records department, and one for her new parents. They put the official stamp on both of the new birth certificates.

"Destroy the old death certificate and take this new birth certificate with you. It will be as if the child never passed away. As far as anyone knows, she was born here in Uppsala. She will live on as Kaya Sue Nilsson."

"Erick … we just changed the course of their lives. After all the tragedy she's faced, this little girl now has a new chance at life. You did a good thing, Sven and Svea will be forever grateful. Thank you, my old friend."

"You're the one who helped me understand how much she needs a loving home. You're welcome, my friend—now, let's leave before anyone sees us."

Erick drove Leif to the train station, they chatted all the way there. Leif looked right into Erick's eyes, "We should get together soon. It would be wonderful to meet your children, and your grandchildren."

Erick was silent for a moment before he explained the dire circumstances.

"Leif ... I only have a few months left. I have stomach cancer. This will be our last goodbye."

Leif didn't know what to say.

"Time runs out for all of us sooner than we think. One day we will all be together again ... Now I understand why you agreed to the plan."

They pulled up to the train station, and Erick walked with him to the train. Leif wiped a tear from his eye. He was heartbroken to learn that he would soon lose his old best friend. With a brief hug and a handshake, they parted ways for the last time.

"May God bless you, and your family."
"Until we meet again."

Leif looked back and saw his Erick standing there alone; he waved to him through the window. A feeling of sadness set in as the train started to pull away. Erick gave him a salute, and Leif saluted him back. He watched as his friend faded into the distance.

On the long train ride home, all he could think of is how excited Sven and Svea would be to hear the good news. He had his dinner on the train and watched beautiful scenery go by. The train traveled north along the Gulf of Bothnia before reaching Umeå, where it turned inland toward Gällivare. He read one of his favorite books until he fell asleep.

The next morning he awoke and saw the sun rising over the horizon. He thought of what a great blessing life truly is. He was thankful that this little girl now had a new beginning with a family that loved her.

When the train arrived in Gällivare, Dr. Leif drove home and got ready to go check on the little girl. Dr. Leif slowly got out of his car when he reached the lodge, he saw Svea running toward him. Svea was thrilled that he had returned and wanted to know what happened.

"Did Erick help you? Did you do it?"
"Settle down now, go get Sven and I'll explain to you both at the same time."

Svea went inside to get Sven, moments later they came outside together. She held on to Sven's hand and was almost pulling him along behind her.

"Let's take a seat here at the round table in the yard."

Dr. Leif deliberately paused for a moment of silence. He started to get a big grin on his face. Svea impatiently tapped her fingers on the table.

"Dr. Lief, please tell us, we need to know what happened!" Dr. Leif opened his bag and took out a large envelope. "Well ... it's official, she is now your daughter!"

Dr. Leif handed them the envelope containing the birth certificate. Svea and Sven stood up and hugged each other, then walked over to the doctor, and put their arms around him.

"Thank you! Thank you, Dr. Leif!"
"We are a family now!"

"Doctor, I've made some little dresses for her while she was resting. She needs some new clothes, but I don't want anyone to wonder why we're shopping for a little girl."

"Well, you don't have to worry about that. Erick and I stopped at a small shop, we bought everything she needed. The clerk helped us with the sizes, and we had them boxed up. It is our gift to her. We got her socks, undergarments, a slip, a robe, and a pair of blue shoes."

"Thank you, Doctor, let's go and see if she is awake!"

They went inside and looked in the bedroom, but saw that the bed was empty. Svea checked in the kitchen, she was not there! Sven was looking around the house, all the while saying, "Where is she? Where is she?"

"Check by the big window. She spends a lot of time looking out towards the hill."

Dr. Leif walked out onto the porch that faces the hill. He saw her behind the house just staring out into space.

In a soft voice, he asked, "Well, little lady, how are you today?"

She recognized his voice and turned towards him. For the first time, her big blue eyes showed a glimmer of happiness. For just a second, they connected—she still didn't say a word.

Dr. Leif called out to Sven and Svea, "I found her!"

The doctor wanted her to know that she is in a loving home. It was important to him that she knew how much they all cared for her.

"Sven, I will go get the gifts from the car."
"Okay, we will meet you in the family room."

When Dr. Leif returned they were all seated on the sofa. He handed the little one a package, and they waited to see her reaction. She looked happy, but she didn't know what to do.

Sven helped her open the box, and they saw the first sign of happiness. They all laughed as she held up each pair of panties and made a high pitch squeal! She tried on the robe and walked around while they all clapped their hands. The shoes were the hit of the day. Once she got the blue shoes on, she rubbed them with her hands to polish them.

They all danced with her in her new blue shoes. When she sat down, she brought her knees up and hugged her new shoes. The next day, Sven told Dr. Leif that she slept in her blue shoes that night.

Once they had opened all of the gifts, Dr. Leif took Sven and Svea aside for a brief talk. He cleared his throat before he began to speak.

"I had a discussion with a friend of mine who is a neurologist, and an expert in psychology. We talked about the little one. We believe she will have a great deal of post traumatic stress. In severe cases, the mind will block out tragic events to protect itself. This tragedy may have been so immense that it causes memory loss … she may have amnesia.

"We need to help her make new happy memories as soon as possible. This will help her to resume a normal life. It's possible that will have some flashbacks, but they should be very brief. We need to start planning more activities for her, things like baking, playing games, or doing puzzles. We need to get her some new books and toys so that she can learn and play."

Dr. Leif stayed to visit for a short time to see how the little one was doing. He was glad just to see her walking around, it surprised him to see her dancing with Sven and Svea. Despite the trauma she had been through, there was a much brighter future ahead.

Sven and Svea were so happy to receive this great news. They all had a wonderful day together. That evening, Svea made a great dinner to celebrate the occasion. The little one wanted to help, so Svea taught her how to set the table.

After dinner, Svea laid out some blankets and pillows on the living room floor, then she brought in the tall chairs from the dining room. She covered them with a king size sheet to make a fort.

"What do you think of that?" Svea asked.

The little one was so impressed, she clapped her hands and crawled right inside.

"When I was little, my grandmother and I made forts like this."
Svea brought her milk and cookies from the kitchen.
"If you want to pick out a book, I'll read it to you."

She quickly ran into her room and came back with one of her new books. They all crawled into the fort together. It had started raining outside and became the perfect cozy little evening. They had such a great time together as a family. As the little one munched on her cookies, she listened closely to every word.

After they finished the story, Sven promised that he and Svea would always be here to look out for her and to protect her.

"You know, little one ... I want to tell you something very important. Svea and I love you very much ... you never need to be afraid, we want you to have a good life. If you would like to stay here with us, you can be our little girl. We will protect you, care for you, and will always be here for you. Together we can be a happy family."

The little one always wanted to have a normal, happy, family life. This is what Anaya wanted too. She stared at them with her big blue eyes. After a moment, she put her arms around both of them and gave them the biggest hug they ever had! For the first time they felt like a real family.

"If you would like to, you can call us Mom and Dad, and we'll call you Kaya Sue."

10. Kaya's New Life

Sven takes care of the ski lodge during the day, and makes skis in his workshop. All throughout the winter season he sells them to visitors at the lodge. Svea has been spending all of her time with Kaya while Sven is at work.

This is the slow time of the year, but the restaurant at the lodge stays busy year round. Svea had started to let people know they are in the process of adopting a little girl, she told her close friends and regular customers at the lodge. She would let them know if the adoption was approved within the next month. Maryann and Corrine heard her talking about the adoption too, which means word was sure to travel quickly! Everyone was so happy when they heard the news.

Svea and Kaya loved to work together in their flower garden behind the house. Until they could introduce Kaya to all of their friends, this was the only place where Kaya could go to be outside. It just so happens that the garden was her favorite place to be.

One evening when no one was around, Svea and Kaya went to visit Sven in his workshop. He was so surprised! He enjoyed showing Kaya all the tools he uses to make skis.

"I'll make a special pair of skis just for you! Stand up straight and I'll measure your height."

Kaya stood real tall with a big smile on her face as Sven took down some notes.

"Let me see now, my little snow angel."
Sven picked up a measuring tape from his tool bench.
"Wow, you are 94 centimeters!"
Kaya proudly looked up at Svea and smiled.
"Someday I'll teach you to ski, you will soar just like a bird!"

Kaya smiled and giggled. Sven was so happy to hear her voice.
She brought so much happiness into their lives.

"I'm happy you came to see me at work. This is where I go
every day."
"We should go home soon and get dinner ready."

Svea and Kaya held hands as they prepared to leave. As he
stood up, Sven bumped into his workbench, one of the tools fell
down and landed on his foot. He let out a yelp and winced in pain!

"Ouch! Oh my, I am so clumsy!"
Kaya ran over and covered his mouth with her hand.
She cried, "No, no, Daddy, you can't be clumsy!"

Kaya put her arms around his neck, and snuggled her face into
his shoulder. She whispered, "Don't ever leave me, Daddy."

Sven forgot about his pain, he picked her up and held her up
high in the air.

"My little Kaya, Svea and I will never leave you—we will be
here for you forever! I love you, and Svea loves you too. We are all
blessed to have each other."

Svea was delighted, her smile was so big it covered her whole
face! She couldn't wait until Kaya won't have to hide any longer.

"I'll close the shop early and help you make dinner. We can all go home together."

He picked up Kaya and carried her as they walked out of the shop; she reached and pulled the string to turn off the light. What a sight to behold, they were now a happy family.

--

Kaya continued to recover a little bit each day. They began to make new memories together. Svea got her a few new tools for working in the garden. Kaya started to get stronger; she enjoyed going outside in the backyard.

Even though the paperwork was complete, they still had to be cautious. No one could see her until after the adoption. If anyone from town saw her they would become very suspicious.

Kaya needed a makeover to keep her from being recognized by the townspeople. Svea got all the things she needed to color Kaya's hair, and give her a haircut. Kaya watched as Svea laid out the towels, hair cutting scissors, and some pretty ribbons.

"Kaya, I want to give you a beautiful new hairstyle! Come sit up here on this chair. We'll make you into a beautiful princess!"

Svea put a cape around her, and Kaya sat very still as Svea started to clip her hair. She looked scared so Svea handed the scissors over to her.

"See, they won't hurt you. I will be very careful."
Kaya nodded her head; Svea talked while cutting her hair.

"I wonder if Dad will recognize you when he comes home from work. You know, you're going to make a lot of new friends here. Soon we'll have a big party for you at the lodge—we will introduce you to all of our friends!"

Kaya knew she was in a safe place and she didn't have to be afraid anymore. When they were all done Svea held up the mirror. Kaya was surprised when she saw her brown hair! She felt so pretty with the pink ribbons in her hair, she put her arms around Svea's waist and hugged her very tightly.

Svea started to hum an old Swedish folk song while she was cleaning up. To her surprise, Kaya joined in with her! She paused and Kaya kept humming right along with the tune. They both nodded their heads as they hummed the melody.

Sven came through the door with new books for Kaya.
"What are my ladies up to?"
He placed the books on the kitchen table.
"Kaya was humming an old folk song with me, she knows the tune perfectly!"
Sven stopped in his tracks as he saw Kaya's new look.
"Wow, your hair is so pretty! Do you like it?"
Kaya nodded her head up and down.
"I think she's happy with her new look, what do you think?"
"Her haircut is very nice, she looks beautiful in every way!"

He was surprised by how much different she looked. Soon they will be having a party for her at the lodge and the people of Gällivare will get to know her. Sven picked Kaya up, and they danced around the living room. As Svea started to hum the folk song again, Sven and Kaya joined in along with her.

As they laughed and danced around the kitchen, there was a knock at the door. Sven set Kaya down and went to check the door.

"Oh, it's Dr. Leif," Sven called out.
He opened the door and Dr. Leif came inside.
"Did I interrupt something?"
"Just a miracle! Kaya is humming an old folk song with us!"

One by one they started to hum the song again. Soon they were all humming and dancing around!
"Good job! I am so happy to see you smiling."

Kaya smiled and ran over to the kitchen table. She began to look at all of the books that Sven brought for her. She was so excited to have new stories to read. She set all of the books on the floor and started leafing through the pages.

Dr. Leif brought a special gift for Kaya too. He pulled out of a gift-wrapped present from his medicine bag. Kaya's eyes lit up as he gave it to her. When she opened it, she shrieked in delight! It was a gardening book all about flowers. Lately she had been spending more and more time with Svea working in the garden.

"I think this will become one of your favorite books."
"It looks like she needs a bookshelf."

Kaya sat down on the floor, and started to check out the whole book page by page.

Kaya had been recuperating for a few months now. Her burns had healed, and all of the bumps and bruises had faded away. With each passing day, she became familiar with her surroundings. She seemed much happier. Her life had started to get back to normal. One day, Svea received a call from Dr. Leif.

"Hallå, Svea! It's time that we make our trip to Uppsala. It's important that everyone sees you bring your adopted daughter home. This will give them the impression that she has just arrived. They need to believe that this is a normal, legal adoption."

They made a plan for Dr. Leif to bring her to Uppsala ahead of time, then Sven and Svea would take another train and meet them there.

"If you and Kaya take the train in the afternoon on Sunday, it should be mostly empty. Sven and I will leave in the evening on the next train. We can take her through the city for some sightseeing too, then we will come back to Gällivare. Kaya knows we have a little trip planned, she is excited to go!"

"That will work out perfectly, it sounds like we have a plan."

"Kaya knows you very well, she will be comfortable making the trip with you. We'll explain that we will be on the very next train, so she won't be afraid. Let us know what time to have her ready."

"Sunday it is. I will call on Sunday before I leave home."
"OK, I'll let our close friends know we'll be out of town."
"Great, I will be there around noon on Sunday."
"We'll be ready, Doctor, Thank you."

After Svea talked with Kaya, she could hardly wait to go on the train. Kaya has been talking more, recently. She has gotten to know Dr. Leif quite well, and likes him very much. Everything went according to plan; Kaya left with Dr. Leif, and later Sven and Svea took next train.

Kaya and Dr. Leif had some time to spare when they arrived in Uppsala. Dr. Leif called his friend Erick to check in. He spoke with Erick's daughter. Unfortunately, she said that he isn't doing well, he has gone in to intensive care at the hospital.

"According to the doctors, he may only have a few weeks left."

Dr. Leif was saddened that his dear friend wouldn't be around for much longer.

"I have someone he would like to meet. I will visit him, but I won't stay for long."

Dr. Leif and Kaya took a taxi to the hospital. They found Erick in intensive care; he didn't know they would be coming to visit. When Leif and Kaya walked into the room, Erick got a big smile.

"Well, Leif, who do you have there?"

Leif was very sad, but he smiled back.

"I'd like to do the honor of introducing you to Kaya Sue!"

Erick was so happy to see the little girl who he helped save.

Leif and Kaya walked over to his bedside.

Erick took her hand, "You are just as beautiful as Leif told me you are!"

Kaya smiled and her eyes got big, she gazed into his eyes.

"You are beautiful too," she softly replied.

Erick looked at Leif, "She will always be a wonderful little lady. Meeting her has really made my day!"

Leif held Erick's hand, "We can't stay long, I have to get her some lunch before she meets her mom and dad. We will head back to Gällivare after some sight seeing here in Uppsala."

Erick held out his hand to Leif and they shook hands. Kaya held out her hand and they shook hands too.

"She is a little light in this big world. I believe she will be a shining example for everyone who gets to know her. I am proud to have met her. Thank you for coming to visit me today, old friend—and for bringing Kaya here with you."

Erick's nurse came into the room with his medicine.
"Erick, it's time for your medicine and some fresh water."
"Take care, Erick," Leif waved goodbye.
"Next time we will meet in a better place!"
Kaya turned and waved goodbye.
"Remember to drink your water, Erick! I love you!"
"Goodbye, Kaya," Erick laughed and waved goodbye.

Sven and Svea met them at the restaurant where they had lunch. Kaya was talking much more than before; Dr. Leif was happy to see her enjoying their trip. Kaya talked about the beautiful flowers and the trees dancing in the breeze.

Out of nowhere she said, "Doctor ... I need some ice cream!"
Leif got her a big dish of vanilla ice cream, and she ate it all.
"I love ice cream," she said, with a big smile.

After lunch it was time for Dr. Leif to catch his train. He left to go to the station and Sven and Svea took Kaya sightseeing. Svea had a great idea, "Let's get Kaya a new dress and coat before we have to go home."

They found a lovely shop with very pretty clothes displayed in the window, a bell rang as they entered. After looking around a while, Kaya found a dress with a beautiful floral print. She instantly fell in love with the dress, it was perfect!

They saw a red princess coat, and Svea found a matching hat to go with it. Kaya never had such a beautiful coat before. She slipped it on and twirled around in front of a long mirror. She loved it, she was so happy with the gifts they got for her.

Kaya was almost dancing down the street as she wore her new red coat. By the time they reached the train station it had been a long day. She became quite tired and slept for most of the trip home. The long train ride home was very tranquil.

When they pulled into the station in Gällivare, they saw a group of people waiting. As they got off the train, the people came closer and began to cheer! When Svea saw the Gällivare Ladies she knew how the news got out.

"Welcome home! Congratulations, Sven and Svea!"
"Hallå," Kaya waved, as she hid behind Svea.

After a short greeting, they climbed aboard the bus and headed back home.

The next few weeks were very busy for Svea. She sent out invitations for a luncheon to welcome Kaya Sue to her new home. It would be held in the restaurant at the lodge. Svea invited all of their friends who had young children.

They could hardly wait to introduce everyone to their new daughter. They were glad that they didn't have to be so secretive any longer. Kaya told Sven that she was a little scared to meet so many new people.

She worried, "What if they don't like me?"
"Don't worry, Kaya, they will all be very happy to meet you. How could anyone not like you? Just wait and see, it will be a very great day."

On the day of the luncheon, Svea told Kaya all about the decorations they were putting up at the lodge. Their staff had been working hard to get everything ready. When they arrived, Kaya looked around in amazement! There were two grand buffets, one for the adults and one for the children. Many games and activities were set up for the kids. There was even a dance floor with a stage and a microphone where the kids could sing karaoke. So many flowers and balloons were sent by their friends, they lined the stage and the entire entryway.

Before long, their friends started to arrive. Kaya stood with Sven and Svea by the entrance and greeted each of the guests.
"Hallå, so nice to meet you," she would say.

The Gällivare Ladies showed up too! They said they had reservations for lunch. Kaya pulled on Svea's skirt to get her attention. She recognized them from the train station.

"Mom! Let the nice ladies stay, Mom…"
"Sure, Kaya, if you say so."

There was a long table where everyone placed the presents they brought for Kaya. There were dozens of books, art supplies for painting and drawing, crayons and coloring books, dolls, puzzles and even materials to make crafts. She had almost everything you can imagine.

Svea was shocked, "I never said to bring presents."
She saw the Gällivare Ladies smile at each other and nod.
"I guess I know how this came about."

Kaya noticed a little girl who seemed lonely and sad, she wasn't talking with any of the other children who were there. Kaya walked over to her and introduced herself.

"Hi, I'm glad you came to my party. What is your name?"
The little girl started to smile, "My name is Leona."
"My name is Kaya—do you want to be my friend?"
"Sure! I don't have many friends ..."
Kaya gave her a hug.
"Okay, we'll be best friends! Come with me, Leona!"

Kaya wanted to share her presents with Leona. She told her to pick out as many presents as she wanted, but Leona only picked out a coloring book. Kaya couldn't understand why she didn't pick out anything else.

"I want you to have the same toys that I have."

Kaya handed her a doll, a puzzle, a few story books, and some art supplies. She helped her carry the presents to her table. Little Leona could not believe what just happened!

When the music started playing, they both began to dance. Leona's parents commented how they never saw her so happy! It was such a wonderful party, Kaya made so many new friends. Everyone had fun playing games and singing karaoke. The Gällivare Ladies took pictures showing all the fun times everyone had at her party.

When Kaya fell asleep that night, she was holding on to a coloring book and crayons. The next morning Kaya told Svea, "Everyone was so nice to me! I think they will all be my new friends."

"See, I told you they would love you. Soon the whole town of Gällivare will know you and love you just like we do."

On Sunday morning, Sven got a big surprise when he picked up his newspaper. There was a big bold headline on the front page, it read, '*Welcome Home Kaya Sue!*'

The article talked all about the lovely party, it mentioned the great time all of the children had dancing and singing karaoke. One of the pictures showed Kaya giving presents to Leona, the parents commented on how kind and caring she was. Svea knew that, once again, the Ladies of Gällivare had to be involved.

The next two months flew by. Kaya stayed busy planting flowers and reading her new books—she didn't even need help from Svea to read them.

11. JP And Kaya Make A Connection

Each day JP delivered the mail at the lodge, and to the house where Sven and Svea lived. Kaya got used to him visiting and started to wait for him to arrive. Other than saying 'Hallå' they didn't say much to each other. Kaya's memories of the past didn't come back to her, and so far JP hadn't recognized her.

One beautiful day, Kaya was reading a book on her blanket in the front yard. Many weeks had gone by. JP pulled up in his postbus and watched her for a while. Today was different, as he saw her sitting there reading, he couldn't help but feel there was something familiar about this little girl. She reminded him of Anna.

He called out to her from inside of his truck.
"Anna!"

She looked up at him right away, with that same look he had seen so many times before. JP's heart skipped a beat.

Was his mind playing tricks on him?
He missed Anna so much.
"This can't really be her," he thought.

Svea came to the front door and called her inside.
"Kaya, it's time to come inside."
JP got out of the postbus and brought Svea the mail.

124

After he delivered the mail, he didn't think much about it. When the next day came, he saw her outside reading once again. He got the same familiar feeling.

"How are you, little one?" JP asked.
Kaya paused for a moment.

He thought that if it really was her, she would remember him. She just ran into the house without saying a word.

He knew he could never tell anyone what he was thinking. However, there was one person he *could* tell: Mr. Magnusson. Ever since the fire, Mr. Magnusson has been all alone—his whole family is in the church cemetery. Knowing this would give him something to live for.

JP could hardly wait to finish his mail route. Once he was finished, he started off toward Mr. Magnusson's house.

Halfway there, JP pulled over to think things through.
"Could it be possible? Could Anna still be alive?"
JP shook his head in disbelief.
"It's not possible, she is in the cemetery."

The grief that overwhelmed JP's heart still caused him pain to this day. He wished that there was something he could have done. He recalled the desperate look on Anaya's face as she told him about her plan.

She said that even if she couldn't save herself, she would save Anna. There was nothing that she wanted more than to give her a new life.

"Even if she was alive, nothing would ever be the same."
"I can't do this ..."
"I will keep your secret, Anaya."

The Norlander's were very close friends with Sven and Svea. They had made many great memories together over the years. They've taken many trips together, and gone skiing with each other more times than they can remember.

Unfortunately they couldn't make it to Kaya's welcoming party. Today will be a special day for everyone, Sven, Svea, and Kaya are going to the lodge to have dinner with the Norlander's. They will get to meet Kaya for the very first time.

"Kaya, some old friends of ours are coming to the lodge today. Their son Derrick will be with them too. He is excited to meet you! Remember to be very kind to him."

"Do I have to?" Kaya pouted.

"Yes, Kaya, Mr. Norlander, his wife Emma, and their son Derrick are very good people. Derrick is nine years old now—he is an excellent skier."

"Did you teach him how to ski, Dad?"
"Yes, I started teaching him when he was five years old."
"Can you teach me how to ski too?"

"Of course, this winter you can use your new skis! You'll meet many new people at the lodge once skiing season starts. People come from all over the world to ski here in Gällivare. There will be visitors from different countries all around the world."

"Tonight you can meet the chefs at the restaurant, Willard and his wife Wilma. I think their little girl Cecilia will be there too. She's three years old now and as cute as can be."

"Last year Sven promised Derrick he could visit the workshop and watch as he works on skis. Maybe after dinner you can give him a tour of the shop—we'll have to leave soon so we can get there in time for dinner."

When they got to the lodge, Sven held the door open for the girls. First they made a stop in the kitchen to introduce Kaya to Willard, Wilma, and their little girl Cecilia.

Willard is a handsome young man and a hard worker. His wife Wilma is always a joy to be around. She is tall and slender with long hair that she keeps pulled back in a ponytail. She is an expert chef and baker, and she really knows her way around the kitchen.

Willard and Wilma truly enjoy working together. They've been known to tease each other and joke around now and then. Their daughter Cecilia is their pride and joy, she is always laughing and happy when people talk with her.

"Hello Kaya, we are so glad to finally meet you!"
"Kathleen told us she met you at the train station. You're just as pretty as she said you are!"
Kaya blushed as she smiled, "It's very nice to meet you."
"This is our little girl Cecilia, we hope you two will be great friends!"
"She'll be happy to have someone to play with."
"Kaya, do you want to stay here and play with Cecilia?"
"Okay Mom!"

Sven and Svea went into the dining room and found a large table where they all could sit together. Soon they saw Emma and Norv arrive, they went to the entryway to greet them. Everyone was so happy to see each other, Emma gave Svea a hug.

"How have you been? Corrine told us about your beautiful little girl, I'm sorry we couldn't make it to the party."

"It's okay, Emma, it's wonderful to see you again! I'm so glad you're here."

"Is Kaya here with you? We can't wait to meet her!"

"She's here, she is in the kitchen playing with Cecilia."

"It's okay, Derrick went to the gift shop. He wanted to get a gift for Kaya."

Sven walked over to Norv and shook his hand.

"How are you, Norv? It's been too long my friend, how have you been?"

"Indeed! I've been doing very well—business is great, our health is good, and I have a happy family. What more could I ask for? Oh! Remember last season you told Derrick he could come and watch you work in the shop? He talked about that the whole way here! He said one day he wants to be a ski instructor."

"Yes, I remember. That boy will be successful at anything he does. He was so focused when I started teaching him how to ski. He's very determined."

With a proud grin, Norv proclaimed, "Just like his mother!"
They both smiled at Emma.
"Come this way, we already have a table picked out."
Svea showed them to their table in the dining room.
"Have a seat, my friends!"

"Perfect, thank you!"

"Later on, can we take Derrick and Kaya to Sven's workshop?"

"Sure, that would be great! I think the kids will enjoy that."

When he returned from the gift shop, Derrick found everyone seated at the table. He greeted Sven and Svea before he sat down. He carefully placed a small box with a pink bow on the table.

"Where is Kaya?"

Derrick was puzzled when he noticed that she wasn't there.

"Don't worry, I'll be right back, I'll go and get her!"

Sven went to the kitchen and found her playing with Cecilia. They both had wooden spoons and were banging them on the bottom of the pots and pans!

"Oh my, Kaya, I hope you haven't been causing trouble!"

"No, Dad, Cecilia and I are having so much fun!"

"Well, come along now, it's time for dinner."

Kaya took his hand and walked proudly beside him.

"I'm so glad you are here with us. Remember to be kind to Derrick, okay?"

Kaya looked up at Sven, "I promise, Dad."

It became quiet when they first got to the table.

"My dear friends, I'd like to introduce you to our daughter, Kaya."

Kaya smiled as she greeted them, "Norv, Emma, and Derrick, I am so happy to meet you. My mom and dad said you are great friends."

"We're so happy to meet you, Kaya!"

"Yes, it's wonderful to finally meet you!"

"Oh, Derrick has a special gift for you too."

"A special gift for me?"

"Yes, because you are such a special little girl!"

Derrick shyly handed the box to Kaya. She opened it very carefully, and inside she found a silver necklace. She picked up the necklace and saw that it had a pendant of a butterfly in flight.

"It's so beautiful, I love it! Thank you, Derrick."

Svea helped her put on the necklace, Kaya was so delighted! It really made her day to receive this gift from her new friend. Derrick was very glad that she liked it.

The waitress came to the table and took their orders, then everyone started talking together. Derrick and Kaya were even talking too.

"I saw your picture in the newspaper from your big party. Everyone in town was talking about it, I think you're famous!"

Kaya told him about the party and her friend Leona.

"I made lot's of new friends, I even have a new best friend!"

"Oh, who is that?"

"Her name is Leona Karlsson, maybe you can meet her too."

Ever since a young age, Derrick's had absolutely loved to go skiing. Once Sven got him started there was no turning back, he was a natural.

"Do you know how to ski?" Derrick asked Kaya.

"I've never skied before ..." Kaya looked down.

"I can teach you, I've been skiing since I was five!"

"My dad is going to teach me, he promised!"

"He is the best, he taught me how to ski too."

"Dad said after dinner, I can give a tour of his workshop."
Derrick rubbed his hands together, "I can't wait!"
"When I go there he lets me pick out the colors."

Before long the waitress brought dinner to the table. They laughed and talked all throughout the evening. They were such good friends; they truly enjoyed each other's company.

Just as Derrick had hoped, they visited Sven's workshop after dinner. Kaya led the tour—she knew the names of all the different kinds of wood and paints. She was even learning about the different tools that he used.

After the tour they went back to the lodge for hot cocoa.
"It's such a cozy evening, what a perfect night."
They sat by the fireplace and told stories of old times.

As the evening went on the kids both started to get tired. Before long they had both fallen asleep on a big plush leather couch.

"Have a look at that," Norv commented.
"Oh my, it looks like they're all tired out."
"I guess we should call it an evening."
"It's really been great, let's get together again soon."

The next morning Kaya came into the kitchen rubbing her eyes and half awake.

"Was I polite for you Mom and Dad?"

12. Corrine Reveals A Secret

The Gällivare Ladies met up with each other on their way to have lunch at the Storgatan Kafé. While passing the church, they saw Mr. Magnusson kneeling at his daughter's gravesite.

"Mag should never have treated Anaya like that, he was no angel himself."
Corrine shook her head in disapproval.
"What do you mean? What did he do?" Maryann asked.
Corrine got a sour look, "I shouldn't have said that."
Carol stopped in her tracks, "Now, you have to tell us!"
"What did he do that was so bad?" Kathleen inquired.

The ladies kept asking her to tell them, but Corrine wouldn't say a word. As they walked to the kafé, it became more and more apparent that they were not going to give up. Val was already waiting for them when they arrived.

Kathleen continued to prompt her, "Come on, Corrine, tell us what you know!"
"No way, if this got out it would ruin his reputation."

They had kaffe and kanelbullar for fika. As ate their cinnamon buns, Corrine got the feeling there was no way out of this.

"Val, you can be our witness."
"We promise, we'll never tell a soul."

The girls all got serious and became quiet. They looked at each other, and all together they vowed, "*I promise.*"

Corrine sat for a while in silence.
"You know, no one is perfect, not even us."
Val looked confused, "Get to the point, what is this all about?"

Corrine placed her hand under her chin and started to tell the story. "This happened about three years before Anaya was born. There was a beautiful French Canadian lady named Carla, she was about to be married in a few days. Mr. Magnusson had a crush on her for a long time, but he had been married to Engrid for about a year. He talked her into meeting him at his hotel one evening. They should have known better, but they put that all aside and met anyway."

Maryann gasped, she was shocked that Mr. Magnusson would do such a thing.
"How do you know this is true?"

"You all know I cleaned Mr. Mag's house three days a week, and I worked the evening shift at his hotel. I was at the front desk one night when Mr. Mag came in with a rose and a bottle of wine. He told me, 'I have a friend meeting me—send her up to room 212 and don't put any names down on the register.' I told him 'Whatever you say.' "

"Just a short time later, Carla came in looking very nervous. She told me, 'I have a meeting with Mr. Magnusson.' I saw her looking around to make sure no one was watching. Then I told her, 'Mr. Mag is waiting for you in room 212.' She took the elevator up, and I ran up the stairs after her to see what was going on."

"I know, I was eavesdropping, but I wasn't going to miss this! I saw her stand by the door for a while, you could tell she knew it was all wrong. She knocked softly and Mag opened the door. He told her, 'I am so happy you're here, I wasn't sure you would come.' I couldn't believe what was happening."

"I am not sure I believe you either," Maryann interrupted. Kathleen hushed her, "Shh! Just let her tell the story."

"I put my ear close to the door so I could hear what they were saying. I heard Mr. Mag say 'You know, I have great feelings for you, Carla.' She said that she felt the same way. I heard some footsteps, and then I heard Carla say 'I can't believe I'm doing this.' I could tell things were getting out of hand."

Corrine looked nervous, she had never spoken a word of this story to anyone.

"I couldn't believe what was happening! Before long I heard Carla's voice again. I heard her say 'This is all wrong, I am getting married on Saturday, I never should have come here! I have to leave now!' "

Kathleen "Oh my, weren't you scared you would get caught?" "Of course, I ran downstairs as fast as I could!" Their eyes were wide as they listened to the story.

"I barely made it to the front desk in time. Carla tried to compose herself when the elevator doors opened, but it was no use. She walked out of the elevator and threw the rose on the floor. She collapsed in tears on a chaise in the lobby. I walked over to her and asked if she was alright. She sobbed, 'No ... I will never be alright ever again. I feel like trash. I just betrayed the man I love to fulfill my lusty infatuation. I don't know how I could do something so stupid! I know he's married too, I even know his lovely wife."

Everyone was in disbelief. They were shocked and saddened. "I remember her, she was such a beautiful lady."

"I still remember the sad begging look on Carla's face. She pleaded, 'Don't tell anyone, please … this is the biggest mistake of my life.' I told her, 'Carla, you are not the first one to make this mistake. No one needs to know, it's none of their business. Put this in the past like it never happened. You are getting married in just a few days. Wipe away those tears, you're going to have a beautiful wedding and wonderful life. Your secret is safe with me, Carla. Forget this ever happened. Leave now so that one will see you.' "

The Gällivare Ladies were speechless.

"The only reason I am telling you now," Corrine justified, "is because Carla and her husband are gone, and now Engrid, Anaya and Anna are gone too. Mr. Mag wasn't perfect. He could have forgiven Anaya, but now it's too late … I hope he can find happiness."

13. Nurturing A Prodigy

Sven was looking for his old favorite sweater in the closet one day. After he took out a few things, he came across Kaya's violin case. Sven called Svea to come and look, and out of curiosity, Kaya tagged along with her.

"Wow, let's open it up!" Kaya was excited.
She carried the violin case out to the living room.

She set it down and brushed it softly with her hands. Sven and Svea watched in silence as she opened the case and very carefully picked up her mother's violin.

Without a word, she started to play a magnificent melody. Sven and Svea were both astonished, it was the most incredible violin performance they had ever heard! When she finished, Kaya smiled and took a bow.

Sven and Svea both applauded, they were so impressed. They immediately knew how important it was that she continued to pursue this great talent she possessed.

They also knew there was only one person in town who she could learn from: Mr. Magnusson.

The next day they got up very early; Sven was getting ready to work in his shop while Svea made breakfast. When they sat down at the table together, they asked Kaya if she wanted to begin taking violin lessons.

"Kaya, did you know that you have a very special talent?"
She smiled and shrugged her shoulders, then put her hands up.
"Sven and I have never heard the violin played so beautifully."

Kaya blushed and her little smile got even bigger. She was very shy, and almost embarrassed to be the center of attention.

"If you want to start taking violin lessons, we have a very special friend who could teach you. He is the best violinist in all of Sweden! His name is Mr. Magnusson."

Kaya was delighted. In her short life, she never had special things to look forward to. She hadn't even been very far from home before. Her life was now changing very quickly.

"Do you want to start taking lessons with Mr. Mag? We can talk to him, I'm sure you'll be able to start taking lessons right away."

"*Yes,*" Kaya exclaimed, "I really love the violin, I promise I'll do my best!"
"We know you will, Kaya. You have been blessed with a natural talent."

A few weeks went by—Kaya continued to watch JP deliver the mail each day. One day when JP stopped by with the mail, he asked Svea if Kaya could ride along in the postbus. He offered to take Kaya to visit Mr. Mag, then bring her back after they finished the route.

Svea thought this was a great idea.
"Sure, I think that would be good for her."
Kaya got so excited!

"It will be good for her to get used to being away from home now and then."

Kaya jumped up into the bus and started to pretend she was a mailman. JP let her wear his hat, it brought back memories that filled his heart with a certain joy that he hadn't felt for a long time.

When they got to Mr. Mag's house, they saw him sitting in his front yard. He waved as Kaya and JP walked up to greet him.

"Well, who do we have here?"
Kaya spoke up right away, "I am your mailman today! Here is your mail Mr. Mag!"
"This is Sven and Svea's daughter, her name is Kaya."
Kaya looked around, "What a big house, it's so pretty!"

Mr. Magnusson's house was not an ordinary house, it was the largest estate in Gällivare. There was a very beautiful garden filled with flowers of every variety. It was unlike anything Kaya had seen before.

"We can go inside if you have time?"
"Do we have time, JP? It won't take long."
Kaya jumped up and down with excitement!
"Anything for you little lady."

They walked through the house and went into the kitchen.
"Would you like some kaffe, JP?"
"Yes, please. Kaya, you can look around a bit while we talk."

Kaya began to wander through the huge rooms. They had very high ceilings with crystal chandeliers. Kaya's eyes got wide as she saw the beautiful paintings hanging on the walls. In one room there was a grand piano, and many other musical instruments. Kaya was in awe when she discovered that Mr. Magnusson had a whole collection of violins!

While Mr. Mag and JP were in the kitchen talking, they suddenly heard the sound of someone playing a violin. They looked up at each other with amazement. Quietly, they walked together toward the music. From the doorway they saw Kaya playing the violin.

Every motion she made was so precise. She had complete control of the violin, in a way that is very hard even for the best violinist. Without a word, Mr. Mag walked over and picked up his violin. In this moment they made a special connection. There was a certain glimmer in their eyes as they looked at each other.

Mr. Mag nodded his head to indicate she should continue, and he started to play right along with her. JP was in for a thrill of a lifetime! Next, Mr. Mag played a very challenging tune, and Kaya played it back perfectly, note for note. Then Kaya played a melody and Mr. Mag played it back! They took turns playing for a while.

It reminded Mr. Mag of playing the violin with Anaya. He started to play the Byssan Lull, a song he used to sing every night while playing the violin for his daughter.

Kaya lifted her violin and started to play it too.
"How could this little girl know how to play this song?"
Mr. Mag was shocked!

They played together note for note. By the time they finished the song, they each had tears in their eyes. Kaya took a bow with her violin at her side. She smiled at Mr. Magnusson and threw her arms up around him!

Mr. Magnusson shared the same lesson with her that he taught his daughter when she was a young girl:

"Kaya, always remember this. *The violin has a soul, it can project emotions—love, happiness, and excitement! If you send your feelings into the violin, and put your soul into the strings, you can create magic!*"

Mr. Mag felt the same love for this little girl that he had for his daughter Anaya. All the memories of playing their violins together came back to him. It was hard to tell if the tears in his eyes were from those memories, or from witnessing Kaya's amazing talent.

"I love you, Mr. Mag!" Kaya chirped, in her sweet little voice.
"I love you too, little lady."
Mr. Mag was so emotional, his voice quivered.
"Kaya... Who taught you to play those songs on the violin?"
She got a blank look on her face.
"I... don't... know..."

JP was just silent, there were no words that could describe what happened. The three of them stood there for a moment. Somehow they knew something very incredible and unexplainable had just happened here.

When Kaya got home that day, she jumped out of the postbus and ran inside to tell the story. Sven and Svea were flabbergasted when they saw this energetic little girl burst through the door!

"Mom! Dad! I played the violin with Mr. Mag!"
She was so excited she could hardly catch her breath.
"He is so great! He is the best violin player I've ever heard."

"His house is so big! He has a whole room that is just for playing violins. He really likes me too! We played the Byssan Lull together."

Six months had gone by and Kaya and Mr. Magnusson had now become close friends. They would get together a few times every week and practice different pieces on the violin.

It's a nice sunny day today, and Kaya is waiting for JP to see if she could ride with him to finish his route. She also wanted to go see Mr. Magnusson. When he arrived, Svea came outside to meet him. He handed her the mail and asked how she's doing.

Svea put her arm around Kaya, "We've been working in the garden today. We planted so many flowers this year that we needed another garden! Kaya is a great little helper, she really loves gardening. We even got her a few books about different flowers. Everything has been going so well, I bring her with me everywhere I go. She has made so many new friends too. Everyone has been so nice to her, she really seems to have a way with people."

JP smiled, "She sure does. Just the way she tilts her head and smiles gets me every time. Would it be okay if she comes with me today to finish the mail route? I promise to bring her back on time."

Svea had noticed how excited Kaya was to go.

"Of course she can!"

Kaya looked up at Svea, "Thank you, Mom!"

"She really likes to spend time with you and Mr. Magnusson. She tells us he's been sad … she said he needs her to make him smile."

"He has, but Kaya brings him so much happiness. He really enjoys teaching her more about the violin. Her visits are something he really looks forward to."

Svea watched as they got into the postbus together. They waved goodbye and JP tooted the horn as they left.

Kaya started to talk non stop, "So, Mr. Mailman, how many letters have you delivered today?"

"I guess around three hundred," he kept his eyes on the road.

Kaya asked, "Were there any birthday invitations?"

"Well, I think someone has a birthday every day!"

"Do you know any of them?"

"Oh, I know most of the people in this town very well."

Kaya looked surprised.

"I've been their mailman for a long time. Over the years you really get to know people."

"JP … do you know those ladies that are all around town? The ones who seem to know everything, even before it happens?"

He laughed out loud, "Yes, I know them. You are pretty smart to have them figured out already, and you are so right."

When they pulled up to Mr. Mag's house JP honked the horn.

"It seems like he is not home, he is probably at the cemetery."

Kaya looked sad, "Can you drop me off at the cemetery, and pick me up here later? I'll be good!"

He paused, "I guess that will be alright. If anything changes, have Mr. Mag call me."

JP drove Kaya to the cemetery to look for Mr. Mag.
"Oh, I see him there … right in the same place. He is always there, I bet he is crying again. I think he will be glad to see me."

Kaya walked up to Mr. Mag, he looked up as she tapped him on his shoulder. He watched for a few moments before leaving.

Kaya threw her arms around Mr. Magnusson.
"I found you! Are you crying again?"
Mr. Mag looked up at Kaya, but was silent.

Kaya continued, "Don't be sad, cheer up Mr. Mag. I am going to go see all the people who live here, I'll be right back."

Mr. Mag knew that he had to cheer up before Kaya got back— he tried to shape up. Before long Kaya came running up to him.

"They don't have flowers; why don't they have flowers?"
"I guess someone forgot?" Mag hung his head low.
Kaya could tell he had still been crying.
"Why are you still crying?"
Mr. Mag struggled to tell her how he felt.

"This is my wonderful daughter, right here. A long time ago we had a disagreement. We parted ways and I never made up for it. I told her I would never forgive her. Now I realize how stupid and horrible I was. I feel so bad … I am so sorry … She had a little girl and I never got to meet her ... I never told my daughter how much I missed her, and how much I love her. Now she is gone forever, and all I can do is come here and cry."

"Mag, didn't anyone ever tell you about forgiveness?"
Kaya had her hand on her hip.
"Just listen to your heart! Your heart will let you know you've been forgiven. You need to remember, we are all like snowflakes, no two are alike. That's how God put us here on earth."

He bent down on one knee next to the gravestone. The Gällivare Ladies were passing by, they stopped when they heard Kaya's voice, and overheard her speaking with Mr. Mag. He listened very intently.

"It takes a lot of love and forgiveness to make a wonderful world. You'll feel so much better if you forgive her, and forgive yourself. It's not too late, trust me Mr. Mag, I know these things!"

"How will she know?" Mr. Mag asked.
"Her angel spirit is here with us."
Kaya lifted her arms up to the sky.
"She will hear you and you will feel her love and forgiveness."

Kathleen, Carol, Corrine, and Maryann had all moved in closer so they could listen.

"God will hear you too! When you forgive her, you will both be forgiven."

Mr. Mag ran his fingers across Anaya's name on the gravestone and sobbed.

"Anaya, my precious daughter … I was so wrong. I was a foolish man with so much pride. I never stopped loving you. I am so sorry, so very very sorry. Please forgive me, Anaya … please, please, forgive me."

"Just be still and wait," Kaya knelt down beside him, "you will feel her love and forgiveness. I'll say a prayer for you Mr. Mag.

"Dear Jesus,

It's me, Kaya. I know I am just one little voice in the whole wide world, but I have faith in you, and I believe you are listening to me. I need your help. My friend Mr. Mag has a very sad heart. Please take away his broken heart so that he won't cry so much. We know his daughter is in Heaven, but Mag needs to know she forgives him and still loves him so he can smile again.

"Mr. Magnusson has a kind heart. I beg you, please, please bless him so he can have a happy heart. Mr. Mag plays the violin at church, and he is there every Sunday. He even taught me how to play *'O Store Gud'* on the violin. This Sunday we are going to perform it together at the church.

"Please try to be there, Jesus, and show us a sign that you heard me. I love you forever and ever, Jesus. Amen."

When they opened their eyes, the sun seemed to be shining down upon them.

"Now you can stop crying and feel good again, Mr. Mag."
They both stood up, Mr. Mag had stopped crying.
"You know, I do feel a lot better."

143

They held hands and walked together through the cemetery. Before long they reached the entrance of the cemetery. Kaya looked up to the sky and then at Mr. Mag.

"I think we need some ice cream. We can call JP from the ice cream shop."

They left together and walked to the Storgatan Kafé. The Gällivare Ladies looked at each other in amazement.

"How does this young girl have so much wisdom?"
Maryann shrugged her shoulders.
"I don't know, she must be very blessed."

"A few days ago, Kathleen and I passed by Mr. Mag's house and heard the most beautiful violin music! At first it was just one of them playing, and then they played along together. It was like being at a concert!"

Corrine had a big smirk on her face, "Oh, you've heard it too! She must be taking lessons from Mr. Mag."

Kathleen perked up, "It's almost like she is replacing Anaya. She came into Mr. Mag's life when he needed her the most."

"I see them together here very often," Carol added, "right by his daughter's gravesite. Mr. Mag is truly heartbroken … have you seen how he looks at the sculpture of little Anna?"

"Yes, it must remind him of Anaya."
"It's a good thing that little Kaya came along."
"Well ladies, we are in for a great performance at church on Sunday!"

Kaya felt sorry as she thought about the graves at the cemetery without any flowers. She remembered that they all said "RIP" on the headstone. Mom was busy in the kitchen, and it was almost time for JP to pick her up.

Kaya got a *great idea!* She ran to the flower garden in the backyard and started to cut some flowers. She thought about how many headstones there were in the cemetery. It didn't look like she had enough flowers, so she just kept cutting more. Before long she had cut them all! She got a big box, filled it up with all the flowers, and waited for JP.

Soon JP pulled up and he was surprised to see Kaya waiting there. She had such a big smile, and was holding the box of flowers. JP called out to her, "You look happy today! That sure is a lot of flowers."

"I'm bringing them to the 'RIP family' in the cemetery!"
JP looked confused, but he understood what she meant.
"Mom is busy, so we can leave now ... it's OK!"

JP helped her into the bus with the big box of flowers and they started to drive to the cemetery. Mr. Magnusson would be meeting them there.

"Those are such beautiful flowers, where did you get them?"
"Oh, I just cut all of the flowers in Mom's garden."

JP got a worried look on his face. He knew how hard they had worked on that garden. He didn't question her, he just let it go. Kaya was so happy that she bounced up and down the whole way there!

When they got to the cemetery, Mr. Mag was shocked to see Kaya with this big box full of flowers. Kaya hopped out of the bus.

"Mr. Mag, I brought flowers for the RIP family!"

Mr. Mag couldn't believe what she was up to. They both watched as Kaya ran around to each of the graves. She put flowers on each of the headstones while saying *'rest in peace loved ones!'*

JP looked down at the ground, then sadly looked up.
"She reminds me of another little girl I once knew."

Mr. Magnusson recalled his memories of Anaya.
"There is something about her, but I can't explain what it is. She sure is very caring and smart for her age."

Soon Kaya returned, ever so happy, carrying the empty box.
"Now the whole RIP family has flowers!"
"Kaya, you never cease to amaze me."
"How are you today, Mr. Mag?"
"I'm having a good day, Kaya, because you brighten my days!"

Kaya took Mr. Mag's hand. "Let's go practice *'O Store Gud'* so we get it perfect. We only have a few days until Sunday!"

"That's right! We can't miss our practice. JP, can you pick her up at four o'clock?"

"Sure, I'll see you then."

When they arrived at Mr. Mag's house they got right down to business. They went to the music room and got ready to practice. After playing through the song a few times, they took a short break.

They talked together about the performance on Sunday. As they discussed the plan, Mr. Magnusson revealed that he had two special violins which they would be using.

"Kaya, I have a surprise for you. I have two Stradivarius violins, they are two of the greatest violins that were ever made. They were handcrafted in Italy many years ago."

Mr. Magnusson pointed toward a special violin cabinet that held only the two violins. They walked toward the ornate cabinet which delicately held the two Stradivarius violins.

"My father was a great collector of violins. He passed them down to me. When I was younger my father and I played these violins together. Since then, the only person to ever play one of these violins was my daughter."

Mr. Mag carefully opened up the cabinet and picked up one of the violins and handed it to Kaya.

"We are going to play these violins together on Sunday."

She examined carefully it, admiring the fine craftsmanship.
"It's so perfect, are you sure we can use them?"
"These two violins were meant to be played on this very day."

At her young age, Kaya could not truly comprehend how valuable and rare these violins really are. There are only a very few

Stradivarius violins in the entire country of Sweden. They picked up the bows and prepared to play the first notes.

Kaya remembered what Mr. Mag had taught her:

"The violin has a soul, it can project emotions—love, happiness, and excitement! If you send your feelings into the violin, and put your soul into the strings, you can create magic!"

As they began to play, the most beautiful and harmonious notes rose up from the violins. It was unlike anything Kaya had ever heard before. The bow floated across strings projecting a very rich, and stunningly brilliant sound. This moment in time became a treasured memory for both of them.

When Kaya got home she found Svea was in the kitchen. She was so excited! She slid onto a chair and began to tell her mom about her day.

"Mom, Mr. Mag and I played two magic violins! We're going to play them together at the church on Sunday!"

"Oh? That will be wonderful! You've been working very hard."
Svea seemed to have something else on her mind.
It may have been her flower garden.

"And guess what? I went with Mr. Mag to the cemetery today. Did you know the whole RIP family is in there? No family is left to bring them flowers. *You'll be so proud of me!* I brought flowers and put them on the graves of *the whole RIP family!*"

Svea knew that Kaya had something to do with all the missing flowers. As she listened, she thought *'How do I handle this?'*

Kaya continued with her story.

"When I gave them the flowers I told them *'rest in peace loved ones!'* You should see, it's so pretty!"

"I am very proud of you my sweetheart. And now I know where all my flowers went!"

"Don't worry Mom, I'll help you plant more flowers. The RIP family is so happy now!"

"Kaya, did you know that RIP stands for *'rest in peace?'*"

Kaya looked intrigued, "Oh? What a lovely name! You're so smart, Mom! I love you!"

With a blank look on her face, Svea replied, "I love you too, Kaya."

14. Sunday, A Day Of Blessing

The sun is shining and it's a beautiful day in Gällivare. The news got out that Mr. Magnusson and Kaya are playing their violins at the church today.

This is their first public performance together and they've drawn the attention of the entire town. Sven and Svea sat in front with Norlander's. The Gällivare Ladies were there too, of course. Whole families came together and the church was completely full.

Toward the end of the service, Reverend Gabriel made the announcement:

"We have a very special blessing today! Mr. Magnusson and his new student, Kaya, will be performing 'O Store Gud' for us. Kaya is only six years old. They will each be playing a very rare Stradivarius violin from Mr. Magnusson's collection."

O Store Gud is a very special song for everyone.
It is a traditional Swedish song, written in 1885.
It is the original version of *'How Great Thou Art!'*

The chapel became silent with anticipation. Mr. Magnusson walked out first, he stood tall and proud. He looked over the congregation, took a few seconds, then lifted his violin. As he started to play, the beautiful melody of *'O Store Gud'* filled the entire church.

People began to wonder, 'Where is Kaya?'

After a few moments, Mr. Magnusson paused, then nodded to Kaya. She slowly walked over to him. She was a little shy because she had never played for a large group before. They both looked at each other, then Mr. Mag lifted his violin and continued playing.

With a nod, Kaya lifted her violin. Just as she was taught, she sent her feelings into the violin, and put her soul into the strings.

From the first note, the congregation was captivated. Each note was crystal clear, the tone was so profound. Mr. Magnusson let her take over—it was a masterpiece!

God's presence was felt by everyone in this heavenly moment. It was so uplifting. Mr. Magnusson raised his violin and began to play along with Kaya. They felt the presence of Angels; the spirit of God's love filled the entire church.

Suddenly a bright beam of light shined down upon the two of them through a tall church window. Kaya turned toward the window, and played the last refrain into the light. Many people were in tears as she finished the final notes.

When she saw this light, Kaya knew that her prayer had been answered. She lifted her hand and waved to the light, then took a bow. To her surprise, a cool breeze swept through the sanctuary and swirled around Kaya and Mr. Magnusson—everyone felt it! They placed their violins by their sides, then took a bow toward the congregation. Kaya turned and ran into Mr. Mag's arms.

The congregation was amazed at what they had witnessed!

Reverend Gabriel announced, "I believe God was in our presence today! We have witnessed a truly inspired performance. On behalf of our special guests, and our heavenly father, I want to thank you all for attending today's service."

He closed the service with Numbers 6:24-26.

"May the Lord bless you and protect you. May the Lord smile on you and be gracious to you. May the Lord show you his favor and give you his peace."

Kaya and Mr. Mag shook hands with the members of the congregation as they were leaving the church, and were blessed with many praises.

"God is watching over her. She is a miracle!"
"We are so fortunate to have this little Angel in our presence!"
"God bless you!"
"Thanks for attending today!"
"God lives here, you know," Kaya said!

For the first time the Gällivare Ladies were speechless. When they came up to Kaya their eyes were red from crying. They each gave her a quick hug and left. Val and Gary were seated in the back, so they were the last ones out. As they left, Val gave Kaya a hug and Gary shook Mr. Mag's hand.

"Kaya, God has blessed you."
"Mr. Magnusson, you and Kaya are an incredible pair."
"We'll be looking forward to your next performance!"

After everyone had left, Mr. Magnusson turned to Kaya.

"Kaya, God sent you a sign today. I saw it, and I felt it. I know he heard your prayer yesterday. I feel like a new life just came into my soul."

Kaya tilted her head to one side, smiled.
"I told you so," she replied.

From that day forward, Kaya held a special place in the hearts of everyone in Gällivare.

15. O Christmas Tree

Winter had started to set in across the town of Gällivare. This would be Kaya's first *real* Christmas. She never had a Christmas tree before. Svea sat on the edge of her bed, and softly brushed Kaya's hair away from her face. She whispered, "Kaya ... Kaya! Wake up, wake up!"

Kaya turned and curled up in her quilt. From under the covers, Svea heard her little voice say, "Mom, I am still tired."

"Kaya, today is the day we go and find our Christmas tree, it will be so much fun! Breakfast is ready and Daddy is waiting for us, this will be a very special day!"

Kaya pulled down the quilt, sat up, and threw her arms around Svea! She jumped out of bed, "Mom, I'm not tired anymore!"

She grabbed Svea's hand and led the way to the kitchen. Dad was drinking kaffe and reading the newspaper. He looked up and smiled, "Good morning, you little rascal!"

Kaya flipped her hair back and put her hand on her hip, "No Daddy, you're the rascal!" They all laughed. They had a contest to see who could finish breakfast first. Sven let Kaya win, of course.

While Svea got Kaya's snowsuit and boots ready, Kaya ran to her bedroom to get dressed. She came back to the kitchen in the blink of an eye. She was jumping up and down so much that Svea had a hard time helping get her snowsuit on.

"You have to quit jumping, my dear, or you will wear out your snowsuit before you can put it on!"

"With all the trees in our world, do you think we can find our one and only beautiful Christmas tree?" Sven asked.

"Yes we can!" Svea and Kaya proclaimed.

"We will find the best tree in all of Sweden! You two finish getting ready, and I will be right back."

Sven went to his workshop to get a special toboggan that he made for this very day. Kaya had never seen it before. It was long enough to hold the Christmas tree, and still have room for Kaya to ride along too. There was a canvas lining on the sides to keep out the snow, and along the bottom.

Kaya was so tiny, but with her jacket and snowsuit on, she looked twice her size. She was all bundled up with only her face showing. They were all ready to go.

Kaya looked out the window, "Where did Daddy go?"
Before Svea could answer, Kaya squealed with excitement! "Mommy, look!"
Kaya ran outside to meet Sven, "Daddy, What is that?"
"It's called a toboggan, I built it just for you!"

Svea came outside too. She had made a special quilt to keep Kaya warm. They tucked her into the toboggan with the quilt, then started to head toward the forest. As they trudged through the snow they pulled Kaya along behind them. Kaya laughed whenever they hit a few bumps.

Sven had walked through the forest and found the perfect tree the night before, but this would be Kaya's first real Christmas, and he wanted her to be the one to pick out the tree.

Soon they reached the forest. For many years, each Christmas, Sven and Svea made this journey together. Until now, they didn't have a little one of their own to share in the joy of picking out a tree.

"Be on the lookout, Kaya! Let's find the best tree. Look for one that is very tall with many branches."
"We will slow down a bit, you will know it when you see it!"

Kaya looked up at the trees as they slowly pulled the toboggan.
"Wow, some of the trees are as tall as a mountain!"
"They've been growing for many years … when I was a young boy, I came here with my dad, and I picked out the Christmas tree!"

Kaya jumped up as they passed a very majestic tree.
"Daddy, I see it! I see the perfect tree!"

Svea walked over to the tree that she pointed out. It just so happens that it was the same tree Sven saw last night. They helped Kaya out of the toboggan; she ran over to the tree and gave it a big hug! Svea got a perfect picture of Kaya hugging the Christmas tree.

Kaya noticed there was a smaller tree that was growing right next to the big one.
"Mom, this little tree told me it wants to be with the big tree. We can't leave it here all alone!"

"Kaya, honey, trees don't talk," Sven told her.

"But Dad, they do talk! You have to be real quiet and listen really hard. They can hear you too, and they even keep secrets!"

Kaya walked to the little tree, with one hand on the big tree and one on the little tree, she looked up at Sven and Svea.

"Look Daddy, the little tree is sad…"
"Where can we put it Kaya?"
"Right at our house with the big tree. We'll put them right next to each other. After all, they are best friends!"

Kaya looked at them with pleading eyes.
"Please Mom and Dad … please? They told me they want to be our Christmas trees!"

Sven and Svea looked at each other and smiled.
"Yeah, I guess we can make it work."
Kaya's eyes lit up and she jumped in the air!
"Thank you, I love them! You just made the trees so happy!"

They sang Christmas songs all the way home with the two happy trees. When they got home, Sven and Svea opened two huge boxes of decorations.

Kaya looked puzzled, "What are you doing?"
"Each Christmas we put up these pretty decorations."
"Come and help us!"

Kaya was in awe when she saw all of the beautiful decorations. She hadn't ever seen anything like it. While she helped to hang up the ornaments, she said "I love this one the very best!" with almost each and every one.

When they finished putting on the decorations, Sven held Kaya up so she could put the star on top of the tree. In a soft whisper, she said a short prayer before placing the star on the tree.

"Thank you God for this star. May the whole world be happy as I am this Christmas with Mom and Dad."

They all stood back and admired their work.
"Daddy, I never saw a tree like this before! It's so beautiful!"

The big tree was decorated with angels, candles, and elegant glass bulbs. The small tree had brilliant white lights, and traditional Swedish decorations made from straw: stars, tomten, julbock, bells, and pinecones.

Svea set out the ljusstake and explained the meaning to Kaya.

"These are the Advent Candles, we light one candle each Sunday in the four weeks before Christmas.

"The first one is the Prophet's Candle, it represents the hope given to us by the Prophets, who told of the coming Messiah for many years before Jesus was born.

"The second is the Bethlehem Candle, which symbolizes preparation for the coming of Christ in Bethlehem.

"Third is the Shepherd's Candle, which represents the joy given to the Shepherds, who were the first ones told by an Angel of the Lord that our savior, Christ the Lord, had been born in Bethlehem.

"Fourth is the Angel's Candle, which represents the peace given by God to all people of the world."

Svea placed the ljusstake in the window, and helped Kaya light the first candle. After it was lit, the light of the Prophet's Candle glowed upon Kaya's face. You could see the wonder and magic of the season in her eyes.

This was Kaya's first real Christmas.
That night she fell asleep under the Christmas trees.

The month of December went by very quickly, as it often does. Soon it was Christmas day. When Kaya woke up, she jumped out of bed and ran to the living room as fast as she could.

"Mom! Dad! It's Christmas!"
"That's right, it's finally here!"
Kaya was so excited that the day had finally come.
"Remember, we have to get ready for company."

Svea was going over her list for the julbord. She wanted everything to be perfect. She had everything they needed: salmon, lutfisk, boiled eggs, beetroot salad, apple, celery, and walnut salad, meatballs with lingonberry sauce, and creamed kale.

"Dad, did you know Mom and I made a thousand cookies? We had so much fun baking. Mom told me I am the best mixer upper! Mom, tell Dad!"
"That's right, Sven, Kaya is the best mixer upper!"
Sven smiled, "I always thought she would be!"

After they finished helping Svea prepare for company, Sven and Kaya went into the living room to take a break. Everything looked so beautiful. The spirit of Christmas filled their hearts and the entire home.

"Dad, is Tomte coming to our house today?"
Kaya sat on Sven's lap, and held his face in her two tiny hands.
"Dad, do you think I was a good little girl? I tried so hard!"
"Well, little lady what do you think?"
A sad look came across her face.

"Daddy, I didn't mean to break your kaffe cup, it just fell out of my hand ... and I'm sorry I spilled the paint at the shop. I tried to clean it up, but it just kept spreading. I tried so hard! I still have Mom's snowflake pin ... please don't tell her! And sometimes I hide your slippers. I like to wear them and pretend I am you ... I can sound just like you too!"

Sven put his finger in front of her face, "Shh, don't worry. We love you just the way you are, and we always will. You are the best little girl in all of Gällivare! Now, let's get ready to have the best Christmas ever!"

"Dad, I really can sound just like you!"
Kaya cleared her throat, and dropped her chin as she lowered her voice. Sven looked shocked as he heard this large voice come from her little body.
"Kaya, be good and help your mom today ... stay out of trouble, and don't pick Mom's flowers! Did you hide the blue paint at the shop?"

They both started laughing so hard.
Svea walked in and asked, "What are you two up to?"
They quieted down and acted innocent.
"Oh, nothing!"

After a few hours went by their guests started to arrive. First the Norlander's arrived, Emma, Norv, and Derrick. Not long after, Leona arrived with her mom and dad, Greta and Ole.

They had a wonderful time telling stories over dinner. Later in the evening they all exchanged gifts. The children were as happy as could be. After opening gifts, they even went outside together and played in the snow. The children had a contest to see who could make the tallest snowman—Leona won the contest!

Sven and Svea had given Kaya her first real Christmas!

16. Three Years Later

Time seemed to pass very quickly. Kaya is nine years old now and she is doing very well in school. She was still spending most of her time with Sven and Svea. As time went on Kaya and Leona became close friends. They would do their homework together, and now and then they would even have a slumber party. They had pajama parties where they made forts, played games, and sometimes had pillow fights. They always had fun together.

One time they cut each other's hair, Leona gave Kaya a short haircut that kept getting shorter! They laughed so hard their tummies hurt. Kaya cut Leona's hair to shoulder-length shag and taught her to shake her head to let it fall in place.

After watching their mothers put on their makeup, they thought it would be fun to try putting on makeup themselves. They found bright red lipstick, put on a thick layer of foundation, used lots of mascara, and put far too much blush on their cheeks.

When they were done, they looked at each other with their bright red lips, dark eyebrows, and rosy red cheeks. They thought it was just perfect.

"Let's show Dad how pretty we are!"

They ran into the living room to show Sven and waited to hear what he thought. Sven looked over his newspaper, stared, and replied, "I think you young ladies need to go wash your faces!"

Kaya was spending lots of time helping Sven in his workshop, she wasn't old enough yet to help Svea at the lodge. She would go to his workshop each day after school.

"Hi Dad, I'm back from school!"
Sven always cheered up when Kaya arrived.
"How did school go today?"
"Just fine, I don't have any homework today."
Sven couldn't believe she was growing up so quickly.
"Do you have any painting for me today?" Kaya asked.
"Yes, I have a very special job for you."

Sven had started to teach Kaya how to paint skis. She is still learning, so they do all of the painting together. Her favorite part was mixing the paint, she loved adding the different colors to get just the right shade.

"We'll put this design on top, and his name on the bottom."
Sven looked real serious as he explained it to her.
"I still have work to do, but we can get started after dinner."
"Okay Dad, I'll go help Mom get dinner ready."

Kaya looked back at Sven as she walked out of the door. When she got to the house, she couldn't find Svea anywhere.

"Mom, I'm home! Mom … where are you?"
Svea called out to her from the back yard.
"I'm out here, Kaya, in the garden!"
"I should've known that's where you'd be!"
"I am planting some vegetables. How was school?"

"Dad just asked me that too, it was great, I love school! No homework tonight. Mom, you look tired. Let me help you,

I'll dig the holes and you can plant the seeds!"

"Thank you, my little angel. When we finish, we can have dinner, I already have everything prepared. We'll have an early dinner tonight, Dad will be home soon."

They planted the seeds, and then watered the garden. This was one of their favorite things to do together. Over the past few years, they had planted many different flowers and vegetables.

When they finished planting they went inside for dinner. Kaya set the table just like Svea taught her.
"Great job, my dear. That's just how we set the tables in the lodge. Maybe you can come and help set tables at the lodge sometime after school?"

Kaya got excited, "I'd love to! I'll always help you, Mom!"
"Maybe this weekend we can go there together."

Before long Sven came home. He hung up his coat and put his hat on the table in the hall.
"And how are my two favorite ladies doing?"
"We're good, I just helped Mom finish planting in the garden."
"Dinner is ready honey, come have a seat."

Kaya was finally living the life that Anaya wanted for her. She had a Mom and Dad that were very happy, loving, and supportive of everything she does. After a tragic beginning, she finally had a normal life—this was just what she needed.

After dinner, Sven and Kaya went to the workshop as they had planned. Kaya mixed the paint and she got the colors just right.

They had such a fun time. Kaya got a little paint on her shirt, but she didn't mind.

"Now this will be my favorite shirt!"
Sven got a kick out of that, "Why is that?"
"Because it will remind me of the time we spend together."

"Kaya, you make me so happy. Each day I wonder what you will do next, and you always amaze me. I will always remember the little things that you say."

That weekend Kaya and Svea went to the lodge. Svea showed her some things that she could help with; she learned how to wrap the silverware, prepare table settings, and arrange flowers for the centerpieces. Before long she could make the flower arrangements all by herself.

"How does it look Mom?"
"It's perfect Kaya, you've done a wonderful job!"

Svea and Kaya made a great team. They made new flower arrangements for all of the tables, and finished all of the preparations for the evening dinner. They even brought the candles out to each table, it was a very elegant sight. They were both proud of the work they had done.

Before going home they went to visit Willard and Wilma. Their daughter Cecilia was there too, she is almost six years old now. In the past few years, Kaya and Cecilia had become very good friends. They would spend time together playing games, and sometimes they even danced on the stage where the musicians would perform, and would pretend they are famous celebrities!

Kaya started going to the lodge each day after school. She would spend a few hours there helping out with things her mother had taught her to do. It seemed like she became an official inspector. She always wanted to make sure everything looked just perfect.

After a few weeks went by, Sven felt that something just wasn't right. He started to miss seeing Kaya after school, she used to visit his workshop every day. The highlight of his day was when she would cheerfully walk through the door at his shop. He would still look at the door now and then, wondering if she might show up.

He decided the best solution was to go and visit her at the lodge. He walked up to the lodge, but wasn't sure where to find her. He checked the kitchen, but she wasn't there. He didn't have to look much further, as he came out of the kitchen they bumped right into each other! Kaya almost dropped a big stack of dishes!

"Oh, Kaya! That was a close call!"
"Oh my, I didn't see you!"
"That was a good catch, you have quick reflexes!"
They both had a good laugh.
"I haven't seen you at the shop lately, how are things going?"

"I love it here Dad! I love the smell of all the good food, but most of all, I love talking with all of the guests. Those four nice ladies come here very often, we're starting to be good friends."

"I'm very proud of you Kaya. I am glad you enjoy your time at the lodge, I've made many great friends here ... and you're right, the food smells wonderful today. Maybe we should have dinner here?"

Sven stayed to visit for a while as Kaya finished up a few things. They walked home together to ask Svea if they could have dinner at the lodge.

It had been a whole month since Kaya visited Sven at the workshop. She realized that she was starting to miss spending time with her dad.

"Dad, do you miss me?"
This question caught Sven by surprise.
"What do you mean?"

"I used to visit your workshop everyday after school. Now I've just been helping out at the lodge, I think I'm starting to miss you."

Sven was shocked, it was almost like she could read his mind.
"Oh? I didn't even notice you were gone."
Kaya scowled, she knew he must be joking.
"Dad, you're just teasing me!"

"You caught me, yes, I do miss you, Kaya … that's why I came to visit you today."

"Aww, I knew you missed me!"
"Kaya, you are my favorite little helper."
Hearing this made Kaya happy.

"I am glad you enjoy being at the lodge. But remember, save some time for good old dad!"
"I'll always save time for you Dad!"

Kaya had spent many days and evenings watching as Sven made skis in his workshop. She knew every step in the process, and admired the fine craftsmanship of his work. He showed her how the measurements are done, and taught her new things each day.

Kaya spent a lot of time with both Sven and Svea, they became a very close-knit family. She made new friends everywhere she went. After her performance at the church, people recognized she was a prodigy. All around town, she was treated like an honored guest.

The very next day, Kaya went to visit Sven at his workshop!

17. A Rumor Around Town

One day Kaya seemed upset when she came home from school. She dropped her books on the table then sat down with a heavy sigh. It seemed something wasn't going well for her today. Kaya held her head in her hands.

"Did you have a bad day, Kaya?"
Svea sat next to her.
"Mom, it seems like people whisper about me."
She sounded a little bit frustrated.

Svea listened as Kaya poured her heart out. She explained how people around town say she looks like some other girl. She even heard them whispering 'that can't be her, she passed away.' "

"I know, Kaya, I hear it sometimes too. There was a bad accident here in Gällivare a few years ago, and a beautiful young girl passed away. It was a great tragedy that affected the whole town. She was a lot like you, she was smart, and talented ... she even looked a lot like you ... when people see you, it reminds them of her. Don't think much about it, most of the town knows you and they love you for who you are."

Kaya cheered up once she understood.

"I guess that makes sense. I was worried that they didn't like me. I thought they were saying bad things about me. I'm glad you explained it, I guess I don't have to worry."

After they talked Kaya went to visit Sven at his workshop. He was putting bindings on a pair of skis when Kaya flew through the door with excitement!

"Dad, Mom told me why people are always talking about me!"
"What do you mean Kaya?"
He was surprised, he didn't know anything was going on.

"I always hear people whispering about me. Now I know why! Mom told me there was a little girl that looked like me who got into an accident."

Sven was always worried that this might happen. His greatest fear was that the life they shared could be taken away.

"It was making me sad, I thought they were talking about me."
"Well Kaya, you can always come and talk to me—"
"Even the Gällivare Ladies said I look just like her."

"Don't let it bother you, Kaya. Remember you will always be our little girl."

Even though Sven tried to reassure Kaya everything would be okay, he became very worried. He started to think of what might happen if her identity was revealed. They had made such a happy life together, they've done everything they could to protect her.

"Kaya, maybe we shouldn't work too late tonight. I'm not feeling very well."

"Maybe you have been working too much, Dad?"
"You could be right. I'll be okay … it will pass."
"Well, let's finish up, then we'll go see Mom."

Kaya walked over to Sven and noticed he was holding his chest. She helped him put away some of his tools, then they closed the shop and walked home together. As they got close to home, Svea could see them through the kitchen window.

"There's my wonderful family," Svea thought.

Kaya was talking with Sven as they walked.

"Aren't you glad I'm visiting the shop again? I promised you that I would!"

"Yes you did, it's great to have you there again ..."

Sven's mind was still wandering. He was very concerned about their discussion and couldn't get it out of his mind. If they ever lost Kaya he would be heartbroken.

"Tomorrow I'll help finish painting that set of skis. They really look great, Dad."

She noticed that Dad wasn't talking too much.

"Who are they for, is it a customer from the lodge?"

Sven started to slow down.

"Dad, are you okay?"

Kaya saw a look on his face that she had never seen before. He started to lose his balance. Kaya took his arm to steady him. He put his hand on his chest again.

"Dad, what's wrong? What should I do?" Kaya panicked.

Sven sat down along the side of the path.

"Get Mom ... Kaya ... get Mom."

Kaya ran toward the house shouting as loud as she could.

"Mom! Mom! Help!"

Svea came running outside.

"What's wrong? What is happening?"

"It's Dad! He—I don't know, he was holding his heart!"
"Stay with him, Kaya! I will get help!"

Kaya stayed with Sven, Svea ran into the house and called 112.
"Dad, you're going to be okay, Mom is getting help."

She knelt down next to Sven and held his hand. After speaking
with the paramedics, Svea came rushing out of the house to check
on Sven. She looked at Kaya and could tell she was very upset.

"Kaya, can you please go get a blanket for Dad?"
Without a word, Kaya took off toward the house.

"Help is on the way, they will be here very soon. You're going
to be okay dear. Remember, you are a strong Swede!"

Kaya came back with the blanket and they covered him up to
keep him comfortable.
"Dad is going to be okay honey, everything will be fine."

After a few minutes the ambulance arrived. The paramedics
rushed over to Sven—they could tell he was not in good condition.
He was dazed, very weak, and short of breath.

"He may be having a heart attack."

The paramedics didn't waste any time, they placed him on the
stretcher, loaded him into the ambulance, and began giving him
oxygen right away.

"We'll meet you there honey, I love you!"
Svea and Kaya follow right behind them.

When they reached the hospital, Svea and Kaya were not able to see Sven right away. After a long wait the doctor came out to give them an update.

"Sven will need to stay here for a few days while he recovers. He's had a heart attack. We will need to watch him closely and run some tests. I am glad you got him here so quickly, he's a lucky man."

"Mom said he is a strong Swede!"
"Your mom is right dear," the doctor smiled as he continued. "His condition has stabilized now. He's been asking about the two of you. Would you like to see him now?"

"Yes, please—thank you Doctor."
Svea and Kaya both looked relieved.

"Remember, he needs rest; please keep the visit short."

Six months had gone by and life was starting to get back to normal. Sven learned to take things a bit more slowly. His doctor instructed him to take a break from any strenuous activities, and to make some changes to his diet. Both of these things posed a challenge for him.

First of all, because Swedes love sweets! Each day both he and Svea looked forward to fika, they would always have a sweet pastry with their kaffe.

Secondly, because they would soon be hosting an international ski competition in Gällivare. This was the busy time of the year, and this year there would be even more visitors than normal. Sven needed to be in his workshop.

Even though he had many orders to fill, he had to follow his doctor's orders and shorten his workday. He prioritized orders for the professional skiers who were coming to compete.

Norv's son, Derrick, always wanted to learn how to make skis. This was his chance, it worked out well for both of them. He started to work at the shop for a few hours each day after school. Derrick had the patience needed to learn the craft, and he soon became Sven's apprentice.

Derrick watched as Sven did all of the woodwork. He learned how to form the skis by steaming the wood. Sven began teaching him the basics of finishing the skis using pine tar and wax. He also learned how to install the bindings. Things were going very well, and the orders were all getting completed on time.

There was one very special order that Derrick was excited to finish. He wanted to get it done before Kaya came to the shop so he could surprise her. Kaya was in charge of the painting, but Derrick wanted to try his hand at painting too.

When she arrived at the shop, she sure was surprised. She was not happy to see Derrick painting, that was her job! Derrick proudly held up one of the skis that he finished painting.

"Look Kaya, I painted the skis for that special order!"

She recognized this pair of skis, her father had just finished work on them yesterday. "Nice job," she flipped her hair over her shoulder with a glaring look.

"You just painted the wrong skis!"

Derrick looked shocked, he realized that she was right!

"You put the wrong name on them!"

Derrick was speechless, he didn't know what to say.

"See, that's why I'm in charge of painting!"

"I'm sorry, Kaya, I'll fix them!"

"No! Dad always has me do the painting—*Dad, help me!*"

The customers were lucky that Sven was still the foreman of the shop. He had a certain way of settling any disagreements that Kaya and Derrick may have. Thankfully, things went well most all of the time.

As he continued to recover, Sven enjoyed spending more time with his family. He started to visit the lodge more often too. There were no more late nights in the workshop, every night they would have dinner together.

After dinner they sang old Swedish songs, and sometimes Kaya would play the violin. At the end of the night, Sven always sang the Byssan Lull. When he was a young boy, his mother used to sing it to him before he would drift off to sleep.

"Kaya, did you know this is the first song I ever sang for you? When we sing it together, it gives me a very happy heart."

Kaya smiled, "I feel the same way. I love you, Dad."

Svea listened as they sang the Byssan Lull.

As time went on, they made several trips together as a family, and visited neighboring cities and towns. Whether going to town

They always made it to church on Sunday. They spent many great days together, making trips into town, and enjoying the natural beauty of the land. In the evenings, they enjoyed singing Swedish folk songs together.

Kaya was growing up, and before long she started High School. They couldn't believe how quickly the years were passing by. If you ask Kaya, she will tell you that she can even ski better than Derick now. During the winter season, they always have many spirited competitions.

On so many occasions, Sven, Svea, and Kaya were reminded that family is the most important aspect of life.

18. Where Is Kaya?

It was a Saturday and the Gällivare Ladies were headed to the lodge for lunch. Kaya was working, she just loved being at the lodge, and the customers loved seeing her too. She made friends with everyone she met. When the Gällivare Ladies arrived, Svea asked Kaya to seat them.

"Kaya, can you seat these ladies at the table in the back? Val and Gary will be joining them, so they need two extra table settings."

Kaya greeted them, "How are you ladies this lovely day?"
They all looked so happy, "We are doing fine, thank you."

"Follow me. I have the perfect place for you right over here. You can see the whole restaurant from here, and there is room for Val and Gary when they arrive."

Kaya handed a menu to Maryann.
"Thank you, Kaya," she replied.
"May I have some water please?" Kathleen asked.
"Of course, coming right up!"

"You do such a great job, Kaya. You add just the right touch here at the lodge!"

Kaya finished handing out the menus to Carol, Kathleen, and Corrine. She went to get water for the ladies and was back in a flash.

"Do you have a lunch special today?" Corrine asked.

Kaya replied, "Yes, today we have—"

"Oh, here comes Val and Gary," Corrine interrupted.

Kathleen stood up and waved them over to their table.

"So nice to see you both today!"

Kaya placed their menus on the table as they were seated.

As Kaya told them about the special, she saw Derrick come into the lodge. He had a searching look about him, Kaya could tell he was looking for her. When he saw her, he got a big smile; Kaya left the table to go and meet him.

"Your waitress will be with you shortly, have a nice day!"

She cheerfully walked to the front of the lodge.

"Hi Derrick! Surprised to see you, would you like a table?"

"Sure!"

As he followed her back to a table, he pulled the sash on her apron and it came undone. Kaya turned back and gave him a slight punch on his shoulder.

"Darn it, Derrick! Don't do that, I have work to do."

Derrick took her hand and he led the way to his usual table.

"I hope you're not too busy today. Do you have time to join me for a slice of the Svea's famous rhubarb pie?"

Kaya looked surprised, "I didn't know you liked rhubarb pie?"

Derrick had a sly look on his face.

"Of course! Kaya, there's many things I like that you don't know about!"

Derrick grinned, "Now, how about the pie, smarty pants?"

Kaya got up without a word and left.

Kaya went to the kitchen to get two slices of rhubarb pie. The Gällivare Ladies whispered to her as she walked by their table.

"I think he likes you, Kaya."
"He sure is a handsome young man!"
Kaya winced, "Yeah, and he knows it ..."

She was happy that Derrick came to visit, but she didn't want him to know that. As they had their pie together, the Gällivare Ladies listened intently—they didn't want to miss anything! Derrick did most of the talking.

"You know, my mom tried to make this pie for me, but it wasn't near as good as this!"
Kaya sat up real straight and looked him in the eye.
"Well, I make pies every day with my mom. She told me someday I will have to know these things."

Derrick got the biggest grin on his face that she ever saw, he took her hand, looked back into her eyes. He softly whispered, "Now I like you even more!"

The Gällivare Ladies commented among themselves.
"Uh oh," Carol whispered, "I think we need to keep an eye on these two!"
Kathleen held up her menu, and glanced over the top.
"Yes we do, I think they are falling for each other!"
"They're young, time will tell," Val added.

After they finished their pie, Derrick flipped down the money for the bill. He even left a good tip for Kaya.
"I have to get back to work. Stay out of trouble, if you can!"

As he stood up, Kaya couldn't help but notice how tall, muscular, and tan he was. He had sandy blond hair and dreamy blue eyes. He turned to Kaya and gave her a big hug.

The Gällivare Ladies felt like they just witnessed a blossoming young love.

As time went on Derrick and Kaya continued to spend more time with each other. Two years had gone by and they both continued to work with Sven and Svea. Kaya would work with Svea at the lodge, and Derrick was still helping Sven in his workshop.

In the evening Derrick liked to visit Kaya at the lodge. Quite often Emma and Norv would join them and they would all get together as a family. The time they spent with each other brought them all closer together.

Sven had taught Derrick everything that he knew. He became very skilled in woodworking. He even made a custom set of skis for himself. After a long day there was nothing he loved more than to go out and hit the slopes.

Derrick knew that Kaya had a secret place where she went skiing, but he couldn't ever find it—this became a great mystery! One day while working with Sven in the shop he decided to ask where she was.

"Sven, I've been wondering, where does Kaya go skiing? When she goes to practice, it seems like she disappears. I can't ever find her!"

Sven looked down toward the ground and kind of chuckled.

"That's her secret, you know! She likes to go out on the slopes all alone. It helps clear her mind, that's how she became such a good skier. I've heard the stories of your competitions, and in the stories I hear, she always wins!"

"Well, you're only getting half of the story. When we were younger I offered to teach her how to ski, but she was dead set that you would be the only one to teach her."

"That's right, she wouldn't let anyone teach her but me!"
"She always told me, *'My dad is my teacher!'* "
Sven and Derrick both laughed.

Sven noticed that Derrick had a sad look on his face, and recalled the feelings he had for Svea when he was a young man.

"I know how much you care about her ... I'll tell you."
Derrick got excited, "Really?"
Sven and Derrick stood eye to eye.
"Yes, but if she asks, you didn't hear it from me."

"There is a small forest behind the lodge where we go to get our Christmas trees. There is a clearing past the forest, it's kind of a secluded area. There is a hill back there and I put in a private lift for her. She practices there almost every day, just follow the tracks in the snow. You have to make it seem like you found her by accident, otherwise she's going to be mad for a long time!"

Sven thought about the two of them, then he got serious.
"It looks like this could be love, maybe?"
Derrick was surprised, "Yes, it feels like love is in the air."

"What about after graduation? Won't you be off to college."

Derrick looked puzzled, he was both happy and sad at the same time. He never thought about real love before.

"I just got an acceptance letter from Stockholm University."
"Congratulations ... I am sure Kaya is going to miss you."
Derrick placed his hand on Sven's shoulder.
"I think I miss her already. It will be hard to be away from her."
"Well, we will all be here. Come back home on your breaks."
"I will—please watch over her for me while I'm gone."

Sven shook his hand "Good luck, she is stubborn, but she knows what she wants. When she is determined nothing can stop her! Go find her, and remember, pretend you found her by accident. Try to look shocked and see what happens."

Derrick carried his skis and wandered around to the back of the lodge. The anticipation was building as he walked through the forest. He started to feel like there were butterflies in his stomach. The snow was deep, he followed the tracks just like Sven told him to do. Soon he came to a clearing, he looked up and saw Kaya at the top of the hill.

Kaya didn't see him yet, so he hid behind a few trees. There were two jumps on the way down. As she prepared to make her descent, he wondered if she could do this.

She checked out her run from atop the great hill. Before starting her descent, she went through the approach step by step. Derrick would remember this sight as long as he lives.

Kaya held her ski poles and bent her knees, then pushed off. She swayed side to side as she started to come down the hill. Her first jump was perfect. She landed gracefully and started gaining speed for the second jump.

When she took off from the second jump, she seemed a little off balance. When she landed she fell very hard and tumbled further down the hill.

Derrick gasped and called out to her, "Kaya!"
Kaya laid there motionless in the snow.

He ran over to her side, she was crying in pain. She sat there covered in snow with tears flowing down her face.

"Derrick, how did you get here?"
Derrick knew he was busted!
"Oh, I was just looking for a place to ski. I didn't expect to find you here, you're so lucky I happened by! Are you okay?"

Kaya cried as she tried to move. She screeched in pain as she held her right leg and foot. Derrick had come to her rescue. He tried to help her stand, but she couldn't put any weight on it. She fell back down to the ground. Derrick saw the frustration and pain on her face.

She tried to stand again, but kept falling and sliding down. Kaya, the independent 'I can do it myself' girl, cried out in pain. He wondered how he could get her back to the lodge. He wanted to let her know that it's okay to ask for help.

"Kaya, you are hurt really bad. Please, let me help you—"
"Oh, just leave me alone, Derrick."
"So, you want me just to leave you alone?"

Derrick shrugged his shoulders.

"Okay ... well, I'll be going then. See you later!"

He turned and started to walk away; still no call for help. He kept walking through the snow. In the distance, he heard her swear, and she never swears! Finally, he heard her pleading voice.

"Derrick, I need you to help me ... you get back here!"
He got a big smile from ear to ear that she couldn't see.
"Kaya, you told me to leave you alone."
"Derrick, I can't walk ... I need help."
"Say please," he teasingly compelled her.
He was about to take her hand, then he pulled away!
"You didn't say please!"
She looked up at him, "Please, please help me!"

"That's more like my girl! I'm going to have to pick you up and carry you to the lodge. You have to hold on."
"Do I have to?"
"Yes, just put your arms around my neck, so you don't fall."

Derrick bent down to pick her up, and she put her arms around his neck.

"Just pretend you like me, and you are giving me a big hug!"

Kaya was lucky that Derrick was there at just the right time. If he wasn't there to help her, who knows what could have happened. He started to trudge through the deep snow. It was a long way back to the lodge.

"You have known me for all these years, Kaya. You can always ask me for help and I will be here for you."

Kaya suddenly felt safe, she rested her head on his shoulder. She was still in a very great deal of pain.

"I hope you know how much I care for you."
Kaya looked up and smiled at him, "I care about you too."

With her arms holding tightly around him, she looked up and their eyes met. Words could not describe how they both felt. He knew the time was right. Derrick stopped for a moment and gently gave her a kiss! To his surprise, she kissed him back!

"Derrick, I think I need a doctor …"
"Hold on Kaya, I'll get you to the shop as fast as I can!"
Kaya winced in pain as he carried her through the snow.
"We'll be there in just a few minutes."

They reached the workshop just as Sven was locking up. Sven was shocked when he looked up and saw Derrick carrying Kaya. He knew that something was wrong.

"Oh my heavens, Kaya! What happened?"
"Dad, I took a bad fall on the second jump."
"Don't worry honey, we will get you to the hospital."

"Derrick, get Svea. Tell her to bring the car around and we'll take Kaya to the hospital. Svea will panic as soon as she hears Kaya is hurt, so do your best to calm her down. Tell her I said to just stay calm, and that Kaya will be well taken care of."

In a flash Derrick took off to go and get Svea. The day had taken such an unexpected turn of events. While they waited, Kaya explained what happened.

"Dad, I can't believe it … I was so scared when I fell. I was out there all alone, and I couldn't walk. Derrick just called my name out of nowhere, it was like God put him there at the just right time."

Sven couldn't believe what had happened. If he hadn't told Derrick where she was skiing, she would've been helpless. The thought troubled his mind. It was a traumatizing experience, but it could have been much worse.

"I was full of snow and furious at myself. At first I didn't want his help, but I don't know what I would've done if he wasn't there."
Sven smiled at Kaya and wrapped his arms around her.
"It's time for you to start trusting people, Kaya."
"Dad, he made me say *'please'* before he would help me."
"As it should be, my dear."

In no time at all, Svea and Derrick arrived with the car. Sven and Derrick helped get her into the car.

"Be careful! Be careful!" Svea repeated.

Sven and Svea sat in the front seat, Derrick and Kaya were both in the back; Sven drove to the hospital. As they went over the bumps in the road Kaya was whimpering in pain.

Two nurses brought out a wheelchair when they reached the Hospital. Derrick parked the car, then met Sven and Svea inside. They waited patiently to hear from the doctor. Svea was so nervous. After they waited for some time, the doctor came to speak with them.

"Doctor, is she going to be okay?" Svea asked.
"Don't worry. She is going to make a full recovery."

"Are you sure? How is she doing?"

"Yes, she is doing very well. In the MRI we saw that she has a small fracture in her right fibula. It's going to take time to heal, so she will be off of her feet for at least the next six weeks. She'll need a cast, and will have to use crutches while she recovers. Derrick, I heard you carried her all the way back when she fell."

"Well Doc, I guess I was in the right place at the right time."
"It's very fortunate that you were there."
"I guess that makes you a hero!" Sven added.

After a long wait, they brought Kaya out in a wheelchair. The cast had been put on, and she had her crutches. In the emergency room they had given her medicine for the pain. They helped her into the car and got her comfortable. It was a quiet drive home.

It had been a long day for everyone. When they arrived at home Svea helped Kaya get ready for bed. Sven and Derrick sat by the fireplace together.

"It's a good thing you found her, Derrick. Thank you."
"I couldn't have done it without your help."
"It seems like fate intervened on her behalf."

Svea took very good care of Kaya as she recovered. During this time, Svea taught her how to do all of the accounting for the lodge. Learning to manage finances for the lodge gave her a sense of responsibility. She took some time to think things over, and decided that when she graduated she would work at the lodge full time.

Derrick started to attend classes in the Department of Law at Stockholm University. He was very focused on his studies and quickly became a favorite student of his professors. Being away from Kaya was challenging for him. Sven and Svea noticed that he had started to call Kaya quite often.

Everyone knew that romance was blooming between Derrick and Kaya. As you may have noticed, the Gällivare Ladies like to keep in touch with everything that is going on. They started having lunch at the lodge at least twice a week so they could keep tabs on Kaya.

So, here they come! Kathleen asked for their favorite table. Kaya had a feeling they would show up today, so she kept the table open. Carol and Maryann were chatting as they were seated. They always seemed to know the latest gossip.

"I heard the Peterson's are going to divorce. He had an affair with her sister, it's splitting up the whole family."

Maryann looked disgusted, "What a creep! He didn't know how lucky he was."

"On a lighter subject," Corrine interrupted, "Sara had her twins yesterday!"

"Oh, I didn't hear, that's wonderful!"

"I knew it was going to be soon."

"Twin girls, Nicole and Novalie, one was seven pounds and one ounce, and the other was seven pounds and two ounces. They're identical twins. Their little brother Adrian won't have anything to do with them!"

The ladies all laughed.

"Oh, he will get used to them in time."

Lately, Kaya noticed they've been asking about Derrick. It was no surprise to her when Kathleen mentioned his name.

"Well, Kaya, have you heard from Derrick?"

Kaya smirked as she handed her a menu.

"He's very busy, but he calls now and then."

Carol looked up at Kaya suspiciously, "Not too busy for his best girl, I hope?"

Kaya replied, "Are you ready to order?"

"No, we need a moment," Corrine shook her head.

"OK, I'll come back," Kaya walked away.

Maryann was quick to add, "I bet they talk every day!"

The ladies all looked at each and smiled with a nod.

Kaya looked back, "Derrick is just a friend, you know."

Kaya had become used to all of her new responsibilities at the lodge. Between her and Svea, everything was very well taken care of. They still planted a beautiful garden together each spring.

Mr. Magnusson and Kaya continued to be the best of friends. They would practice their violins together weekly, and even started to play at the church once a month. This became a very special occasion for the townspeople.

Between working at the lodge, gardening, and practicing her music, Kaya had a very full and happy life. Helping Sven in the workshop was still one of her favorite things to do.

Now and then, she would recall her dad saying:

"Remember, save some time for good old dad!"

19. Scenic Overlook

It's Derrick's third year in college, and he came back during winter break. Everyone was so happy to see him again. During break, he worked at the lodge as a ski instructor. He is really an excellent teacher. All the girls signed up for lessons, whether they need them or not! Sometimes they would pretend to fall so he would catch them or help them up. They flirted with him to no avail.

Every year Derrick plans a one day hike into the mountains to visit a scenic overlook. This year, five people signed up for the hike. His friend Mark would be joining him for the first time, along with two other couples. A young couple, Jan and Jeff, and an older couple, Helen and Charlie.

Jan and Jeff are in their late twenties and are in perfect shape. Jeff is very kind, he has brown hair and is six feet tall. Jan has blond hair and green eyes. She is a lovely young lady, with an independent mind and nature.

Mark is a happy-go-lucky single guy, with highlighted blond hair, perfect teeth, and a smile that could turn on a crocodile! He is the most athletic one of the group.

Helen is a gentle and loving older woman with gray hair and blue eyes. She is pleasantly plump and very religious. She's married to the love of her life, Charlie. Sometimes he can be stubborn as a donkey—he is always right, even when he is wrong! He is bald but still has gray hair around the edges. He has a beer belly from the good old days that jiggles like jello when he laughs! He was a handsome man when he was young. He is still a very good looking man for his age.

Derrick had given everyone a list of supplies they need to bring for the trip. He checked in with them in the morning before they left for the day. It would be a one day trip, it takes about three hours to reach the overlook. They all wore warm winter clothes, boots, a scarf, and gloves. They each brought lunch, a flashlight, and any medicine they may need for the day. Derrick brought a camera to take pictures.

It was an early morning in Gällivare. The sun was shining through the clouds on the horizon. Kaya came to visit and see them off on the journey. Mostly, she wanted to say goodbye to Derrick.

Kaya told the hikers, "You will love it, it is so beautiful up there. Have a good time, you are in good hands."

As she spoke to Derrick, she gazed into his eyes with a serious look, "Please be careful, and promise you'll call me later."

"I will, I promise. We will be back before you know it."
Charlie smirked, "Looks like something's going on here!"

Kaya blushed as Derrick gave her a kiss goodbye in front of everyone! Before they left, Derrick brushed back his hair and put on a warm toppluva hat.

"Alright everyone, are you ready to go?"
"Yes!" they replied in unison.
"Great, let's be on our way."

Everyone was in a good mood and enjoying the hike. Jan and Jeff were holding hands as they walked along. Mark was taking pictures with Derrick's camera. He got a close up of a Golden Eagle flying near by with the mountains in the background.

The air was fresh as they journeyed into the hills of the mountain. They couldn't believe how silent it became. After about two hours, Charlie complained that he was tired, and needed to take a rest.

"We're halfway there, we are making good time. We can take a short break here," Derrick told the group.

Helen asked Charlie, "Did you bring your inhaler?"
Old Charlie dug through his pack, but he couldn't find it.
"Looks like I forgot it."
Charlie got a half-mad look on his face.
"Helen, why didn't you put it in here?"

"Well, Charlie, I can't keep track of *all of your things* ... you told me you put it in there!"

Jan and Jeff both got a knowing look and smiled at each other. A few snowflakes started to fall from the sky. Derrick was surprised, he thought they would have good weather throughout the day.

"Best we're on our way," Derrick looked out across the sky, "it looks like there may be some snow coming."

Derrick knew the time frame of the trip, so he started to move at a faster pace. He wanted to get to the overlook within an hour. Mark liked the fast pace and he started to sing.

"Vi gå över daggstänkta berg"
— We walk over the dew sprinkled mountains.

Soon Jan and Jeff joined in the song. It was a lovely sound to hear. It felt like the mountain was listening as their voices sang out.

As time went on, the snow started getting heavy and the wind picked up. Derrick knew this was not a good sign. He needed to get everyone to a safe place. Derrick remembered there was a small cave under a ledge about a half a kilometer from where they are now.

Helen told Derrick, "Charlie's getting tired. What can we do?" Derrick told everyone to stop and listen.

"This is what we have to do, Mark and Jeff, you two stick with Charlie and help him keep up. I have a strong rope that we will all hold onto. We will stay close together."

Jan and Helen went first, right behind Derrick. The wind was getting worse and Derrick feared it could cause a whiteout, time is of the essence.

"There is a cave nearby where we can take shelter. Let's go as fast as we can."

Jan looked concerned, "Are we going to be in danger?"

Derrick tried to keep everyone calm, he didn't want anyone to panic. "Just keep up a fast pace. If we can make it to the cave before the whiteout, we'll be fine and we can wait it out."

The snow started coming down more heavily and the wind continued to get stronger. They all held onto the rope to stay safe.

Derrick could still see the path, and he knew his way to the cave. After a while Derrick's phone rang, it was Kaya.

"Derrick, are you on the way back yet?"
"No, it's been slow going because of the snow."

"The weatherman said the jet stream sent a blizzard right over us! Can you find shelter somewhere?"
"Don't worry, we're going to take shelter in a cave nearby."

"We are all at the lodge. All of the staff are here, along with Willard, Wilma, and Cecilia. They all came here to be safe. The wind is so bad that we can't go outside!"

"Kaya, I have to go now, I'll call you later."
Derrick hung up the phone.

The wind suddenly began to blow very hard. Now they had to deal with a whiteout! Mark and Jeff had fallen a little bit behind, they were holding on to old Charlie and helping him along.

"The cave should be here, I just have to find the entrance."
He walked a few steps and dug in the snow.
"Not there …"
He searched for the entrance, trying to recall where it was.
"I know it's here …"
Helen was shivering, "It's so cold, I'm freezing!"

He asked Jan to help him dig as he checked a few places. They dug as quickly as they could, until they finally found the entrance.

"We found it!" Jan yelled out.

The entrance of the cave emerged from the snow. It took a moment to clear the snow before they could go inside. Derrick tried to check their surroundings before he went inside; the snow was all he could see. He went in first to make sure that it was safe.

One at a time, they made their way into the cave. It was dark and cold, but they felt fortunate to be out of the wind. They lit up the cave using two flashlights and a small lantern. It was small, circular in shape, and had a pathway that went further back.

"Everyone, stay close together for warmth and try to relax. We're going to be here until the blizzard passes. This would be a good time to have your lunch, but save some for later."

Helen sat next to a rock, "I hope we can warm up now."
"At least we are out of the wind," Charlie replied.
Derrick feared they may be here all night.

Old Charlie wasn't very hungry and he didn't feel good either. Helen reminded Charlie to take his medicine.

"Do you have your nitro pills in your pack?"
"I think I put them in," Charlie looked a little confused.

Helen looked everywhere, she checked his pack, and even emptied it all out.

"I thought you did too, but I think you left them at home."
"Maybe I won't need them," Charlie replied.

Jan and Jeff loved how Helen watched out for Charlie. Everyone hoped that he was right, and that he wouldn't need them.

Derrick got another call from Kaya. He could hear in her voice that she was worried. Kaya told him that many of the townspeople came to the lodge to stay safe during the storm.

Kaya asked, "Did you find the cave? Are you safe?"
Derrick told her they made it to the cave.
"We will have to wait it out here. The wind is so strong that we don't stand a chance."
"Just stay there … later we will try to send help."
"It's very cold here, and I can't see anything outside."

"Don't do anything stupid, like going outside and not being able to see to get back in."

Derrick laughed, "So you do think I'm stupid? Thanks for the compliment!"

"Well, you know what I mean, I'm worried about you."
"I'm glad to know that you care … I'll call you later."

Old Charlie was not doing so well. Helen tried to make him as comfortable as she could. She found some aspirin and gave him two.

"Helen, you are so good to me. All these years, you put up with me. I went from a handsome lover to a grumpy old man. I love you, my sweetheart. I love you just as much as the day we got married."

Helen held his hand as she told him, "Well, old Charlie boy, we've both changed as the years flew by. I wasn't so easy to get along with when I was younger. God is watching over us, in sickness and in health. We've been blessed with a lifetime of love."

Everyone was touched by what they heard.

Mark walked over to Helen and Charlie.

"I hope I find a love like that someday, it's hard to find!"

Jan and Jeff took a good look at each other and vowed to let that be an example for them. They all huddled closer together to help keep warm. Derrick thought it would be a good time for everyone to take a nap and regain their energy. Charlie was the first one to fall asleep, he had his arm around Helen.

Derrick kept one of the flashlights on so they had light. He laid down to rest for a while, and he fell asleep too.

After some time passed by, they woke up again. They could still hear the wind howling outside, which made it seem much colder.

Derrick thought of how he could safely get everyone back home. He called Kaya; she had become very worried. She was upset that he was stuck out in the storm. She told him that everyone was still at the lodge.

"We're all trapped here until the storm is over. Everyone is here, even the Gällivare Ladies. The wind is so bad, we had a hard time closing the door! Derrick … how are you going to get out of there?"

"We need to be patient and wait for the storm to pass. I just hope Charlie will be okay, he seems to have forgotten to bring his heart medicine."

Kaya pleaded with him, "Please stay safe Derrick. Don't go outside, you won't even be able to stand up in this wind. Promise me you will stay inside."

"I promise, Kaya. I just don't know what we'll do if Charlie needs help."

"Svea is talking to Val and Gary, they came to the lodge when they saw the storm coming. Once the storm lets up, they'll go out in the helicopter and find you. For now, you just have to stay put. You will make it back here safely."

"Thank God for Val and Gary! Don't worry, Kaya ... I'll be here, waiting for your call."

The snow started to come down very heavily, everyone was braced for the storm. Sven built a fire that warmed up the whole lodge. They all started to feel much more comfortable. Even with the wind howling outside, the lodge seemed very warm and cozy.

People gathered all around the huge stone fireplace, and told stories to pass the time. Svea got out blankets, Wilma made hot cocoa, and Willard made sandwiches for everyone. Kaya and Cecilia helped serve the sandwiches and hot cocoa.

Kaya sat down with Val and Gary, she talked with them about Derrick and the others who were trapped in the cave.

"Derrick goes on this hike every year, but no one knew this storm was coming. They are all trapped out there—Mark, Jan, Jeff, Helen, and Charlie. I'm so worried, Derrick said that old Charlie forgot his heart meds, and he seems to be having a rough time."

Val and Gary both had a worried look.

"We'll get them out of there as soon as we can, but right now it's too dangerous. We have to wait until the wind slows down to a safe speed. If the snow doesn't let up, we may even have to wait until morning. Tell him to listen for the wind to let up. When we're nearby, he will be able to hear the helicopter."

"Thank you, Gary. I am so worried about him."
Kaya was trying to hold back her tears.
"I hope the storm will pass soon ... we will find them."
She felt better after talking with Val and Gary.

"I'm glad you are here ... I'm so worried about Derrick. I don't know what we would do without you."

Carol, Kathleen, Maryann, and Corrine listened in on every word. They had never seen Kaya so worried and upset like this before. When she finished talking to Val and Gary, she took a seat at a table by the kitchen. She put her arms on the table and rested her head. The Gällivare Ladies went over to comfort her.

"Don't worry, Kaya, Derrick will be okay."
"Are you sure he is just a friend?" Corrine asked.
"Oh Corrine, just let her be," Kathleen insisted.

Kaya sighed, "I have known Derrick since we were kids. We've become so close over the years. He teases me now and then, but I would miss it if he didn't. All I know is that I want him home safe. I can hardly wait to see him again."

"He will be back before you know it."
"That's right! For now, you just need to stay busy."
"How about making some popcorn?"
"Oh, that sounds good. Should I make popcorn for everyone?"

They all answered together, "Yeah!"

So off to the kitchen Kaya went. She tried to cheer up, but Svea followed her and saw she was still crying. Svea went to talk to her. She held her close, just like the old days.

"My dear Kaya, you will always be my little girl. Everything will be just fine ... I think you have deeper feelings for Derrick than you know. This looks like love to me!"

"Don't be silly Mom, we're just friends!"
"Well, we can talk about it later, at another time."
Kaya smiled, as Svea wiped away her tears.
"Looks like you have a lot of popcorn to make, I'll help you."

Back at the cave, Derrick was explaining that, once the storm lets up, Val and Gary will be coming to rescue them. They had to hold on until the wind slows down and the snow lets up.

"Gary is going to have a hard time finding us. He won't be able to see the cave with all the snow covering it up. We need to do something to give him a sign."

Helen got an idea and spoke up.
"Charlie has a red flannel shirt on under his vest and coat. We could use it as a signal?"
Charlie agreed, "It's my favorite shirt, but we can use it if it means we will get out of here."

"Thank you, Charlie. I think that will work, they should be able to see it from the helicopter. I'll get it from you in the morning after we've cleared out the entryway. It won't be long now and we'll be on our way home."

As time went on Helen realized that Charlie was in really bad shape. He was very cold, and was starting to have a hard time breathing.

He told Helen, "I need more pain pills."
She gave him the last two.
"Help is on the way, hon. Try to take a nap."

She gave him a kiss, "Remember, today is our anniversary! Dream of our wedding day."

A few hours went by and the storm was not letting up. The wind was bellowing outside of the cave. Derrick knew that the helicopter could not fly in these strong winds.

"We are going to have to settle in for the evening. The wind is so strong out there, I don't think it will let up until morning. I'll keep track of the time overnight. In the morning, we'll need to dig ourselves out. Once we clear the entry way, we will raise up Charlie's red shirt as a signal for Val and Gary. Then we'll listen for the helicopter to arrive. Ration any food you have left to keep up your strength."

Helen let Derrick know that Charlie was getting worse.
"I'm worried him, he's very pale, and almost turning blue."
Derrick could hear the concern in her voice.
"He is breathing a little hard too."
Derrick tried to reassure her that Charlie would be okay.

"We aren't too far away from the lodge. In the morning, Val and Gary should be here as soon as the sun comes up. They will bring you and Charlie directly to the hospital. Jan will go along with you, then Mark, Jeff, and I will head back on foot."

As the night went on, Jan started to cry. Mark overheard as she told Jeff, "I hope the morning comes soon, my feet are frozen."

He commented, "Yeah, my lunch is frozen too! I'll never eat a frozen peanut butter sandwich again, as long as I live."

Derrick kept track of the time throughout the night. He struggled with a feeling that he had let everyone down. The storm came as such a surprise, there really wasn't anything he could have done. Nonetheless, their lives were in his hands.

Derrick had turned off his phone during the night. It was a long and cold night for everyone. They all huddled together to help keep warm. Fortunately, when the morning came, Derrick was able to make a quick call to Kaya.

"We are all okay here, it sounds like the wind has let up too."
"I'm so glad to hear your voice!"
"Are Val and Gary ready to go?"
"Yes, we all spent the night here at the lodge."
"We've got a red shirt to hoist up in a tree as a signal."
"Okay, I'll let Gary know. Get home safe, Derrick."
"We will listen for the helicopter."

They were in such a bad situation—the phone call was brief and to the point. Derrick woke everyone up; Jeff sat by the entrance of the cave and listened carefully for the helicopter.

Before long he jumped up with excitement!
"I think I hear it! Listen ... do you hear that?"
They all gathered around and listened.
"I hear it too!" Helen replied.

Helen helped Charlie take his flannel shirt off, and put his vest and jacket back on. They both wrapped up together in their blanket to keep warm. Derrick tied the shirt to a rope to use as a signal.

"Let's get moving and dig ourselves out of this cave!"
Jan looked afraid, "I can't, my hands are numb."
"It's okay, I'll dig for both of us!" Jeff replied.

Mark, Jeff and Derrick all started to dig through the snow. Mark seemed to have boundless energy, within a few minutes they had cleared all of the snow from the entrance of the cave. The sun started to shine in—they had survived, and made it out of the cave.

Derrick found a high branch on a tall tree next to the cave. He used the rope to hoist up old Charlie's red flannel shirt. When they saw the Helicopter, they all started waving their arms to get Val and Gary's attention.

The helicopter circled overhead a few times as Gary looked for a safe place to land. With fresh snow covering the mountain, he couldn't find any stable ground. He decided they would need to bring the helicopter in close enough to lower the ladder.

Val waved to everyone as they lowered the helicopter near the entrance of the cave. Everyone was standing outside except for old Charlie. Val sent down the ladder, but she worried there would not be enough space them all.

Derrick directed the rescue from the ground.
"Jan and Helen, you two go first. Can you climb the ladder?"
"My feet and hands are frostbitten, I will be careful."
"Are you sure you'll be OK?"
"Yes, I can make it, I need to get out of this cold!"

Jan started to climb up the ladder. When she reached the top, Val took her hand and carefully helped her inside. Derrick noticed that Helen looked worried.

"Helen, are you alright? Can you climb that ladder?"
"You bet I can!"
She was determined to get help for Charlie.
"Ask them to send down a stretcher for Charlie."

As Derrick looked up at the helicopter, he realized they couldn't all fit inside. The most important thing was for them to get Charlie to the hospital.

"Helen, once Charlie is on board, tell them to go."
"You want us to leave you behind?"
"We will be okay, we'll make our way back on foot."
With a nod, Helen began to climb the ladder.

As Helen boarded the helicopter she started to feel some relief. They were finally getting out of that cave. It had been a long and very cold night. Val sent down the stretcher for Charlie.

"I'll get the stretcher ready here for Charlie."
Derrick shouted so Mark and Jeff could hear him.
"Can you two help carry old Charlie over here?"

Mark and Jeff walked to the entrance of the cave where Charlie was waiting. He was unable to stand up on his own.

"Don't worry old Charlie, you're getting help. Everything is going to be okay!"

"Derrick has a stretcher waiting for you."

"We will carry you over there, you will be getting help in no time at all."

Mark and Jeff stood next to Charlie, and together they picked him up. They carried him through the snow over to the helicopter. Derrick had laid out the stretcher and the safety harness. He helped get Charlie wrapped up and buckled in.

"Are you ready, Charlie?"
"As ready as I'll ever be!"

Derrick gave Val a signal that he was ready. The stretcher started rising back up to the helicopter. Once they got Charlie inside, Helen sat next to him and held his hand.

"We're safe now honey, just take some deep breaths. We are on the way to the hospital. I'm right here with you. I love you."

Val could tell that Charlie was in very bad condition. He was having a hard time breathing, so she started oxygen for him right away. As they lifted off, a great flurry of snow rose up all around.

"Welcome aboard the Big Red," Gary shouted back to his passengers, "I turned up the heat for you, and we're on our way to the hospital."

Derrick, Matt and Jeff watched as the helicopter flew off in a cloud of snow. As it faded into the distance, Derrick explained that there wasn't enough space for everyone. Having decided to make the journey on foot, they started their trek back to the lodge.

In the helicopter, everyone was safe and starting to warm up. Jan watched the snow outside through the big windows.

"I've never seen so much snow."

"No one expected a storm like this, I'm glad you're all safe."

"It sure is beautiful, but now I know how dangerous it can be."

It was a quick ride to the hospital. Gary landed on the helipad outside, and the paramedics came rushing out. They brought Charlie in and Helen followed right behind them. They brought a wheelchair back for Jan because she was having a hard time standing.

"Mission accomplished!" Gary announced.

"Now, let's get back to the lodge!"

When Val and Gary made it back to the lodge, they saw Kaya was in tears. She was right next to the phone, waiting for it to ring. Svea did her best to console her. She became more worried as time passed by. Finally the phone rang and Kaya jumped to answer it.

"Derrick, where are you? Are you OK?"

"Don't worry, we're on our way back now."

"Please be careful, I can't wait until you're home safe!"

Suddenly the phone went dead.

"Mom, something happened … he hung up!"

"Don't worry Kaya, the battery probably went out."

Svea hung up the phone and held both of Kaya's hands.

"Everything is going to be alright. Why don't you make him a rhubarb pie? By the time it's baked, he will be home."

Kaya looked around and noticed how many people were watching her. Corrine, Kathleen, Carol and Maryann had all been listening in on their conversation. She did a double take when she realized that Val and Gary were there too!

"You're back! I wish Derrick would have come with you in the helicopter! He's so stubborn."

"We didn't have enough room for everyone, but they are all together—Mark, Jeff, and Derrick. They'll be OK, it won't be long."

"Please pray for them," Kaya pleaded.
Val asked everyone at the lodge to join them for a prayer.

"Please everyone, gather around—we have a need for prayer at this time. Let's pray for Derrick, Mark, and Jeff.

"Dear Heavenly Father,
We pray to you now to ask for your help. Please watch over Derrick, Mark, and Jeff on their journey home. Please guide them safely back to us. Bless them with your love and care. In Jesus' name, amen."

Kaya smiled through her tears. She knew that her mom was right, she needed to keep herself busy. Baking pies sounded like a great idea.

"Thank you, Val … I'm going to go make some pies."

As she walked toward the kitchen, there was a loud banging on the door! Kaya ran to see who it was. To her surprise, Mr. Mag and JP stood before her covered with snow! The cold wind was blowing, and snow came swirling through the door.

"Hurry, come in," Kaya's excitement fell.
They stepped inside and brushed off the snow.
"We heard the helicopter pass overhead—"
"We knew something was going on, so here we are!"

"It looks like everyone is here ... Kaya, why are you so sad?"

"Derrick went on a hike and got caught in the storm. He was bringing a group to the scenic overlook, just like he does every year. They got trapped in the storm and took shelter in a cave."

Hearing this, JP and Mr. Mag became concerned.

"Has anyone heard from him today?"

"I just talked to him a moment ago, he's on the way back now."

"I'm sure he will be here soon, Kaya," JP replied.

"Swedes are a strong and hearty bunch," Mr. Mag added.

"That's right! He will be back here sooner than you think."

Hearing this from Mr. Magnusson and JP, Kaya felt a little bit better. She went with her mom into the kitchen, they decided to make enough rhubarb pies so everyone could have some. They worked together preparing and baking the pies.

When they worked together, Kaya and Svea made the perfect team. First they mixed the flour, sugar, salt, and butter, along with a hint of apple cider vinegar. Next they sprinkled the water on top and slowly mixed it in. They followed an old recipe that was from Svea's grandmother, it was a favorite of everyone at the lodge!

Once the dough was ready, they lined up all of the pie tins in a long row. Svea rolled out the dough, and began to fill the pie tins. Meanwhile, Kaya began to mix the filling. She combined the rhubarb, sugar, lemon, almond extract, and tapioca starch. Finally, they added the secret ingredient—just as the recipe called for!

Soon the big ovens were packed with rhubarb pies. Everyone could smell the pies baking, they had made the best out of the situation; it almost seemed like a special holiday! Thankfully all of their friends were safe, it was truly an incredible storm. The only thing left was for Derrick, Mark, and Jeff to arrive.

Kaya and Svea cleaned up the kitchen while the first batch of pies were baking. After they put the second batch in the oven, they went out to join all of their friends. Sven was talking with some of the skiers who regularly visit the lodge. The Gällivare Ladies were telling entertaining stories of their antics from years ago.

Kaya couldn't concentrate on what people were saying. Derrick was all that she could think of. She kept a close eye on the door while waiting for him to arrive. A few times she actually thought that she heard Derrick's voice, but he wasn't there. She would stop in her tracks and look at the door, but it didn't open.

As she turned to walk back into the kitchen, she heard Derrick's voice again. This time she knew it was him! Kaya ran over to the door and opened it. The wind and snow came blowing into the lodge, and Derrick, Jeff, and Mark just about fell through the doorway!

"Derrick, you made it!"
He looked up and saw all the people gathered at the lodge.
With a big grin he shouted, "We're here!"

There was a great cheer throughout the lodge to welcome them home. Kaya gave Derrick a great big hug! Everyone was so happy that they made it back safely. Still loaded down with all their gear, they were making a considerable effort just to hold each other up!

"Jeff is going to need some help, he took a bad fall on the way back. He hurt his right leg on a sharp rock. Mark and I almost had to carry him half of the way back! Mark is a hero in every way, we wouldn't be here without him."

Sven and Svea helped Jeff to a seat.

"I'll call Dr. Leif and let him know you need help."

Svea got through to Dr. Leif right away.

"Even if I could make it through this storm, it sounds like he needs an x-ray. It may still be a few hours until the roads are clear."

"Good thing Val and Gary are here. We will get him to the hospital right away!"

Sven made plans with Gary to take Jeff to the hospital. After the first trip, he had parked the helicopter right in front of the lodge. They were so happy to be back at the lodge; it had been a harrowing experience for them all.

Before they left for the hospital, Kaya and Svea served fresh baked rhubarb pie to everyone. It was almost right out of the oven! The townspeople had always tried to figure out their secret recipe, especially the Gällivare Ladies. It was a secret that Kaya and Svea would never tell!

After warming up, Derrick and Jeff prepared to leave.

"You're a lifesaver, Gary, we're lucky you're here!"

"It's all in a day's work, we'll be there in no time at all!"

Derrick and Mark helped Jeff out to the helicopter, and lifted him aboard. Kaya was nervous to see them go, but Svea reminded her they'll be right back. On the way there, Jeff apologized to Derrick for falling and getting hurt.

"I'm so sorry this happened, I should've paid more attention."

"Don't worry my friend, you'd have done the same for me."

"I'd carry you all the way, and you're a lot bigger than I am!"

When they arrived at the hospital, Gary moved into position for the landing. Their great adventure was finally coming to an end. Back at the lodge, Val had called the hospital to let them know that Jeff was on the way.

"At least your girlfriend is here, she'll be very happy to see you! Let the staff know you are looking for her, they'll help you."

"Well, it looks like this is your stop—"
The staff brought out a wheelchair for Jeff.
"Give us a call and let us know what's going on."
With Jeff safely inside, Derrick and Gary were ready to go.
"Alright Derrick, let's rock!"

Gary put on some classic rock and roll music, and turned the volume up loud! They took off in Big Red and headed back to the lodge. Derrick loved every minute of it!

When they arrived, they found Mark telling all about the cold night they spent in the cave. He got a little sentimental when he talked about Helen and old Charlie.

He held his hand over his heart, "Now that is true love. I hope to find it for myself one day ... and to have enough sense to know when I do!"

Derrick and Gary showed up just in time for a nice hot meal. They looked a little worse for wear, they were tired, and concerned for Jeff and old Charlie.

Lunch at the lodge was served buffet style. After such a distressing trip, it was exactly what they needed: a chance to visit and get cozy by the fire. Kaya sat next to Derrick and wanted to hear about everything that happened. The Gällivare Ladies asked a few questions too.

"Derrick, did you miss Kaya?"
"Did you ever think you might not make it back?"
Derrick replied with a shy smile, "Of course I missed Kaya. Deep down I knew that if I didn't make it back, Kaya would never forgive me—I couldn't allow that to happen."

"Aww, Derrick, that is the nicest thing you ever said! You know, I do care about you."

Svea knew there was something special between them.
"We're very happy to see you two back together again."

The phone rang and Sven went over to answer it.

"Jan, how are you and Jeff? Oh sure … that's good … yeah … did you see Helen and Charlie? … I was afraid of that … God bless him … Oh? … So when is he coming home? … That is great! OK, we'll call and check on him in the morning."

Silence came over the room as Sven hung up the phone. Everyone had been wondering what happened to Charlie.

"I talked to Jan, she has some frostbite on her fingers and toes, but the doctors took good care of her. Jeff had a deep gash on his leg, he needed over twenty stitches! It will take some therapy to get him back on his feet. The doctors are going to keep both of them overnight."

"Sven, what about Charlie?" Svea asked.

"Well, the worst news is that old Charlie lost his favorite red flannel shirt. I hear it's still flying high out on the mountain! He is doing well though, he is a tough old bird! He will be in the hospital until sometime next week."

Val was relieved to hear that he was OK.
"That's the best news I've heard all day!"

"This will be a day that we will never forget!"

20. Last Year of College

Derrick will be graduating this year, with honors, and will receive his Bachelor of Laws degree. Time seemed to pass by so quickly, another year had gone by. There is a job waiting for him at Mr. Magnusson's Law Firm. One of the lawyers at the firm, Mr. Hansson, will be retiring soon. Derrick will take his place and join Val and Gary who also work at the firm.

Derrick and Kaya have been keeping in close touch with each other. He calls her at least twice a week, and they've spent many hours talking. It's clear to everyone that they miss each other very much, but Kaya will not admit she misses him.

Kaya has continued to take on additional responsibilities at the lodge. Her Dad told her that someday the lodge will belong to her! In the last few years, she's started to take care of the business needs, accounting, and handle the special events.

Kaya has been working at the lodge for over ten years now. She's made friends with all of the townspeople, and regular guests. Visitors from neighboring countries have told her stories of Switzerland, Germany, Italy, Norway, and many other places—she loves to hear of their adventures! In many ways the lodge has become a second home for her.

As time went on Mark and Derrick became the best of friends, they're almost like brothers. Mark likes to tease Derrick, and told him that if he doesn't ask Kaya to marry him, then he will! During the winter season, they've come to the lodge together many times to go skiing. They always enjoy telling the story of how they got stuck in the blizzard.

Kaya was talking with Svea while she made notes for an upcoming graduation party that was booked at the lodge.

"Mom, I have the details sorted out for the big graduation party. The date is set, and I've started making all of the arrangements. The colors will be red and gray; I've ordered all of the flowers and decorations. They have a recipe for a special punch, it sounds really good. I think we should try it out ahead of time. The band is all set, they will perform on the middle stage of the banquet room.

"We've finalized the menu, and all the food has been ordered. Our best waitresses will be serving the guests. The kitchen helpers will keep close watch and clear tables after each course. They've requested fine dinnerware. Decorations and balloons will be in place two hours before the guests arrive."

Svea was so impressed, she had watched little Kaya grow up before her eyes. She appreciated how responsible and professional Kaya had become. Kaya knows everything it takes to run the lodge.

"Wow! I am so proud of you, Kaya."
Kaya was so happy, it showed in how she carried herself.
She asked Svea, "Did Derrick call yet?"
"Not yet, but it's still a little early."
Svea noticed her expression change.
"I think you care for him more than you admit."
"Mom, I do not! Why would I miss him?"
"Oh? I didn't say you missed him—do you?"
"No! He teases me all the time."

Svea knew there was more to the story than Kaya was letting on. She noticed how much time they spent together. They would take off now and then and to go skiing together, and make trips into town.

"Kaya, let's sit down here and have a talk, between mother and daughter. You know, everyone needs someone to love, and to be loved. Your heart and mind will let you know if it's true love. At some point, you are going to have to trust Derrick. Listen to your feelings."

Kaya felt kind of mixed up, "How can I just trust my feelings? What if I do, and then he changes? I don't know what to do."

Svea pointed to Kaya's heart, and gave her a tap.

"Listen to your heart. Your heart will tell you everything you need to know! Think about how you can look at him and almost read his mind. Think about how when you are apart, you miss him so much that your heart aches to see him again and you can't wait to hold him in your arms. He feels the same way. I've seen that special look, when you and Derrick look into each other's eyes. That look that makes your heartbeat a little faster."

Kaya squinted her eyes and tilted her head.
"How do you know all this stuff?"
Svea got a dreamy look of love on her face.

"That is exactly how I knew that Sven loved me! We both felt the same way. Don't be afraid to give Derrick a chance. You can still keep your independence. You know, he only teases you because he wants your attention."
Kaya brushed her hair back, and took a long breath.

"Somehow, you really do seem to know everything! You are the best, Mom, I love you. I needed to hear this from you. But this still doesn't mean I miss him!"

Derrick entered the lodge and stood in the doorway with a huge smile that made his dark blue eyes twinkle. He was home on winter break and felt like he was on top of the world! Today is the day that could make him the happiest man in Gällivare. He searched the lodge looking for Svea, and quietly snuck into the kitchen. He found Svea preparing venison steaks; she just started mixing the seasonings in a large pan. Svea was so busy that she didn't see Derrick come in.

Derrick walked up behind her and yelled, "Svea!"
She jumped with fright, and the pan fell to the floor!
"Darn it, Derrick!"
"I'm Sorry, I couldn't resist!"
"If you ever do that again I'll ban you from the kitchen!"

Derrick started helping to clean up the mess, he knew he was in trouble. He didn't mean to cause her to drop it, he apologized as best he could.

"Look what you made me do! What is wrong with you?"
"I'll explain! Slow down, don't worry."
He timidly hid behind his hands.
"It's important, I promise! Come on, let's go sit at a table."

Svea didn't know what was so important that he would interrupt her cooking, and cause such a mess. She reluctantly followed him to a table and they took a seat. Svea folded her hands and waited intently. She saw a look on Derrick's face that she had never seen before. She got worried and grabbed his hand tightly.

"Derrick, did something bad happen? Is everything okay?"
"Svea … you've known me ever since I was a youngster."

Svea interrupted him, "What did you do? I'll get the best lawyer in town! Oh wait, I forgot, you are a lawyer—being a lawyer, whatever you did, you should have known better! You shouldn't be so full of mischief!"

Derrick was shocked!
"Don't worry Svea, just listen. It's not bad news!"
She paused for a moment to hear him out.
"You know Kaya and I have been friends for all of our lives."
"That's right, you two aggravate each other to no end."

"She has punched me in my shoulder more times than I can recall … but when I was away at college, I realized how much I missed her. She finally told me that she misses me too!"

Hearing this made Svea laugh. She has tried to get Kaya to admit she missed Derrick so many times!

"I miss her voice. I remember the way she tosses her long blond hair back when she's mad. In her strong voice, she would say, 'Don't you dare ever do that again,' demanding an apology on the spot! In our ski races, she always has to win. When we were kids, she would say 'My dad told me I am a winner!' She's so determined."
Svea shook her head, "Yeah, he did tell her that."

"She's pushed me into snowbanks and laughed at me when I fall on my skis, but she's always willing to fix me up when I get hurt. I miss everything about her. I miss the stance she takes when she's checking me out, trying to figure out if I'm telling the truth, or playing a joke on her. I miss walking through the forest together, making snow angels. I miss working in Sven's shop ... I miss being here with Kaya."

Svea knew how close they had become over the years. "Derrick, why are you telling me all of these things?"

"Svea ... this may come as quite a surprise. I love Kaya ... I'm here to ask you for your blessing ... I want to ask her to marry me! I can't imagine life without her. *Please say yes!*"

Svea was silent, she looked into his eyes and she saw a sincere look of love, a forever love. Svea took his hand.

"I knew that someday this would happen. Honestly, I can't imagine you two without each other. You have my blessing, Derrick. I pray that God will bless you both."

Derrick jumped up from his seat, "Hallelujah!"
As Svea stood up to give him a hug, he took her hand and twirled her around!
"Thank you, Svea! Thank you!"

The Gällivare Ladies had just arrived at the lodge for lunch. They were puzzled when they saw Derrick twirl Svea around. A waitress greeted them.
"Welcome Ladies, would you like to sit at your regular table?"
"What's going on here?" Corrine asked.
"We'll sit here so we can hear better."

Maryann motioned toward Derrick.

"I feel like we just missed something," Carol commented.

"Listen up girls, and take notes," Kathleen added.

They all wanted to figure out what was going on. Derrick, and Svea both sat back down at the table. He ran his hand through his hair, he was beaming with excitement!

"Svea, can you do without Kaya this weekend?"

"Sure, I can. There are other girls who can cover for her"

Kathleen whispered to Carol, "Take note, Kaya will not be at work this weekend."

Derrick started to explain, "I talked to Val and Gary and made a plan. If Kaya wants to go, they will fly us to Kiruna in the big red helicopter!"

The ladies were all ears as they listened.

"Write that down! Why didn't Val tell us about this?"

"We'll all stay at the Grand Hotel," Derrick continued, "Val and Gary will take us wherever we want to go."

Carol looked shocked, "Corrine, did you hear that? They're going to a hotel together! How can Sven and Svea condone this?"

"I don't know—here comes our waitress, pretend to be busy!"

Maryann kept it brief, she ordered for all the girls.

"We'll each have the lunch special, and kaffe, please."

Svea was amused by how anxious Derrick looked.

"I'll ask her if she wants to go, when does she start work?"

"She starts in about 30 minutes. She should be here soon, but you never know, she could arrive any minute."

"Oh no, I'm so nervous!" His face became pale, "What if she says no? What if she doesn't love me as much as I love her?"

"You'll be fine. I'll get you some lemonade, wait here."

Derrick started talking to himself after Svea left. As he was talking, the Gällivare Ladies were still listening in.

"Okay … nothing to worry about, Derrick. If she says *'yes'* then we leave for Kiruna at one o'clock on Saturday, and everything is right in the world. If she says *'no'* then life as I know it will cease to exist … no pressure."

Carol took notes, "Saturday at one o'clock."
Corrine started making a plan.
"We'll split up, so we don't miss anything."
"What a surprise!" Maryann exclaimed.
Kathleen interrupted, "Shh! Svea's coming back."

When Svea returned, she saw Derrick talking to himself. She couldn't believe how nervous he was. She patted him on his hand, and gave him the lemonade.

"I know how much she missed you while you were away in law school. I remember when you called, and sometimes would only talk for a little bit, but you would both stay on the phone. The line was silent for such a long time. You didn't need words to explain the feelings, they were expressed in the silence. I saw the look of love on her face."

Just then Svea saw Kaya walk through the door. She didn't have time to give Derrick any last minute advice.

"She's here! Stay calm and collected, I feel good about this!"
Kaya waved to Svea and Derrick.
"Hi Mom! I'm a little early, has it been busy?"
Svea pulled out a chair for Kaya.
"No, not yet, but it will be later in the evening."

Kaya sat down in the chair next to Derrick, it seemed a little bit out of the ordinary. She felt that something was going on.

"Hey Derrick, are you here for lunch?"
He ran his hand through his hair.
"Yeah, I stopped in to see Svea. I was hoping to see you too!"
"What do you want to eat? We can visit since it's slow today."
"I'll have a cheeseburger and a soda, please."
Kaya winked at Derrick, "I'll be right back."

Derrick tried to stay calm while he waited. Kaya went to the kitchen to put in his order, then came back to talk to Derrick.

"Is everything okay? You look worried."
Derrick smiled as he replied.
"Worried? I am perfect now that you are here!"

Kaya got a teasing look on her face, "So, did you come here just to see me? What are you up to? Do you think you can get me a few drinks and go skiing, so you can win and laugh when I fall?"

"That was the old Derrick, but you do look hilarious when you fall. The new Derrick has changed, and he is quite lovable."

"Oh? I'll believe that when I see it!"
Kaya looked at her watch to check the time.
"I better get to work—Mom, where is my apron?"

"It's okay, he's been waiting here for you. Just stay and visit with him, it's very slow right now."

Kaya smiled as she sat across from Derrick. She started to suspect there was more going on here than she knew. Derrick got a shy smile on his face.

"Okay, looks like I can stay and talk with you. You're in luck! Well, new smart lawyer, man about town, what should we talk about?"

The Gällivare Ladies were still listening in.
Corrine whispered, "Looks like trouble to me—"
Kathleen shushed her again, "Shh, just listen."

Kaya noticed the heartfelt look on his face.
"I need to talk to you, Kaya. Look at me, have I ever said a bad word to you?"

Kaya was confused by the question.
"No," she shook her head.
"Well, give me a moment and hear me out … please?"
Kaya challenged him, "Why?"

Derrick knew this was not going to be easy. He ran his hand through his hair and pulled his chair closer.
"Please? It will mean a lot to me."
Kaya paused for a moment to think.
"Okay," she knew this was something serious.

Svea smiled from across the room, Derrick smiled back.
Carol whispered to Corrine, "Did you see that?"
Corrine whispered back, "Oh, I sure did."

Derrick had been planning this trip for several weeks now. It all came down to this.

"Kaya, I want to take you to Kiruna for the weekend to see the Aurora Borealis. From up close, it will be so beautiful. They say you can even hear the whoosh of the lights overhead! You are the only one I would ever want to take there. We can stay at a very elegant hotel, go sightseeing, dining, and dancing. It would be so much fun! No hanky panky. We both need a break, and it's only for a weekend. I'll bring you back safe and sound, just promise not to injure me! So, what do you say?"

Kaya looked blank, she didn't know what to say.
After a pause, she slowly replied, "I ... I just don't know."
Kaya looked toward Svea, she gave her nod and smiled.
"This is so much to think about!"

Derrick went on to tell her the plan for sightseeing, and how Val and Gary would take them to Kiruna in the big red helicopter.

"I talked with Val and Gary, they'll come with us to the Grand Hotel in Kiruna. We'll stay there and have a great dinner. After dinner, they will drop us off in Abisko to see the northern lights. They'll have their own plans, but will come back to pick us up."
Maryann whispered, "Oh, this is so romantic!"
Carol pointed, "Look, he is holding Kaya's hand!"

Derrick held both of her hands and gazed into her eyes. This meant so much to him. It was the most important moment in his life!

"I already asked Svea if it is okay. She said it's up to you. Please say you will go with me ... please?"

"Oh Derrick, you look so pathetic!"
Kaya laughed, Derrick still looked confused.
"Of course I'll go! How can I say no?"
He smiled with excitement, "Really?"
"Yes, Derrick, I'll go with you."

They all started to celebrate, the Gällivare Ladies stood up and gave them a round of applause! Kaya started blushing and Derrick kissed her in front of everyone.

Derrick slept well that night. He went to bed with a smile on his face. Everything was right in the world.

He had finally shared his great secret!

21. Visiting Kiruna

Kaya was so excited that she could hardly sleep. She stayed up talking with Svea until late in the evening. The next morning, Kaya came bustling into the lodge. Svea had arrived early, she greeted Kaya as she hurriedly walked through the door. It was still early in the morning and they were the only ones there.

"Good morning, Mom."
"Good morning, Kaya. You are a little late."
"I'm sorry, I overslept and I got a little bit sidetracked!"
"Don't worry, I have something for you. Wait here!"

Svea returned with a large box. Kaya wasn't expecting any surprises, her face lit up as she started to open the box! Inside she found a beautiful new ski jacket. It was white and light blue, and the hood was trimmed in white fur.

"I love it, Mom!"
Kaya slipped it on and danced around.
"Just wait, there's more, I have another surprise!"
Svea gave her a second box.
"Oh, Mom! What did you go out and do?"

She became a little emotional as she opened the box. From inside she lifted up a matching set of ski pants. She looked at her mom and tilted her head adoringly. Svea felt so proud of her.

"Mom, they are so beautiful!"
She held them up to check the fit.

"Look, there is something else in the box too!"

Kaya laid the pants over a chair, then checked in the bottom of the box. She found the most perfect ski boots she had ever seen. They were white and light blue, trimmed with white fur, and came up to the knee.

"Thank you Mom, they are perfect! I can't believe it!"
Svea was delighted to see her daughter so happy.
"I picked them out specially for you, they match the jacket."

As she went to put them on, Kaya noticed there was one more surprise hidden inside of the boots! She found a pair of white ski gloves inside. They had white fur trim that matched the jacket, pants, and the boots. She was almost in tears, everything was so beautiful! She hadn't had anything like this before.

Svea held out her arms, "Come here, my darling."
They both gave each other a big hug!
"Thank you Mom, I love it! It's all so beautiful!"

"Your dad ordered this for you for Christmas, but he couldn't wait. He said this is just the right time. We're both so happy for you. We trust you and Derrick, and we hope you have a wonderful trip!"

"I'm so lucky to have you and Dad. You're such great parents."
"There's just one thing I am afraid of ..."
Svea noticed that Kaya looked troubled.

"I've never flown anywhere before ... I've never been on a helicopter! I really don't think *flying* is such a *good idea.*"

Svea put her hand on Kaya's shoulder, "Don't worry, my dear. You will be safe and sound with Val and Gary. Helicopters don't fly very high, and they can land almost anywhere. Just enjoy the sights, forget about that fear, Derrick will be right by your side. Now, get to work! You're off at eleven o'clock."

"Mom, do I look okay? Can you tell I cried?"
"No, you're as pretty as you always are."
They both gave each other another big hug.
"You mean the world to me, Kaya."

Later on, the Gällivare Ladies came to the lodge for lunch. Kaya was very perky and energetic as she approached their table.

"Hi! How are you ladies of the town today?"
They looked at each other in silence.
"We are as good as we can get, I guess."
"What would you like for lunch?"
"I'll have the caesar salad, tea, and rhubarb pie."
"Good choice!"

The other ladies all decided to have the same. When Kaya turned to leave, Kathleen tugged on her apron.

"You look so pretty today, is there anything going on?"
Corrine looked up and waited for her to answer.
"I have the weekend off! Have you ladies ever—"
Svea interrupted, she knew what they were up to!
"Kaya, I'll take care of these ladies, there are some other customers waiting."

Kaya stood with Sven and Svea waiting for the helicopter to arrive. Soon they started to hear it in the distance, it was getting closer. The Gällivare Ladies were inside pretending to have a meeting. They heard it too and went outside to watch.

"Now, this should be good!" Maryann proclaimed.
"Let's split up so we can cover all sides."

Kathleen coordinated the plan, "You and Carol take one side, Corrine and I will wander around."

When the helicopter arrived, it slowly descended and landed in front of the lodge. Kaya was a little nervous earlier, but when she saw the big red helicopter she got excited!

"I've never been in a helicopter, it looks so incredible!"
"Gary calls it Big Red, it's his pride and joy!"

The Gällivare Ladies tried to blend in with the crowd that had gathered in front of the lodge. With the way they keep track of everything in town, taking notes and pictures, they could almost get a job with the newspaper. When you see them, you never know if they might be undercover!

Carol got a great picture of Kaya and her parents as the helicopter was landing. When the engine stopped, Derrick jumped out. When he looked at Kaya and his mind went blank. Her long blond hair fell in such beautiful curls; the white fur on her ski jacket encircled her lovely face. She looked like a real Lapland princess!

Derrick thought, "I think I just fell in love all over again!"
He walked over to Sven and shook his hand.
"I've wished for this day for a long time, Derrick."
"She sure takes my breath away."
"Real love will do that, I still feel that way about Svea."

Kaya smiled at Derrick as he took her hand. Derrick helped
Kaya climb into the helicopter, Corrine got a photo of that one! He
sat down next to her; Sven and Svea wished them good luck as they
all said goodbye.

They have known Val and Gary for such a long time. It made
them comfortable to know Kaya and Derrick were in good hands.

Val reassured Svea, "Don't worry, not even for a moment!
They are safe with us, it's an honor to look after them."

"We'll be at their beck and call," Gary added!

They all got buckled in and prepared for takeoff. Everyone
waved to Sven and Svea from inside of the helicopter. They each
had a headset so they could still talk with each other, Gary had some
beautiful Swedish love songs playing softly through the headsets.

The time had come, they were all ready for take off. As the
helicopter lifted up off the ground they waved goodbye to Sven and
Svea one more time. The sound of the motor made Kaya nervous.
When she looked at the blades turning overhead she became a little
scared. Derrick reassured her that everything would be okay.

"Just hold on to me and try to enjoy the ride. Soon we'll be
able to see the mountains in Stora Sjöfallet park."

Kaya always felt safe when Derrick was with her. She held on to his arm as the helicopter rose up into the sky. Everyone in the crowd was waving to them.

"Oh, I see the Gällivare Ladies waving at us!"

Derrick got a big grin on his face, "Well, wave back!"

Kaya waved back to everyone in the crowd.

"What a wonderful couple," Kathleen said, as she waved.

Maryann jumped up and down, saying "I love it! I love it!"

Svea heard them, she smiled and walked into the lodge.

The world below them became very small as they rose up into the sky. Derrick pointed out the people riding on the ski lift. It was Kaya's first time flying, she was amazed to see the world from so high up above.

As they left town Gary gave them a small tour. He flew around the whole city of Gällivare, Kaya recognized all of her favorite places. After leaving town, they flew west and saw the great beauty of the mountains. Then, on the way to Kiruna, Gary took them on a tour of the small towns that were nearby.

Gary made an announcement when they arrived in Kiruna. He circled the area a few times as they prepared to land. When Gary angled the helicopter it caused Kaya to slide over into Derrick.

Kaya was scared, "Gary, don't let me fall out!"

"Don't scare the poor girl," Val scolded him.

Gary laughed, "Okay, I'm sorry!"

Their anticipation was building as Gary began to bring them in for the landing. Kaya looked out and saw the hotel, their arrival in the big red helicopter was generating a lot of attention. People started to gather to watch the helicopter land.

"I called before we left, we'll land right in front of the hotel."
Kaya held tight to Derrick, "I'm so happy we're here!"
Derrick smiled and held Kaya's hand.
"We have a wonderful weekend ahead, Kaya!"

Kaya admired how exquisite the hotel was, it seemed like a scene from a fairy tale. Derrick got out of the helicopter first, then held out his hand to help Kaya down. He looked like a handsome prince; together they made a breathtaking couple.

The townspeople all gathered around to see them. It was not every day that you would see a big red helicopter flying through town. Derrick and Kaya smiled and waved to everyone, the crowd gave a big cheer as they walked by! Kaya heard the questions and comments from people in the crowd.

"Who are they? Are they Royalty?"
"She is so beautiful! What a wonderful couple!"

Gary spoke with the bellboys who came to carry their luggage. As they approached the hotel, they were welcomed by the doorman.

"Welcome to the Grand Hotel, Mr. Norlander!"

The lobby of the hotel was very elegant! It spanned two floors, had large stone pillars, and was decorated with many beautiful pieces of art. They were met by a receptionist.

"Welcome to the Grand Hotel! Right this way, follow me and I will show you to your rooms."

Val and Gary followed behind Derrick and Kaya, the bellboys were right behind them. They took the elevator up to the top floor where they had very charming and spacious rooms.

"We are at your service, just call if you need anything."

"Thank you, everything looks perfect!"

"Lunch will be served in the ballroom when you're ready."

It was sure to be a very memorable evening. They met with Val and Gary and went down to the ballroom together. The hostess curtsied as they entered the room.

"Good afternoon, your guests have just begun to arrive."

Kaya got a puzzled look on her face. She was not expecting there to be any other guests! They followed the hostess into the elegant ballroom, she wondered who was here.

Magnificent chandeliers lit up the room. The tables had crystal candelabras and beautiful flowers. It started to become clear that Derrick had planned a very special event!

At a long banquet table she saw fancy place cards with the name of each guest. Kaya read the names: Mr. Magnusson, JP, Dr. Leif, Elda, Mark, Val, and Gary.

"I can't believe it! Derrick, are all these people here?"

Before Derrick could answer, Mr. Magnusson responded!

"We sure are, Kaya!"

JP was right behind him, "We're all here for you!"

Dr. Leif and Elda walked in.

"Mr. Magnusson wanted us all to be here!"

Mark, Val, and Gary came in together.

"This will be a night to remember!" Mark announced.

Kaya was seated next to Derrick. With a soft loving look on his face, he took her hand and held it for a while. Val nudged Gary's foot under the table, and gave him a knowing look.

Val whispered, "Have you noticed how many people are watching us?"

Gary took a look around the room.

"Oh, you are right!"

"Let's start a conversation about famous married couples!"

They both laughed.

The waitresses brought bread and hors d'oeuvres to their table. Mr. Magnusson had requested a special Italian wine for the occasion, Montepulciano d'Abruzzo. They talked about the years Kaya and Derrick spent together growing up. Everyone laughed so hard they cried as they recalled all the tricks that Kaya and Derrick played on each other.

Kaya wished that Sven and Svea were there. She shared an old memory of her dad saying, "Don't write Derrick off, Kaya. He is a fine young man and a very hard worker. I respect him, and I believe someday you will too."

Once they had finished lunch, Derrick began to tell the guests about their next stop. They will be going to Abisko National Park to see the aurora borealis. He had been planning this trip for many weeks now.

Before they left for Abisko, Mr. Magnusson announced that he would like to make a toast to Derrick and Kaya. They all raised their glasses together.

"A toast to young love, may it last forever! Skål!"

22. Stars Of The Night

Everyone followed them outside to the helicopter and waved goodbye as they took off. Derrick and Kaya waved back; this time Kaya wasn't as scared. The town of Kiruna faded into the distance as they looked out of the window.

On the way there, Gary started singing a rock and roll song and having a good time. Soon Val started singing with Gary, then Derrick and Kaya joined in too!

Derrick told Kaya, "See Kaya, this can be a lot of fun!"
He kept his arm around her to help her feel safe.
"We will be there in a few minutes," Val announced.

After a few of Gary's favorite rock and roll songs, they were almost there. Derrick brought heavy blankets to keep them warm, and two big lanterns to light their way. He got ready to unload them from the helicopter while Gary found the right place to land.

Everyone had big smiles as they landed in a clearing on the north-eastern face of Mount Njullá.

The sun began to set, filling the sky with brilliant shades of pink and violet. The ice on Lake Torneträsk reflected the beautiful shades of the sunset and the northern lights.

"We'll be nearby, call if there's an emergency."
"Thank you, see you in an hour!"

Derrick climbed down to the ground first, then helped Kaya step down from the helicopter. Wind from the helicopter caused a flurry of snowflakes to swirl all around them. They each carried a bundled up blanket under their arm, Val handed them the lanterns.

Val waved, they were off to do some sightseeing too.

Derrick led the way as they walked along, "Kaya, I found a special place for us to watch the aurora borealis. You will love it!"

He was so excited to show Kaya the place that he picked out. He stopped talking and then, with his hand on his head, he looked into the distance.

"I think it's this way—"
"Derrick, are we lost?"
"No, don't worry, I am an expert in navigation!"

Kaya laughed, she always questioned his sense of direction. They looked up at the beautiful sky as they walked along together.

"This is the best place in the world to see the aurora borealis!"
"It's such a beautiful sight, it looks so magical!"
"We're almost to the place that I picked out."
His eyes searched from right to left.
"Oh, there it is! From now on this will be our rock."

They approached a very large rock that protruded from the foothills of the mountain. Derrick climbed up first, then set down his lantern and blanket. Kaya handed him the other lantern and blanket, then he helped her up. After unbundling the blankets they sat down together and watched the sun set behind the mountains.

The Secret of Gällivare

As the sun went down the northern lights began to shine so brightly, their reflection was cast across the surface of the ice along with shadows of the great mountains. High above the peaks the many shades of green waved gracefully like a wispy green genie. The waves of color danced all across the star-studded sky.

Kaya sighed, "Oh, Derrick ... I love this!"
"The stars are so bright tonight too."

"You're right, I've never seen so many stars! I just—" Kaya paused in the middle of her sentence. "Derrick ... I hope you didn't bring me here to tell me that, since you're a highly influential lawyer now, you're going to sue me for harassment, or defamation of character. If you do, I'll never talk to you ever again!"

Derrick had a grin on his face as he listened. The borealis lights lit up her eyes and gave a certain luster to her hair. He held her face in his hands and gave her a kiss on the cheek!

"Kaya ... I would never sue you! I wanted to bring you here to tell you that—oh, I'm so nervous ... I want to tell you ... that I love you! Kaya, I want you to harass me for the rest of my life!"

"Why?" She gave him an odd look.
Derrick went on to explain.

"I missed you so much while I was away at college. I realized that I need you in my life. I remembered all of the times we've spent together, the snow fights and the ski races and had. How even though you were so competitive, sometimes you would let me win a race. I remembered when we were kids. When we first met, I was nine and you were six years old. I held out my hand, but you slapped it and ran away. I didn't understand at the time."

Kaya looked sad, "I'm sorry, Derrick, I was never around many people before. I felt so alone, I didn't know how to make new friends. I still have a deep feeling of sadness with me all the time."

"Kaya, don't carry that sadness with you any more. When we first met, I didn't know it would be the beginning of a lifelong friendship. Every time I tugged at your ponytails or made fun of you, I fell more in love with you."

Derrick was next to tears; he moved a little closer
"Kaya, what I am trying to tell you is—"
He took the ring out of a small box.
"I want to ask you to marry me."
With a smile on her face, a tear ran down Kaya's cheek.

"Kaya, will you marry me? Can we spend the rest of our lives together, and have a long happy marriage?"

Kaya replied without a second thought.
"Yes, Derrick! I will marry you!"

He was so nervous that his hand was shaking. The ring slipped out of his hand!

"Oh no! Kaya, I dropped the ring!"
"Don't worry, we're going to find it."

They stepped down from the rock and walked toward the spot where the ring landed. As they started to brush away the snow, Derrick slipped and they both fell into a pile of snow.

Kaya made a snowball and threw it at Derrick!
He caught it in flight!

When the snowball fell apart in his hand, to their surprise, the ring was inside!

"Look, it's the ring!"
They both laughed with joy!
"Now … Kaya, will you marry me?"
"Of course I'll marry you!"

Derrick put the ring on her finger, then brushed the snow from her face. As they kissed in celebration, a bright wave of green light flashed across the sky.

"Oh, Derrick, I love you so much! I am so glad we will always be together. I wish our parents would have come with us. I've got an idea! Remember when we were younger and we used to always make snow angels?"

"Well, what are you waiting for? Come on!"
They laid down in the snow and waved their arms and legs.
"It's like we are flying through the sky!"
Derrick helped Kaya up, "Let's put halos on them!"

Covered with snow themselves, they put halos on their snow angels. Kaya started a snow fight and they playfully tossed a few snowballs at each other. Afterward, they sat down together and watched the great beauty of the borealis lights.

"Kaya, look! A shooting star!"
"It's a blessing from Heaven!"

So in love, they watched the borealis lights together.

Meanwhile, at the hotel, their guests were all visiting with each other. Somehow the secret got out that Derrick was going to propose! The staff already knew because Mr. Magnusson mentioned it when he made the reservations. Everyone was waiting to hear what happened, they were so excited for Derrick and Kaya to return.

It was so elegant, Mr. Magnusson had asked for the best of everything. The tables were lit up by candles and had large flower sprays at each end. The staff was just beginning to set up a buffet dinner for when Derrick and Kaya returned. Five violinists had just arrived, who would soon be playing at the stage in the ballroom. Everyone staying at the hotel wondered what was going on.

Before long Val and Gary returned to pick up Kaya and Derrick. Little did they know, they had decided to keep their engagement a secret until later in the evening.

The helicopter flew overhead, then made a circle and landed right near Kaya and Derrick. Val noticed the two snow angels lit up by the lights of the helicopter.

"Oh Gary, look they made snow angels!"

They smiled at each other as Kaya and Derrick climbed aboard, carrying their blanket and lantern. They sat down and got buckled in without a word, then remained silent as they took off from Abisko. Val and Gary started to wonder if something might be wrong. Trying to ease the tension, Gary started to sing a bit too loudly; Val told him to tone it down.

Upon reaching the hotel they were still strangely silent. People smiled and waved as they walked through the lobby. Derrick went upstairs to the room and changed into formal wear for dinner. He wore a finely tailored black tuxedo along with a white shirt, and a black bow tie.

While he was gone, Val let Kaya know that she had a special gift for her. Before they entered the ballroom, she stopped Kaya to give her the present.

"Svea asked me to give you this, she wanted it to be a secret."
"Oh? That's my mom, she thinks of everything!"
Tears of joy came to Kaya's eyes.
"Thank you, Val. I wish Mom and Dad could be here."

Kaya didn't see that Derrick was just returning when she got into the elevator. He looked for her, but she was nowhere to be found. The hostess brought Derrick, Val, and Gary to the table where their friends were waiting. The guests all made small talk as they waited.

Upstairs in her hotel room, Kaya opened the gift that was sent by her mother. She couldn't believe it, Svea had picked out the perfect dress and shoes to match! She picked up the dress up and gave it a tight hug, then held it up in front of a tall mirror and swayed from side to side. Svea always knew the right thing to do.

She slipped into the dress, it fit like it was custom made. She took a moment to touch up her makeup, and rearrange her hair so her long curls would fall just right.

"Now I'm ready, everything is perfect!"
Kaya twirled around in front of the mirror like a princess.
"Oh, Mom, I miss you so much right now!"

She put on the periwinkle shoes, they had short heels, so they would be comfortable for both walking and dancing. Everything was just like she always wanted. It was time for her to rejoin Derrick and their friends.

Kaya pushed the button to call the attendant who escorted her to the room. There was a knock at the door and she went to open it. There stood a young man, Kaya was caught off guard.

"I'll show you back to your table Ma'am."

They took the elevator down to the second floor. Once they got to the stairs, Kaya went on by herself.

"I can find my way now, thank you."

From the top of the stairs, she saw that Mr. Magnusson was waiting for her.

"Here she comes," he announced!

Everyone watched her as she walked down the stairs. Her periwinkle dress had a scooped neckline, and the bodice fit her perfect figure. The bell sleeves flared to the wrist, and there was a gradual flare below the hip line.

Mark commented, "Wow, Derrick, she looks like an angel!"

Derrick met her at the bottom of the stairs and took her hand. She took a moment to greet the guests, they were all charmed by her striking beauty. It was a truly a moment they would remember forever. They approached the banquet table and Derrick helped with her chair so she could be seated.

Val asked Kaya, "Did you have a good time?"
Everyone anticipated news of the proposal!

"It was so beautiful! The lights waved like giant ribbons flying through the sky. They shined across the mountains and reflected off the surface of the lake. It was so glorious, it took my breath away!"

Kaya paused for a moment, and tilted her head.
"Then Derrick fell into the snow, taking me with him!"
They all started laughing, even Derrick.

Mr. Magnusson made an announcement that the buffet was ready. As they had dinner, Gary talked about his pride and joy, the big red helicopter! He explained how it was custom ordered, with all of the emergency rescue equipment, cherry red paint, plush custom seats, and state of the art navigation system.

He looked so proud while explaining how Val painted 'Big Red' on the side of the door.

23. Hotel Security Has A Problem

The guests were having such a wonderful dinner together. The hotel security unexpectedly came to speak with Mr. Magnusson.

"Excuse me, Sir, could you please come to speak with us?"
Mr. Magnusson politely excused himself.

They entered the lobby together and they began to explain.
"I'm sorry, Sir. It appears that we have a problem."
Mr. Magnusson looked concerned.

"First we noticed somebody looking in the windows. Then we saw a few others hiding by cars in the parking lot."

"Find out who they are, and what they're up to."
Who could this be? He wondered.
"Once you find out, bring them to me."

Kaya was curious about what was going on, she watched for him to return. When he returned to the table, she inquired what was going on.

"Nothing that I can't handle," he smiled.

Dr. Leif was telling JP how glad he was to see Kaya grow up to be so happy and healthy. Mark was telling stories about dates that didn't turn out well. He told one about a blind date that was so bad, he excused himself to the men's room, left her on the dance floor, and never came back!

A short while later, the security guards came back to speak with Mr. Magnusson. He left the banquet and followed them to their office. They had rounded up four ladies, including the one who was in the bushes looking through the window!

"I told her not to look in the window, that we'd get caught." Corrine grumbled.
"Hush! Don't get us into more trouble than we're already in!" Kathleen interrupted.
"For the record, I don't know them," Carol insisted!

"This one tells us her name Maryann, she was in front acting as a greeter. She was doing a pretty good job of it, I must admit. This one gave us quite a chase! She ended up hiding under a car in the parking lot. She wouldn't give us her name, but we found her driver's license. Her name is Corrine."

"Then we have Carol, she was taking pictures of the violinists as they arrived. She offered to help them carry their equipment so she could get inside. Last of all, this one, who was peeking in the window, is Kathleen. It seems she was taking notes about the guests in this notebook."

"What should we do with them? Should we book them?"
"No … I know these ladies."

Mr. Magnusson looked them over, they were a sorry looking group! He was relieved that the Gällivare Ladies were his only concern.

"They can stay, if they promise not to cause a problem."
"We promise," they answered in unison.

They were so happy that Mr. Magnusson invited them to stay. If he had security take them away, it would've been a very unhappy trip back to Gällivare.

Maryann was elated, "I knew you were a grand old man!"
Kathleen was cleaning her glasses.
"It really is tough to see from the window."
Carol was relieved, "I've never been to jail yet! Thank you!"

Mr. Magnusson led them to the grand ballroom. He asked a hostess to help find a table for the ladies near the band.

"Welcome, come in and join the party!"
As they walked to the table, Corrine nudged Mr. Mag.
"Are they engaged yet?"
"We'll have to wait and see! Enjoy the buffet!"

Kathleen whispered to Maryann, "I sure hope so, or we came all the way here for nothing."

Mr. Magnusson spoke with the receptionist, he paid for their rooms at the hotel that evening.

Derrick and Mr. Magnusson saw the violinists getting ready to perform. They all wore very classy white tuxedos. The quintet started to play a Swedish love song—Kaya's attention was captivated.

She looked at Mr. Magnusson, he smiled and winked at her, then he pointed toward the doorway. Kaya looked over and saw

Sven, Svea, Emma, and Norv all walking into the ballroom together. She and Derrick ran over to meet them and gave them each a great big hug!

Svea smiled, "Oh Kaya, you look so beautiful in your dress!"
Kaya had tears in her eyes.
"Thank you, Mom! I love it, it's perfect!"
Derrick's eyes lit up, "I am so happy you're all here!"
"We wouldn't miss it for the world!"

Their guests had all stood up to welcome them, they clapped and cheered. The room had such a festive spirit!

Mr. Magnusson made an announcement:
"Next, Ladies and Gentlemen, we have a very special song to celebrate this great evening. This is dedicated to all of our loved ones who are here with us tonight."

Derrick stood up and asked Kaya to dance.
"Kaya, will you do me the honor of sharing this dance?"
She nodded, "Yes."

Derrick led her to the center of the ballroom floor, they stood directly under a magnificent crystal chandelier. He twirled her around and pulled her close against him.

He whispered, "I have the ring!"

The guests all watched so intently, they became very silent. Kaya and Derrick danced so gracefully, it was so romantic! When the song finished, he twirled her around and around, then took her hand and they both came to a stop.

Everyone stood up and cheered! The performance was so beautiful, it set the stage for what was next to come. Derrick suddenly knelt down on one knee, and everyone became silent.

It was such a breathtaking moment!

One of the violinists handed him a microphone. It was so quiet you could hear a pin drop. Derrick looked up at Kaya with such love and affection.

"Kaya, I've known you since we were very young. Over these many years, somewhere along the line, I fell in love with you … it wasn't always easy, you are very independent. You are so special to me. I hope you share the same feelings for me that I have for you."

They stood face to face, looking so in love.

"Kaya, will you marry me? Will you be my wife, and promise not to break my heart, or hurt me in any way?"

"Derrick … I don't know …"
Kaya paused for a moment.
"I don't know when I started to fall in love with you, but I did."
She paused again, "Yes, I will marry you."

The entire ballroom let out a great cheer! This was what everyone had wished for. Their parents had such great smiles on their faces. Mr. Magnusson called for a toast.

"Blessings to you both! A toast to everlasting love! Skål!"

After the toast, Kaya approached one of the violinists. He handed her a violin, then Kaya and Derrick returned to the center of the ballroom. She took a bow.

"Derrick, I wrote this very special song for you. It's called *'Stars of the Night'*—I hope that you love it as much as I do."

Mr. Magnusson was telling the guests how talented she is. "She is like a daughter to me, you know! " He loved to see Kaya play the violin.

Before Kaya raised her violin, she remembered her greatest, and most important lesson:

"The violin has a soul, it can project emotions—love, happiness, and excitement! If you send your feelings into the violin, and put your soul into the strings, you can create magic!"

With the first wave of her bow, she had her audience under a spell. While she played this beautiful love song, she began to dance, her dress seemed to flow along with the melody of the music.

At the end, she placed her violin by her side and took a bow. Everyone stood up and gave a roaring applause! Derrick and Kaya gave each other a big hug and a long kiss.

Kaya and Derrick each had a special dance with their parents. Kaya danced with her father, and Derrick danced with his mother. Having their parents there made everything just perfect. Of course, Val and Gary knew they would be there, but they had kept it a secret!

It was a day that they would all remember forever.

24. Back To The Lodge

It was a Sunday morning and everyone was still at the hotel in Kiruna. Before they returned home, Val called a special meeting with the Gällivare Ladies. She wanted to tell them how important it was that they keep the engagement a secret. They had to give Derrick and Kaya time to share the news on their own.

"Remember, it is up to the bride and groom to tell people of their engagement. You have to keep it a secret until they choose to make it public. Do you promise?"

"Yes, we promise," they all nodded in agreement.
Corrine added, "Our lips are sealed!"

Once they finished their meeting, Val and Gary brought Sven and Svea back to Gällivare. After dropping them off, they returned to Kiruna to pick up the future bride and groom.

Svea went into the lodge to check how everything was going. The Sunday brunch crowd had just arrived after church. Everything seemed to okay, she went to check in with Willard and Wilma.

"Don't worry, Svea, we can handle things here."
Willard and Wilma assured her that everything was fine.

In the afternoon hours, Svea saw Kathleen and Corrine came in for lunch. After a while, Maryann and Carol joined them. They must've thought that if they came in separately, they wouldn't be noticed! They sure seemed to be staying on top of things.

Sven was there too, he relaxed and read the newspaper from his favorite place, next to the big windows by the fireplace. Svea sat with him and went over the dinner menu to keep busy. It was a peaceful moment.

After a while, Svea heard the helicopter in the distance. It started to come closer and closer; the Gällivare Ladies heard it too! Sven and Svea went outside to greet them, they waited for Gary to land the helicopter.

Svea waved to them, "Welcome home!"
Kaya got out first and gave her parents a big hug.
"Welcome home, Son," Sven and Derrick shook hands.
"Thank you, Sven!" Derrick replied.
"Come on inside, everyone!"

Together, they all walked into the lodge and had lunch. They talked about the wonderful evening that they had in Kiruna. Derrick and Kaya talked about watching the beautiful aurora borealis lights in Abisko. The engagement party was next on their minds.

"Mom, can we have the engagement party at the lodge?"
"I'm sure it will fit in the schedule. When should we have it?"
"I think just two weeks from now."
"We won't have much time to send invitations."
"We can get the guest list done today."
"I can't believe that Derrick and I are getting married!"
"I always knew you would, someday!"

Meanwhile, the Gällivare Ladies watched and listened as they enjoyed their lunch. If anything was going to happen, they were not going to miss it!

Kathleen pointed, "Carol, did you see that ring?"
Carol was swooning, "Isn't it lovely? I wish it were mine!"
"Did they announce their engagement yet?" Corrine asked.
"No, I still don't know."
"I think they're keeping it a secret until the engagement party."

The ladies weren't in much of a hurry. After they had finished lunch, they stuck around to have kaffe. Very shortly, to their surprise, they saw Norv and Emma arrive at the lodge. All together the family started going over the plans for the engagement party. The ladies were just within earshot of their conversation.

"Well, Kaya and I finished the guest list."
Svea and Emma looked over the list together.
"Let's get the invitations in the mail on Monday."
"Maybe JP can help? He can make sure they arrive on time."
"Good idea, Svea! Looks like we're going to be busy."

Their parents were so happy to work together on planning the big party. Little did they know, the whole town would soon be buzzing with news of Derrick and Kaya's engagement. They only had one week to finish all the plans.

Svea wondered how many people would come to the party.
"Until they RSVP, we won't have a count of guests."
"We should estimate on the high end," Emma suggested.

Svea took notes while Kaya and Derrick shared their ideas.
"We want to have banquet style seating."
"Very informal, so everyone can feel at home."
"Mom and I will work on the menu. Emma, can you help too?"
"Sure! Should I order a special cake?"
Derrick's eyes lit up, "That's a great idea!"

"What about a toast, Sven? It is tradition!" Norv added.

"You're right, I'll order champagne and work on my speech!"

"Perfect," Derrick replied, "we'll begin on Sunday at five o'clock in the evening. Tell the staff at the lodge they are welcome to stay and celebrate with us!"

Maryann hid behind her menu, "Five o'clock girls, got it?"

25. The Engagement Party

The next two weeks went by in a flash. It is now around three o'clock on Sunday and the lodge is already bustling with activity. Kaya looked up and saw four men come through the door with large flower arrangements.

Svea looked surprised, "I didn't order any flowers."
The delivery men lined up side by side, stood straight and tall.
"Compliments of Gällivare Blomsterhandlare, Ma'am."

Each of the arrangements had a white ribbon with *'Congratulations on your Engagement'* written in royal blue lettering. When Svea asked, the delivery men reiterated that there was no charge. They left after making the delivery.

Derrick and Svea looked over the flower arrangements.
"Well, I think the news has already gotten out."
Kaya was both puzzled and surprised.
"They are perfect, I love them."
She felt the soft petals and smelled the flowers.

The staff helped get the flowers in just the right place. After they had moved the last of the arrangements, another florist arrived! They brought more beautiful flowers to celebrate Derrick and Kaya's engagement.

"Greetings, we're from Tre Kronor Blomsterhandlare. We've brought flowers for your special occasion, they're our gift to you."

They were mostly roses, along with some white orchids. They placed one on each of the long tables, and three on the main banquet table. Their informal event had turned into a very elegant evening. The flowers complemented the white linen tablecloths; blue candles illuminated the tables.

One by one their friends began to arrive, and soon the room was filled. They all talked with each other about Derrick and Kaya, and made small talk: the weather, the new job, the new girlfriend.

As time went on more people continued to arrive, many more than they expected. There were not enough seats at the tables, so the staff helped bring in more chairs to accommodate the guests.

Mr. Magnusson and JP waited until the last guests were seated, then took their place at the main table. Everyone was surprised by how many people showed up. The Gällivare Ladies were sitting near the front, so prim and proper. Maryann had an inquisitive look, and she seemed to be questioning the other girls.

"Kathleen, did you keep the secret? Did you tell anyone?"
"Oh … only a few close friends," Kathleen looked away.
"How about you, Corrine … Carol?"
Corrine looked down toward the floor.
"Well, I did tell four of my neighbors."
Maryann knew they were in trouble.
Carol had a guilty look, "I tried so hard, but I let it slip out."
"What about you, Maryann? Who did you tell?"

"Well, I'll be perfectly honest. I saw an old friend who works at the market. We were just catching up on a few things, and … I didn't mean to say anything, but I think a few people overheard us talking."

Mr. Magnusson had a feeling that he knew how everyone found out. He knew that they had something to do with it! He looked at them with a 'What did you do now?' look on his face. The ladies glanced at each other, then smiled waved.

Everyone settled in, they started to anticipate the great announcement. Derrick came to the front of the room. He brushed back his hair, then straightened his tie. He was confident, but a little unsure if he had found the right words. He became a little nervous as he started to speak.

"When you received your invitation to this special evening, you may have already known what was coming next in my life. After graduating from law school, surely there must be a great new job on the horizon. If that is what you guessed, then you are right."

The Gällivare Ladies were confused and concerned.
Kathleen nudged Carol, "What's he going on about?"
They had told everyone this was an engagement party!
"I don't know … I don't know what's going on."

"It's true, I now have a great new job practicing law at Mr. Magnusson's Firm."

He paused for a moment.

"Thank you, my dear friends and family. It means so much that you've all come here tonight to show your support. Tonight we're gathered here to celebrate the best day of my life. Not my new job, but something much more important!"

The Gällivare Ladies let out a big sigh of relief.

"Last Saturday, we caused some commotion here at the lodge when Val and Gary picked us up in their helicopter. They flew Kaya and I first class to Kiruna, where we had a joyful luncheon together with some surprise guests. After lunch, we took flight for a second time, they brought us to Mount Njullá, in Abisko, where Kaya and I admired the beauty of the aurora borealis. While looking out over Lake Torneträsk, I asked Kaya for her hand in marriage!"

He looked at Kaya affectionately, she stood up next to him, with tears in her eyes.

"And I said *'Yes!'*"

Their friends and family all cheered and clapped their hands; Derrick wiped away her tears and gave her a kiss.

"As we begin this next great chapter in our lives, I want to thank all of you for sharing in the wonderful times we've had over the years. It's a great honor to have your friendship and your support. It is the greatest honor of all, Kaya, to have you for my wife. My love for you will last for all eternity!"

The cheers and applause continued as he finished his speech.

"Congratulations," Mark called out, "we always wished you two would quit picking on each other and fall in love!"

Sven came to the front and shook Derrick's hand, then prepared to give his speech. He looked over the crowd, they were all familiar faces. It became very quiet.

"In this room, we have a very exceptional young lady. You've all witnessed her great talent, she is a musical prodigy. She has empathy for all people, and walks closely with the Lord—I know that he watches over her.

"I have seen Kaya and Derrick grow up, and I've watched as they fell in love. It took a long time! Sometimes she would say, *'I'm so mad at him!'* I would tease her, and say *'I think he loves you.'* She would stomp her foot and walk away!"

"After the many years of growing up together, these two love each other so much, it touches my heart. Whether they're helping me at the shop, or Svea at the lodge, they are always there for each other. This love was meant to be. I speak for everyone here—we all wish you a blessed marriage and wonderful future together. A toast, to Derrick and Kaya!"

Willard popped the cork on the champagne as Sven finished his speech. The waiters and waitresses already had champagne on ice at every table. The champagne was poured, and everyone rose to their feet for the toast.

"To Kaya and Derrick, may they be forever in love! Skål!"

A great cheer echoed through the hall, everyone was so happy for them. It seemed that Kaya, Svea, and Emma were filled with a special sense of joy.

The band started playing a beautiful love song. The guests all cheered for Derrick and Kaya as they made their way to the center of the floor for a dance.

Their friends commented while watching them dance.
"What a perfect couple!"

"They are so in love, and it shows!"

"This will be a wedding you do not want to miss!"

Soon all of their friends had joined them, they danced all throughout the night. It was a great evening for all, filled with great stories and celebration.

Maryann even got Mr. Magnusson to dance with her!

26. A Magnificent Wedding

It was a Sunday afternoon, Svea had just finished making kanelbullar and kaffe for fika. They invited Emma and Norv over to help Derrick and Kaya plan the wedding.

Norv told Sven, "Derrick picked a wonderful young lady, she's as perfect as anyone could be. We will always love and protect her."

"We feel the just the same about Derrick. He is so kind, and such a hard worker. You know, that young man is always so patient with her. He is very caring in everything that he does."

"Surely, they're two of the luckiest people in all of Gällivare!"

Kaya and Derrick mentioned that they've reserved the church for two o'clock on June 25th. Mr. Magnusson is good friends with Reverend Gabriel, he pulled a few strings to get the date they wanted.

Svea seemed a little bit anxious.
She asked, "Do you want the reception at the lodge?"

Derrick replied, "Svea, you're the mother of the bride. We want you to enjoy the day, you shouldn't have to worry about anything. Let's have the reception at the Magnifika Hotel, I am sure that Mr. Magnusson would reserve it for us."

Sven agreed, "That's a great idea, Derrick. I will check with him tomorrow."

Kaya and Derrick's parents had wished for this day for such a long time. Working on the wedding plans brought them so much joy. Emma took notes as they discussed the arrangements.

"How about flowers, did you decide on the colors yet?"
"We're thinking about white and periwinkle."
"Should I schedule a meeting with a florist?"
"Yes please, thank you, Emma!"
"You're welcome, I'll set up a meeting for you and Derrick."
"What about the wedding cake?"
Derrick looked blank, "I think Kaya should decide that one."
Kaya looked over to her Mom, "Mom, can we have pillars on our wedding cake? I want it to be very elegant."
"If that's what you want, that is exactly what you will have!"

Kaya got so excited, in a cheerful voice she announced, "We're going to have pillars on our cake! I always wanted to have pillars on my wedding cake!"

Suddenly, there was a knock at the door.
"I wonder who that could be?"
"We weren't expecting anyone else."

Sven opened the door and there stood Mr. Magnusson. He opened the door wider so everyone could see.

"Mr. Magnusson, please come in! Have a seat and join us for fika, I'll get you kaffe and a kanelbulle. We're discussing the plans for the wedding."

"Thank you, I guess I'm right on time."

Mr. Mag smiled, he walked inside and took a seat at the table. Sven quickly returned from the kitchen with a hot cup of kaffe and a kanelbulle.

"I am so happy that everyone is here."
Mr. Mag took a sip from his cup of kaffe.
"I wanted to have a talk with you about the wedding."
Kaya was surprised, "Mr. Mag, I didn't know you wanted to help plan the wedding?"

"Kaya, at this stage in my life, spending time with you is one of the few things that brings me happiness. Watching you grow up has been such a blessing. You're like a granddaughter to me."

"And you make the perfect grandfather!" Svea replied.

"Thank you, Svea," Mr. Magnusson let out a chuckle, "I am so happy you've all let me become a part of the family."

Sven gave Mr. Magnusson a pat on the shoulder, "Everything happens for a reason, I believe this was all meant to be. You've brought so much happiness into her life."

"Our times playing violin together will always be my favorite memories. You know, I don't think there is anything left that I can teach her! She has passed me up now."

"I don't know about that," Kaya chimed in, "I am not canceling my lessons any time soon!"

They all laughed together.

"Sven, I'd like to do something special for Kaya and Derrick. If you will permit, I would like to pay for the entire wedding. I would consider it to be a great honor."

Kaya spoke up before Sven could answer.

"Mr. Magnusson, we're so lucky to have you in our lives. I've come to love you so very much. You're always there for me when I need you. We all understand how much you care for us, but the wedding will be expensive. We can't let you pay for everything!"

Mr. Magnusson shook his head, he stood up and walked over to Kaya and Derrick, then put an arm around each of them.

"I am an old man, Kaya … my family is all gone. I have no one left to spend my money on. You two are my world now, and I am going to pay for your wedding! All I need to hear is, *'Thank you!'*"

Everyone was silent.

"Mr. Magnusson, I know you better than anyone, you've always been so kind to me. Thank you so much, we will always remember how much you've done for us. I'll always love you, and you will always be just like a grandfather to me."

Sven, Svea, Emma, Norv, and Derrick all cheered.
Mr. Magnusson announced, "This will be a wedding that Gällivare will never forget!"

The next day Mr. Magnusson called Kaya and wanted to meet at the Storgatan Kafé. It was their regular meeting place, they've gone there for many years now.

"Good morning, Kaya!"
"Good morning, Mr. Magnusson!"
"Can we meet at the kafé to discuss plans for the wedding?"
"Sure, I am surprised you called so soon."
"We have lot's of work to do, Kaya."
"I'll get ready to go!"
"Great! I'll reserve our table, my driver will pick you up."

Kathleen and Carol just happened to be arriving at the kafé for fika. They had been out shopping for new shoes. After the hostess seated them, they ordered kaffe, mazariner, and hallongrotta cookies.

"Oh, my feet are so tired from walking around town."
Carol grimaced as she lifted up her foot.
"I'm going to slip off my shoes for a while."
"Don't get tired out on me Carol, we not done yet."
"I know, we've got to find the perfect heels for this wedding."

"I love shoes, I must have twenty pairs by now." Kathleen bragged, "have you heard anything more about the wedding?"

Carol looked disappointed, "Not yet, but it's too soon. It's only been a few days so far. Any day now this town will start buzzing with activity."

Kathleen had a dazed look in her eyes, like she was day dreaming of being at the wedding.

Carol shook her arm, "I just saw Mr. Mag's personal car!"
Kathleen's eyes got big, "What? Where?"

Mr. Magnusson came inside, he walked by with the hostess.
She seated him at a big round table. As they do best, Carol and
Kathleen started listening in.

"Kaya will be here soon, can you bring flowers to our table?"
"Right away, Mr. Magnusson."

Kathleen perked up, "Wow, do we have great timing or what!"

Mr. Magnusson noticed the ladies were there, he smiled and
nodded his head. Just shortly after, his driver arrived with Kaya and
parked the limousine in front of the kafé. The driver walked over to
open the car door for Kaya, then took off his hat and opened the door
to the kafé. Carol and Kathleen were impressed.

Mr. Magnusson stood up and greeted her.
"What do you have planned today, Mr. Mag?"

He had papers, photos, and his laptop spread out all across the
table. He was ready to get down to business, he talked to Kaya like
she was his daughter.

"I have the name of a famous designer from Milan, Italy.
I would like to have him design your wedding dress! I can call him
now to make the arrangements. What do you think?"

When they heard this, Carol and Kathleen were astonished!
Kathleen accidentally dropped her spoon and drew a bit of attention.
She bent down to pick it up, still listening to hear Kaya's response.

Kaya didn't know what to say, she seemed confused.

"Mr. Magnusson, how can you afford to do this?"

Mr. Mag laughed, "My dear Kaya, I could buy this whole town if I wanted to! We don't have to worry about money. Consider it repayment for all the times you cheered me up when I felt so sad. If it's okay with you, Kaya, I'd like to call him right now."

"Okay, you know what's best!"

Carol and Kathleen couldn't believe it. With just a few clicks on his laptop, he called Antoni Bagati to discuss the wedding.

"Ciao Antoni! Come va?"

"Ciao, Mr. Magnusson! Everything is well, la vita è bella. How can I help you?"

"We have a wedding in Gällivare on June 25th. Can you fit it into your schedule?"

"Fantastico, che bella sorpresa! Deve essere un matrimonio molto speciale!"

Kaya couldn't understand what Antoni was saying.

"Rallenta, Antoni! Slow down, you're talking too fast!"

"Oh, fantastic, what a great surprise! It must be a very special wedding!"

"Yes, it is! That is exactly why I called you. The bride's name is Kaya, is like a granddaughter to me. I want you to design her dress, and the dresses for the bridesmaids. I also want special dresses for the flower girls, and decorations in the church."

"Anything for you, Mr. Magnusson!"

"Perfect. Can you be here by next Friday?"

"We have a fashion show here in Milano next week, but I've already completed my work. My associates can handle everything, I will clear my schedule for you."

"The entire top floor of the Magnifika Hotel will be reserved for you. No other guests will have access to that floor. We will be ready for you on Friday."

"Grazie, Mr. Magnusson, my team and I will be there. We will need plenty of room to set up machines and make patterns for the dresses. No one shall see the dress until wedding day. Let the bride know we are bringing many fabrics and laces, there will be many fittings. She should begin to imagine what type of dress and veil she would like."

"I knew I could count on you Antoni! My travel agent will contact you to schedule the flight. When you arrive, I will have two limousines waiting for you at the airport, and transportation for all of your equipment. Grazie, Antoni."

Carol forgot all about her sore feet
"Did I hear that right, they're getting a designer from Italy?"

"Yes! It sounds like he will arrive on Friday. We need to tell Corrine and Maryann." Kathleen had a one-sided smile, "I have a feeling he will be very handsome."

Kaya's eyes lit up, she knew Mr. Magnusson would have big plans, but didn't know what to expect.

"Antoni is one of a kind. He designed my wife Ingrid's dress when we got married. Just wait and see Kaya, you will be amazed!"

"If you chose him for your wedding, I am sure he is exceptional. We'll have to decide on the flower girls next."

"You and Derrick are both going to be very busy! But right now, we need ice cream!"

Kaya laughed, "Hey, that's what I always say!"

Mr. Mag noticed that the Gällivare Ladies were listening in.

"I bet you ladies would like some ice cream too?"

"Yes, we were … I guess we've been caught."

"We all love ice cream, we may as well join the celebration!"

"It sounds like you're planning a spectacular wedding."

Mr. Mag motioned for the waitress to come over to the table.

"Ma'am, we would each like to have an ice cream sundae."

"Two sundaes coming right up."

"Please bring sundaes for these two ladies as well."

With a conspicuous smile, Carol and Kathleen both waved to the waitress.

The next week was so hectic, Svea and Kaya had been to almost every shop in town. They had to find a strapless bra, white nylons, and a perfect perfume for the occasion. She met with hair stylists, makeup artists, florists, cake designers, and jewelers.

Everywhere they went people stopped to talk, wish them luck, or even take a picture. At the jewelry shop, they saw Corrine and Maryann looking in the window and waving.

Kaya told her mom, "I see those ladies almost every day now, they are always so nice to me."

Svea laughed, "Yes honey, they're almost like reporters! Just wave and smile."

Kaya was looking for a solid gold ring for Derrick. She almost found the perfect one. She started looking at gifts for the wedding party too. She picked out four diamond cross necklaces, one for each of the bridesmaids.

As they left the shop, Kaya was daydreaming about her wedding dress. She couldn't believe that her dress was going to be custom made by a famous designer!

"Antoni is designing the flower girl's dresses too. I can't wait to see how they turn out, it's will be such a beautiful wedding!"

"You're very fortunate, Kaya. Your wedding is going to be wonderful, but we've got a lot of work to do!"

On Friday morning Mr. Magnusson called his travel agent to check the status of the flight. He was told that the flight from Milan was on time, and will be arriving at three-thirty. His agent took care of all the transportation, he scheduled two limousines for Antoni and his team, and three vans to transport all of the equipment. The would be ready and waiting at the airport.

Next he called his driver and told him that he was ready to go to the hotel. Upon his arrival, he called in the best of staff and let them know they would be caring exclusively for Antoni and his team. He insisted that they are to have the best of everything.

"The entire top floor is blocked off to all other guests. No one is permitted access to the top floor, or allowed to enter the room where the designers are working. Except, of course, for Kaya and Svea. Antoni and his team will have an open expense account, and the concierge needs to be available for them at all times for any needs they may have. In the evening they have time off for sightseeing in our beautiful city of Gällivare. Please see to it that they all enjoy their stay."

Shortly after Mr. Magnusson addressed the staff, he received a call from his travel agent. Antoni and his team had arrived at the airport and will soon be on their way to the hotel.

Somehow word had gotten out that a famous designer would be in town, and that he was going to be staying at the Magnifika Hotel. The Gällivare Ladies wanted to see what he looked like, so they staked out the hotel.

It was a little after four when Antoni arrived. The limousines attracted quite a bit of attention, the townspeople watched curiously as they parked in front of the hotel.

The bell boys came out and lined up by the entrance, prepared to take their luggage. In front of them, Mr. Magnusson stood patiently as he waited to welcome Antoni.

With Mr. Mag distracted, Corrine set their plan in motion.
"Okay girls, this is our chance! Just walk inside casually and no one will notice."
Carol pointed to Maryann and Kathleen.
"You two go in first, then Corrine and I will follow."
They started to walk toward the entrance.

Corrine called out to them, "Remember, if you get caught we don't know you!"

Maryann and Kathleen walked into the lobby, took a seat, and started reading a newspaper. Everyone was so busy that they went unnoticed. Corrine and Carol went inside next.

The drivers got out of the limousines, then walked over to the passenger side to open the door. The townspeople all wondered who was inside. Antoni and one of his helpers stepped out of the first limousine. Mr. Magnusson stepped forward to greet them.

"Ciao Antoni, welcome to Gällivare!"
They shook hands, and gave each other a quick hug.
"Grazie, thank you for the warm reception!"
Antoni gestured toward his helper.
"Mr. Magnusson, this is Alessandra, she is my assistant."
"Very glad to meet you, did you have a pleasant flight?"
"Everything was excellent, thank you."
"Let's go inside, we have a lot to discuss."

The ladies watched as Antoni walked through the lobby. He was very well dressed and had an air of confidence. Maryann whispered to Kathleen, "He is so handsome!"

He briefly spoke to the receptionist, then noticed that the ladies had been watching him.

"Good afternoon, Ladies."
He tipped his hat and then walked to the elevator.
All Corrine could say was "Wow!"

Next a train of bellboys came through the door with carts of luggage, sewing machines, and other supplies. Mr. Magnusson led them and the rest of Antoni's team to their rooms on the top floor.

While Antoni and his staff got settled in, Mr. Mag called Kaya to see if she could join them for dinner. He wanted her to meet Antoni, and the seamstresses who she will be working with for the dress fittings.

When Kaya arrived at the restaurant, she saw that Mr. Mag, Antoni, and his staff were already seated at a table. Mr. Magnusson waved to Kaya as she walked in and they all stood up to meet her.

"Welcome, Kaya, I'm so glad that you could make it. It's my pleasure to introduce you to Antoni Bagati!"

"Antoni, this lovely young lady is Kaya, our bride to be!"

"Ciao, Kaya! So happy to meet you, you will make a wonderful bride!"

"Thank you, Antoni. Thank you so much for changing your schedule to be here."

"Have a seat, I will introduce you to my team."

As they sat down at the table, Kaya noticed how closely they watched her, how she walked, and how she was seated. Antoni began to introduce her to his team.

"Kaya, this is Olivia, she has worked with me for seven years. She is the best seamstress in all of Italy!

"Giulia has been with us for five years. She is an expert pattern maker, and can bring even the most challenging designs to life.

"Annika is a visionary, she always perfects the details and adds her special touches. She's been with us for over six years now.

"Alessandra is my personal assistant, and has worked with me forever! She sources all of our materials and takes care of almost everything. She's like my shadow, she is with me everywhere I go!

"Ladies, this is Kaya. It's our job to make her a beautiful and very happy bride! When she is happy, we are all happy!"

"I am so thankful you're all here, it is very nice to meet everyone!" Kaya was blushing.

Antoni lifted his glass and made a toast, "To a lovely bride to be, we wish you many years of happiness, good health, and many lovely children!"

In the time leading up to the wedding, they were all so very busy. There were a few great surprises along the way! First the Norlanders held a bridal shower for Kaya with all of Derrick's family. Then Sven and Svea held a party for her with many of their close friends from over the years. The bridesmaids even had a bridal shower for her at the lodge and invited all of her friends!

Kaya had spent many weeks working with Antoni and his team on the dresses. The bridesmaids visited the hotel many times for fittings, everything was coming along just beautifully.

When Antoni was around town people always called out to him, they would say 'Hallå Antoni!' as they passed by. He would tip his hat and flash his infectious smile as he greeted them, 'Hallå, fina damer!' He always appreciated the friendly nature and good hospitality of the Swedes.

Svea and Emma spoke with their relatives in town to find the flower girls for the wedding.

First was Tatijana, an adorable child with lots of personality and confidence who loves to dance. Her mother was in Svea's wedding, and they've been friends since they were young.

Second was Eva, she is very smart for her age and a great singer. She is one of JP's granddaughters, she also loves to read, so he always brings her new books.

Third was Sara, she is Elsa's niece, and a very charming young girl. Her family loves to ski and has visited the lodge for many years. She enjoys talking to the waitresses and playing games with Kaya.

Fourth is Lilly, a beautiful child with blue eyes and long blond hair. She is Emma's niece, she is always very happy and couldn't be more excited for the wedding!

They had found the flower girls just in time. Kaya was at home when the phone rang, it was Antoni, he wanted to schedule a meeting with the flower girls and their mothers to go over the design, and take their measurements.

The next day they all met at the Magnifika Hotel. Kaya, Svea, and Emma arrived early to go over some details with Antoni. When the flower girls arrived, their mothers all sat the little girls down and told them how to behave when during measurements and fittings.

"Now listen up girls, this is important. When we come here to work on your dresses we all have to be on our best behavior. Hold very still when they take your measurements. If you don't your dress won't fit right!"

Tatijanna asked, "Mom, is he famous for sewing clothes?"

"Yes, Tatijanna, he is a very famous designer! They have come here all the way from Italy to make each of you feel like a beautiful princess!"

Eva asked, "Mom, is he cute?"
"Yes!" All the moms agreed on that one.
Eva's mother explained how important it is that they're well behaved, "Now remember, no complaining, and running or playing games. Do what they ask, and be very nice."

"Okay, we'll be nice," Eva promised.

They went inside and Antoni briefly introduced each of the members of his team. He pointed out how important they are to everything that he does. He gave them a tour, and explained each step of the process of making a dress. They got to see all of the beautiful fabrics that were being used for the dresses.

Guilia, Annika, and Olivia started taking measurements for the girls dresses. Meanwhile, Antoni and Alessandra talked with Kaya, Svea, and Emma to review plans for the decorations at the church. Kaya mentioned that she wanted to have tall candles at the end of the pews. They gave Antoni the information for the florists so he could coordinate their plans.

After the meeting with Antoni, Svea, Emma, and Kaya went to the kafé to have lunch with Derrick and Mr. Magnusson. Just by coincidence, the four Gällivare Ladies were seated one table over.

Kathleen was excited, "Now we'll get the latest news!"

The ladies waved to them as they sat down, Derrick started to feel like they were being followed! Mr. Magnusson began to look over his list.

"Well Derrick, let's see where we stand. Have you been fitted for your tuxedo yet?"

"My father and I have an appointment on Saturday."

"Why don't we go together? Sven could join us."

"That's a great idea, I'll let the tailor know."

"Wonderful! Now, Kaya, how are things going young lady?"

"Well I must say, Antoni is incredible! I love the design he's made for the dress, it's one of a kind, everything is just perfect!"

"Glad to hear that, I'd expect nothing less from Antoni."

Mr. Mag adjusted his glasses and looked down the list.

"How about the wedding cake, have you placed the order?"

Derick looked bemused, "I never knew there were so many different options!"

Emma laughed, "You should've seen these two, they tried every kind!"

"Fortunately the bakers were very nice to us."

"It's going to be so beautiful, we're even going to have a fountain! Can you believe it?"

"Very good. That's another one we can check off the list!"

Mr. Mag leaned forward as he continued to read the list.

276

"I was thinking, there may not be enough room inside the church for everyone. We should set up extra space outside of the church, and broadcast the wedding on a big screen. Then people outside can watch the ceremony."

Derrick and Kaya looked at each other, then both replied at the same time, "Really?"
"Yes, you never know who might show up."
"I guess the church is a little bit small."
"Perfect, it's settled then!" Mr. Mag updated his notes.

Svea smiled, "It's coming together, all is well."
"What do you think, Kaya?" Mr. Mag asked.
Kaya got up and gave him a big hug.
"I'm so happy, this is a dream come true!"

Carol was out shopping for a dress to wear to the wedding. While she was searching for the perfect dress she ran into Maryann.

"Carol, what are you doing here?"
"Oh nothing, just a little shopping."
"You didn't get a wedding invitation, did you?"
"Not yet, but it should arrive in a few days."

Neither of them had received an invitation yet, but they both were out shopping for dresses to wear to the wedding.

"I'm sure you're right, they'll want to have us there."
"We know more about them than they can remember!"
"That's right, they wouldn't miss the chance to have us there."
"Yeah, our invitations should be in the mail by now."

"We must be in the last batch they sent out."

"That must be it! Let me know when you get one."

"You too, if you get one and I don't, I'd be really upset!"

Later in the day, Maryann started to get very worried. She was concerned that their invitations had not arrived, and the wedding was coming up so soon. Out of desperation, she called all four girls and asked them to come to the kafé for a meeting.

"Well, my dear friends, the wedding is three weeks away now. I'm worried they couldn't fit us in. So far, we have not been invited."

Corrine interrupted, "This is so sad, how could they forget us? Everyone is going to be there!"

Kathleen frowned, "The people who got an invitation are bragging about it all over town, I feel so left out."

Carol spoke up, "Don't worry girls, every problem has a solution. Let's put our heads together and figure this out."

The ladies started to think of ideas. One way or another, they simply had to get invited to the wedding.

"We could pretend to work for the church," Maryann thought.

"Oh right, like that would really work," Corrine replied.

Next Carol thought she had a good idea.

"We can pretend to be Kaya's long lost relatives!"

Kathleen brought her back to reality.

"That won't work, they know who we are! Maybe we should just crash the wedding reception?"

Corrine had a light bulb moment!

"I've got it, we can get a job as reporters!"

Maryann looked skeptical, "Reporters, from where?"

"The Gällivare Gazette, of course!"

Maryann put her arms up, "Oh Corrine, I'm so glad I let you hang out with us!"

The ladies looked impressed, "This is a great idea!"

They took some time to work out a plan—Maryann explained that she would take care of everything. The next day she called the Gällivare Gazette and asked the secretary if she could speak with the owner, Mr. Karlsson. She claimed to have exclusive information on Derrick and Kaya's wedding, and managed to schedule a meeting with him.

The following week, the ladies all met at the offices of the Gällivare Gazette. They walked in together and went to the front desk to speak with Märta, Mr. Karlsson's secretary.

"We're here for a meeting with Mr. Karlsson. We have an appointment, so he is expecting us. Please tell him Maryann is here."

The secretary called Mr. Karlsson to let him know they've arrived. A moment later he came out from his office.

"I didn't know there would be four of you!"

Corrine tilted her head, "Yes, there are four of us!"

Mr. Karlsson motioned for them to follow him, "Okay girls, come right in and have a seat. Your reputation precedes you, how can I help you today?"

Maryann spoke up, "We want a job, all four of us. It will just be a temporary position."

Mr. Karlsson stood up and walked around his desk.

"Why? I thought you had something to tell me about Derrick and Kaya's wedding?"

Corrine looked Mr. Karlsson right in his eyes, "Your newspaper needs us!"

Mr. Karlsson looked a little puzzled and concerned.

"Mr. Karlsson, as you are aware, this is the biggest wedding our town has ever had."

Maryann stood up and took over the conversation.

"We've known Derrick and Kaya since they were both little kids. We want you to hire us as reporters to cover the wedding, and the reception. We'll take pictures, write headlines, and get comments from guests. We'll be the eyes and ears of the Gazette. Mr. Karlsson, what do you think?"

Mr. Karlsson looked over the top of his glasses.

"This is not what I expected, let me think this through."

Carol tried to appeal to him, "We are good at what we do!"

"Like you said, our reputation precedes us!" Corrine insisted.

"We know where to be and when to be there!" Kathleen added.

"That's right, we're always in the right place at the right time!"

Mr. Karlsson paced the floor a few times and considered what he may be getting himself into. He rubbed his bald head and wrinkled his forehead.

"If I do this, you're going to have to sign a contract stating that you won't do anything illegal, or anything that the newspaper could get sued for—and that you won't embarrass our town! Like you say, you have a reputation."

Maryann agreed on behalf of everyone, "We promise. We will be on our best behavior."

Mr. Karlsson held up his hands, "Hold on now, I haven't agreed to anything yet!"

"Will it help if we had a personal reference?" Carol suggested.

He glanced at the four of them, "Well … yes, that might help."

"Okay, since you know us so well, how about you write us a letter of recommendation? Then this will all go more smoothly! We can read it to you, then you can hire us, and we'll be on our way."

Mr. Karlsson looked befuddled. He leaned back in his chair and pulled down his vest. He remained silent as he tapped his fingers on the desk. The ladies didn't know if this was going to work or not.

"You ladies don't give up, do you?"

They looked at each other and shrugged their shoulders.

"That's right, we won't let you down, Mr. Karlsson!"

Mr. Karlsson shook his head in confusion.

"Well, I guess I'll have to take the risk. You're hired."

Their faces lit up with excitement!

"No matter what they say about you, Mr. Karlsson, you are a great man!"

They all thanked him, "Thank you! Thank you!"

"Don't make me regret this. Come back tomorrow to pick up your Gazette press credentials."

When they left, Mr. Karlsson began talking with his secretary.

"Märta, why do I feel like I've just made the biggest mistake of my life?"

The little flower girls were sitting on a bench in the hallway at the hotel. They were waiting for the final fitting of their dresses before the wedding. The door opened and Antoni called them in. They bounced off the bench and went inside together. He was happy to see the girls, they've become used to spending time with him.

"Okay girls, settle down! My helpers will bring your dresses to you, then your mother will bring you to a dressing room so you can slip into your dress. Come out when you're ready and we will check everything over."

As each of the little girls received their dress they went to the dressing rooms. Antoni heard them saying, "Oh Mom it is so pretty! How do I look, Mom? Look I can twirl!"

In a few moments they were all ready to go. The girls stood side by side and checked out their dresses. Antoni called Eva over first. He had her turn around while he inspected every seam. He asked her to lift her arms as high as she could, and try bending down to check the fit.

"Are you comfortable, Eva?"
"Yes, I never want to take it off!"
She hugged his leg and whispered, "I love you!"
Sara was next, she was so thrilled to be in the wedding.
"I feel just like a princess, I'll be the best flower girl ever!"
Her dress also fit just perfectly.
"I wish you could stay here forever," she told him.

Next came Lilly, she couldn't stop dancing around.
"Do you have a little girl like me, Antoni?"
"No, I am not married yet, but I hope that someday I will."
Lilly looked sad, "I'll marry you Antoni!"

Antoni laughed, "You're too young, my dear! You need to be with your mom for a few more years."

Finally, Tatijanna gracefully stepped forward, she turned around like a little ballerina!
"I love my dress, it is so beautiful! Do I get to keep it?"
"Yes Tatijanna, it was made very specially just for you!"

Antoni carefully inspected the dress.
"Can you teach my mom how to sew like you do?"
Antoni laughed, "We'll see, Tatijanna."

The girls were all twirling around in their new dresses and giggling. Antoni got them to pose for a picture, then they went with their mothers to change back into regular clothes. As they left they all waved goodbye and blew kisses to Antoni.

Up next was the final fitting for Kaya's wedding dress, Svea and Emma accompanied her. She went inside and changed into her dress, then came out and gracefully stepped up onto the platform. Antoni was taken back by her beauty.

"Bellissima! It's perfect, Kaya! Absolutely perfect!"
Antoni and Alessandra looked over every detail of the dress.
"Kaya, you compliment my design just perfectly! How do you feel? Is it comfortable when you are moving around?"

"The dress is just perfect, Antoni! I feel so heavenly. It's even more beautiful than I ever imagined. All my friends wish we could trade places."

Kaya was filled with joy. Svea was overcome with emotion seeing her little one all grown up, she took a few photos to save the moment. Kaya loved posing for the photos in her beautiful new wedding dress.

"Can we take a few photos for my portfolio?" Antoni asked.
"Sure, that's fine."
"Alessandra, can you take some photos please?"
"Okay, I'll go and get the camera."

"Derrick is going to be so surprised! It's been such a delight to work with you, Antoni."
"This is one of the finest dresses that I have ever made."

"I am so honored. Thank you, Antoni."
"You're welcome, tou have a great new life ahead of you!"

One day while delivering the mail, JP stopped in to have fika with Mr. Magnusson. They talked about the wedding, it was just days away now. Mr. Mag mentioned that he wanted to get a very special wedding gift for Kaya.

"You know that place on the hill outside of town, where there was a fire all those years ago? No one has been up there since the fire. I've been thinking … I could put that land to good use. I would like to buy it."

JP looked shocked. "Why would you want to do such a thing?" Mr. Mag began to explain.

"You have to look at it in a different way. It would be a change for the good of the whole town. We can make it a place of music, happiness, and culture. There is enough land to build a school where we could teach violin lessons. We can build an amphitheater with a retractable roof, and have open-air concerts. It would be a orchestra under the stars! It's a perfect location!"

JP took a step backwards, "Wow, Mag, you are talking about a very big investment!"

Mr. Magnusson laughed, "JP, I have more money than I could spend in my lifetime. I want to make sure Kaya never has to worry. My daughter Anaya was trapped in an abusive marriage. My daughter and granddaughter both lost their lives … and it was my fault. I will never be able to tell her I'm sorry, but maybe this will help make it right. Kaya has the talent and the intelligence to make this dream come true. She can play even better than I can. She has given me a reason to live. Now I can help her build a future performing the music that she loves. I've decided that I want to do this, JP."

JP was speechless, "I'm proud to be your friend."

Mr. Magnusson went to the Gällivare Kommunhus the next day and spoke with a clerk at the office of the register of deeds. He asked to talk to someone about buying property. An older man came out to help him.

"Hello Sir, How can I help you?"

Mr. Mag explained, "There is some land on the hill outside of town where there was a fire many years ago. No one has been there ever since. I want to buy it."

The old man took a step back and took a deep breath.
"I remember that fire, it was heartbreaking. There was a beautiful young lady and child who died in that fire. Everyone in town still remembers them."

In a broken voice, Mr. Mag replied, "Yes, it broke my heart as well. That was my daughter and my granddaughter."

The old man became very saddened.

"I'm so sorry for your loss, I can't imagine what you went through. Give me a moment to get the deed for the property."

He returned with the deed and all of the paperwork that Mr. Magnusson needed.

"Well, it appears there was no will and no survivors. This property is currently registered to the city. You will need to speak with a judge to make the sale legal. If you come back tomorrow before court starts, about nine o'clock, the judge will have time to see you. Show him a copy of the deed and explain what happened to your daughter. He will be able to approve the sale of the property. His name is Judge G. Gavel."
"Nine o'clock tomorrow, Judge G. Gavel. Thank you."

The next day Mr. Magnusson returned to the Kommunhus. After briefly speaking with the receptionist, he went in to meet Judge G. Gavel. The judge looked up from his paperwork and watched as Mr. Magnusson entered his office.

"What can I do for you Mr. Magnusson?"

Mr. Mag placed the deed on his desk.

"I would like to buy this property. It has been abandoned for many years."

The judge started to look over the deed.

"The young lady who lived there was my daughter."

"I'm so sorry," the judge paused and looked down.

"Do you have all of the documentation?"

Mr. Magnusson took out his daughter's birth and death certificates, showing that he was indeed her father. Judge G. Gavel carefully looked over the papers.

"I remember that day, it was such a tragedy. I can't imagine the pain that it must have brought you. I am very sorry for your loss."

"Healing that pain is the reason why I am here. We are going to turn this land into a place of music and happiness. I plan to open a violin school and concert hall there, it will be dedicated to my daughter Anaya."

Judge G. Gavel picked up the papers from his desk, tapped them on the edge and set them on his desk.

"You are a good man, Mr. Magnusson. Everyone in this town respects you. I look forward to attending one of your concerts! Since you are the only living relative, the land will go to you. To make it legal, the purchase price will be one krona. I will notarize the papers, but we need two witnesses."

Judge Gavel called two ladies into his office, they watched as the papers were signed and notarized the documents.

"You are now the new owner of this property."
He put papers in a large envelope and gave them to Mr. Mag.
Mr. Magnusson smiled, "Thank you, your honor!"

The Judge watched as Mr. Magnusson walked away, knowing that this was a very important time in his life. He may never come to terms with what happened, but he had found a way to turn it into something better.

27. Meeting At The Church

As an official reporter for the Gazette, Maryann contacted Reverend Gabriel to schedule an appointment. They wanted to plan ahead to be sure they got the best photos on wedding day.

Reverend Gabriel was waiting for the ladies outside of the church. When they arrived he led them inside. They made a point of acting very professionally. They each had a notepad, a camera, and a Gällivare Gazette press badge.

Maryann, "Thank you for meeting with us today, Reverend Gabriel. We have been recognized as the top reporters in Gällivare. Mr. Karlsson has hired us to cover the wedding, he wanted only the best for the big event! We need to plan ahead to ensure we get all of the photos we need—that is why we are here."

Corrine chose to be out front to cover their arrival.
"I'll take pictures from in front of the church when the bride and groom arrive."
Maryann found a place at the front of the sanctuary right in the center, so she could watch the service.
"I will blend right in, no one will even know I'm here."

Carol decided to cover the back, so she could get pictures as they came through the church doors. Kathleen found a spot on the right, so she could take photos as everyone walks down the isle.

They felt better prepared once they had decided where each of them would be. If they didn't get good photos, they would be in big trouble with Mr. Karlsson.

Reverend Gabriel went over the schedule for the service and the ladies took a few notes. Afterward, he walked outside with them.

Maryann stopped in front, "Mr. Mag ordered a big screen television that will be right here!"

"Oh that's right, I will get photos of everyone who is watching from outside." Corrine pointed up toward a tall oak tree. "If I climb that big tree over there, I can get the perfect angle!"

"Good idea, Corrine!"
Reverend Gabriel started to get worried.
"I don't think that's a good idea, what if—"
"Oh don't worry Gabriel, we're professionals!"
The ladies started to call the Reverend by his first name.
"You won't regret this! Thank you, Gabriel. "

Despite his worries Reverend Gabriel knew that the ladies meant well. He checked his watch to see how much time was left before the rehearsal.

"Glad that I can help you ladies. If you have any questions please let me know. I have to go now and get ready for the rehearsal."

"Thank you, Reverend. Have a nice evening."

The ladies lit up with excitement when Reverend Gabriel mentioned the rehearsal! They knew it was today, but didn't know what time it would be.

"Kathleen, did you hear what he said?"
"I know, it's perfect timing."
"Well since we're already here, and it's starting soon—"
"I am sure Derrick and Kaya won't mind if we stay!"
"No, they won't mind! It wouldn't make sense to leave now."

The ladies quickly convinced themselves that staying for the rehearsal was the right thing to do.

Before long cars started pulling up at the big front doors of the church. The little girls and boys in the wedding party hopped out and ran around outside in front of the church. They had fun playing games with each other to pass some time. When Kaya and Derrick arrived they all settled down.

Once the bridesmaids and the groomsmen arrived everyone went inside to begin the rehearsal. Reverend Gabriel started to explain the order in which they would walk down the isle.

"After all of the guests have been seated, the parents will take their place in the front row."
The Reverend started to address the groomsmen.
"First the groomsmen will enter from the right side of the sanctuary. Mr. Magnusson, Mark, and Jeff, you will all stand to the right of the altar."

He looked toward the children, "Now, don't be alarmed when the music starts." Gabriel motioned toward the pipe organ in the back of the sanctuary.

"Bridesmaids, Leona, Cecilia, and Elsa, you will walk down the aisle first. Go one by one and walk very slowly. Remember to leave some space between each other. When you reach the end of the aisle, you will stand to the left of the altar."

"Next two of the flower girls will enter the sanctuary, escorted by two of pagers. The boys will carry baskets of rose petals, and the flower girls will toss the rose petals as they walk down the aisle."

"Then comes the moment everyone is waiting for! The wedding song will begin, and the bride and groom will walk down the aisle together. Behind them will be two more flower girls, and two pagers. They'll be in charge of the train of the wedding gown. Do you have any questions?"

"I think we are all ready to go," Derrick replied.
"Great, let's start the rehearsal!"

Norv and Emma were seated next to Sven and Svea. Norv was so proud of Derrick, he took charge of getting the boy's tuxedos, and attended to all of the extra details. They listen to him and follow his orders, he did his best to make it fun for them.

The bride and groom, the bridesmaids, and the little ones all went to the entrance of the sanctuary. The groomsmen took their place to the right of the altar. Reverend Gabriel gave instructions as they began the rehearsal.

"Okay ladies, first Leona, then remember to leave a space. Next Cecilia, and then Elsa. Lovely! Now the flower girls with their pagers—Eva and Lucas, then Tatijanna and Oliver."

The boys walked tall and proud as they held the baskets for the petals. Kaya heard Eva tell Tatijanna, 'I bet I can throw more petals than you!' in a teasing tone.

"Now Kaya, as the bride you will stand here at the entrance, Derrick will meet you here. You will start walking when the music changes. Everyone will stand before you start to walk down the aisle. Remember to wait for everyone to stand, and remember to walk slowly. Last of all, behind the bride and groom, we have Sara and Erick, along with Lilly and Jethro. Your job is to keep the train straight. It is very long, so we will have one pair on each side. Unless it gets caught, don't pick it up, and don't go flipping the train up and down."

Kaya went to the entrance of the sanctuary and waited for Derrick. They started walking down the aisle together for the first time. They heard Svea and Emma whispering to each other.

"They make a perfect couple."
"I can't wait to be a grandmother!"

As Derrick and Kaya walked down the aisle, the flower girls and pagers followed behind them—Sara, Erick, Lilly, and Jethro. Everything was just perfect, Reverend Gabriel was very happy. The little girls had so much fun pretending to throw petals. Erick and Jethro were perfect little gentlemen, after a few practices, they had it down.

"You've all done a great job. Tomorrow will be a perfect day for Kaya and Derrick. Now we have a special dinner for everyone in the church dining hall."

After working so hard to plan every detail, there was a joyous feeling in the air. It brought Kaya and Derrick great happiness to see everyone gathered together before the big day.

Mark had brought his girlfriend along with to the rehearsal, they seemed to be so happy together.

"Kaya, I'd like to introduce you to my girlfriend Sheri."
"Oh, it's so nice to finally meet you!"
"Sheri this is Kaya, Derrick's fiance."
"I'm so glad to be here, thank you for inviting me!"
"You're welcome. Mark can't stop talking about you."
"Oh, that is so sweet!"
"Well, you two have a good example for me," Mark added.

Kaya noticed that Elsa looked kind of down. She knew that she had to talk to her and figure out what was wrong.

"Elsa, is everything okay? You seem a little bit sad."

"Oh, I've just been thinking a lot lately," Elsa looked down at her hands, "I don't have a special guy in my life." She looked back up at Kaya, "I've started to wonder if I will ever find Mr. Right."

"Don't worry Elsa, I know he's out there looking for you. It will happen when you least expect it! Remember, you have all of us girls and we all care about you."

Leona and Cecilia walked over to Kaya and Elsa too. The girls talked for a while and helped Elsa to cheer up. She realized how lucky she was to have such great friends. Gathered together in a small circle, they all held each other's hands.

"We will always be here for each other."

"I am really thankful for all of you," Elsa smiled.

"Me too, we will hold on to these memories forever."

Kaya was just delighted, "I am so happy that I have *real friends* like you!"

After having dinner at the church everyone returned home for the evening. Derrick was back at home with Emma and Norv. It was the very last night before their wedding day. Kaya, Sven, and Svea were looking at old photos and reminiscing about old times.

Suddenly Kaya got a sad look on her face, out of nowhere she asked, "Dad ... are you going to miss me?"

He replied with a grin, "Not really ... why would I miss you? I'll just get less gray hair."

Kaya became quiet—Sven let her pout for a moment, then he held her hand.

"Kaya, I hope you know how much we truly love you. Of course we will miss you! You will still be helping Mom at the lodge, and I hope to see you in the shop painting skis. Your life will be different, but we will always be a part of it."

"Mom and Dad, I want to thank you for putting up with me. Mom, I am still sorry about that time I picked all your flowers, and brought them to the cemetery for the RIP family. Dad, I hope you will forgive me for mixing the wrong colors now and then. I will always love you both. You're two of the most caring parents in all of Sweden!"

Sven and Svea both smiled at each other.

"Oh, Dad! Do you know what we should do tonight?"

"No," Sven shook his head.

"Before bed, let's sing the Byssan Lull, just like we used to. It is my very first memory!"

"We used to sing together every night!"

"Our memories make me so happy. I remember when I was scared of the fireplace. You picked me up, held me tight and rocked me. *I felt safe,* I knew that nothing would ever hurt me."

Kaya's recollection of the times they shared was very touching. As she listened, Svea remembered how she cared for Kaya when she was very little.

"God blessed us with you, Kaya. God has a special reverence for you. We all saw His blessing shining down upon you the first time you played the violin at church on that very special Sunday. The whole church saw it happen. This whole town loves you, and has recognized you as a child of God."

It was a very pleasant and peaceful evening. They all stayed up late talking about the special times they've shared. They recalled her welcome home party, which was featured in the Gällivare Gazette, her first Christmas, and the time when Sven started teaching her to ski. The time passed by quickly, as it always does. It started to become late and Kaya got a bit sleepy.

"You look tired my dear, maybe we should call it a night. It's getting late and we have a big day tomorrow."

"Okay, I'll go put my pajamas on and get ready for bed. But before we go to sleep, let's sing the Byssan Lull."

After she got ready for bed, Svea tucked her in just like she had so many times before. Her mom and dad sat on each side of her. Kaya felt a great peace come over her as Dad started to sing the lullaby which she loved so dearly. Then Mom began to sing too, and Kaya joined in. It was such a beautiful and harmonious sound. They gave her a hug goodnight.

Kaya looked up and simply said, "Thanks for loving me."

28. Morning On Wedding Day

It was early in the morning and the sun was rising across the town of Gällivare. The big day had finally arrived! The wedding will start at four o'clock. Svea wanted to go to the church to see how things were coming along.

"Kaya, should we go check on things at the church?"
"Sure, I'd love to see what is going on!"
"You'll be surprised to see what it takes to create a wedding."

When they arrived, they were shocked to see van after van lined up in front of the church, six florists were delivering flowers!

They had placed flower arrangements in front of the church, and great arches of flowers along the entrance. Inside there were flowers leading into the sanctuary, sprays of flowers and tall candles at the end of the pews, and beautiful arrangements around the altar.

There was so much going on! A crew of workers was setting up a huge screen outside for people to watch the ceremony, and setting up the sound system. Antoni's team was busy at work coordinating the decorations. Kaya was so happy that she started to cry.

"Pull yourself together now Kaya, you don't want red eyes in your wedding pictures. This is your day my dear, it's the beginning of your new life!"

Suddenly there was a flash from a camera! Carol snapped a photo of Kaya, then she was gone. Outside Corrine was talking one of the crew members into leaving a ladder for her under the big oak tree. Flash! Carol got a picture of that too.

After making sure everything was on track at the church, they returned home for breakfast. Sven, Svea, and Kaya all had breakfast together.

"You know, this isn't really the last breakfast you will have with us. You and Derrick are always welcome here."

Kaya scrunched her nose, "I know that, you silly goose! I'll still be around, you can't get rid of me that easy."

Antoni called and let them know everything was on schedule. The bridesmaids had arrived at the hotel and were getting their hair and makeup done. They would arrive at the church by one o'clock.

At ten thirty, Antoni will be delivering Kaya's wedding gown. The hair stylist and makeup artist would arrive at eleven o'clock. The wedding party will have their pictures taken in the courtyard behind the church at two o'clock, and the wedding will start at four.

Antoni's limousine arrived at the house right on time. Olivia and Alessandra came with him to deliver the wedding dress. He almost looked more nervous than Kaya, his dark hair tousled down on his forehead. He helped the ladies out of the car and they carried the dress to the door.

"Be careful, make sure the dress doesn't touch the ground!"
Kaya answered the door in her blue satin robe.
Antoni took a step back, "Buon giorno! Where should we place the dress?"

"This way to the living room, follow me."
Kaya led the way and they followed her.
"It's so nice of you to deliver my dress!"

"Anything for you, Kaya. By the way, I have a special gift for you. These hair clips are made with akoya pearls, they were ordered by Mr. Magnusson. Give them to your hair stylist and she will know what to do."

Kaya was delighted, "They're so beautiful!"
Antoni glanced at his watch.
"I have to get back to the church, I'll see you there."

The hair stylist arrived early to make sure everything would be perfect. In the weeks leading up to the wedding they had practiced Kaya's hair style several times. They decided on a cascading half up half down updo with bohemian curls on the sides. In the blink of an eye, she transformed Svea's living room into a hair salon.

Kaya watched as she created the perfect masterpiece. First she curled her hair, then back combed it to add volume. Next she formed the middle base and then finished the sides. She paid so much attention to detail, she made sure every hair was perfectly placed. All the while, they talked and laughed about how it feels to fall in love.

As she pinned up the curls piece by piece, Kaya showed her the pearl hair clips from Mr. Magnusson. They were so amazed, the akoya pearls were a such a pure and brilliant white, with very subtle hints of silver. They complimented her style so beautifully.

After her hair was finished she moved on to doing her makeup. She was so fascinated by the airbrush, her makeup felt so light, it gave her such a luminous look. Once her eyelashes were done, Kaya got a feeling that was hard to describe.

"It looks just perfect! You are so lucky, Kaya ... no one has ever had a wedding quite like this. I am so glad to be a part of your wedding day!"

Kaya couldn't wait to see how she looked! After makeup she slipped into her gown, Svea helped her with the back.

"Hold still while I button up the back of your dress ... these buttons are so small, this will take a moment."

Svea set the veil upon Kaya's head, her stylist carefully clipped it into place. They were all glowing with excitement! Before she looked in the mirror the stylist reminded her, 'No tears, don't streak your makeup.'

When she saw herself in the mirror, she couldn't believe how elegant she looked. The special moment had finally arrived, she was really going to get married!

"Oh Mom—I look just like a princess! I love it, I look like a real bride!"

"Kaya, you are a real bride!"

As time for the wedding drew closer the whole town started bustling. Mr. Magnusson had spared no expense, it will be the most beautiful ceremony that the town of Gällivare has ever seen.

The Gällivare Gazette ladies were the first ones to arrive at the church. Carol and Corrine were outside waiting for the bridal party to arrive; Maryann and Kathleen were inside.

Corrine saw a white limousine approaching in the distance, she had her camera ready as it pulled up in front of the church. She took a photo as she wondered who would be inside. When the door opened she it was Derrick and the groomsmen, Mr. Magnusson, Jeff, and Mark. She got pictures of them as they walked inside. Derrick had a white tuxedo with tails, and a white bow tie. The groomsmen all wore black tuxedos and bow ties.

The next limousine arrived moments later, it was the bridesmaids. Corrine snapped photos of each of them in their beautiful periwinkle dresses. As they walked through the big church doors, they bumped right into Antoni! They laughed and looked so happy to see him, together they gave him a big hug. Carol grabbed her camera. Flash! She got it!

Just moments later, the two more limousines arrived at the church. "I can't believe this," Corrine said to herself. She knew that the wedding would be big, but this was just the beginning!

The four little flower girls hopped out, Eva, Sara, Lilly and Tatijanna. Their dresses had full organza skirts with just a hint of periwinkle. They each had a beautiful updo encircled by a crown of periwinkle flowers. They looked just like little angels in their ballerina length dresses and sparkly periwinkle ballet slippers.

The young pagers stepped out of the next limousine, Lucas, Erick, Oliver and Jethro. They followed right along behind the flower girls. They wore black tuxedos with a pristine white shirt, and a bow tie. They walked tall like fine gentlemen and carried themselves with pride. Carol had a big smile, 'I got it,' she told Corrine.

Some of the guests began arriving at the church early, they couldn't wait for Kaya to arrive. The little boys were excited to see the big red helicopter they heard so much about.

Val and Gary were on the way to pick up the bride in the helicopter. Soon Kaya, Sven, and Svea all heard the helicopter approaching in the distance. Sven went outside to watch as the they landed. Val and Gary stepped out to go and check how things were coming along.

"How are we for time?" Gary asked.
"We're on schedule, we have an hour and time to spare."
Val looked nervous, "I doubt we'll have time to spare..."
"How is Kaya doing?" Gary asked.
Val left them to talk, "I'll go and check on her."

Val went inside and saw that Svea and Kaya were all ready to go, they were just taking care of the details. Kaya had packed a bag with all of her last minute supplies.

"Mom, could you please ask Dad to take this bag?"
"I'll take it Kaya," Val offered.
"Thank you, I'm so glad you're here!"
"You're so beautiful, your dress is stunning!"
"Thank you, Val! I think we need your help with the train."
Val brought the bag to Sven and came back.
Everything was perfect, they were all ready to go. Svea and Val held the train of the dress to keep it off the ground. Sven opened the front door as they walked outside. When they got to the helicopter,

Gary held the door for Kaya. Svea helped arrange her dress inside the helicopter, the train was so long that it covered the whole seat.

They stood back and took one last look, Kaya was ready to go to the church! They took their seats and prepared for takeoff.

"Okay, we're ready to fly!" Gary called out.
Val smiled, "Let's go, you can't be late to your wedding!"

The helicopter rose up into the sky and they were on their way. In just a matter of minutes they arrived at the church. Gary prepared to land, then carefully set the helicopter down in front of the church. Kaya saw the wedding party gathered outside waiting for her arrival.

"Just stay calm, Sven and I will be right here with you."
"Okay ... I love you Mom, thank you for all your help."

Sven stepped out and held his hand up to help Kaya. First one foot touched the ground, then as her other foot came down, one of her sparkling periwinkle high heels slipped off! Sven saw it fall and bent down on one knee to pick it up. He carefully placed it back on her foot.

With a giggle Corrine snapped a photo! Svea and Val helped with the train of her dress, and Sven held her hand as she took a few steps. The pager boys were there to take over. They held up the long train as Svea straightened her cathedral veil. Kaya looked back to make sure the pagers were ready.

"Are you ready?"
They all smiled, "We're ready!"

Kaya walked up the stairs toward the door of the church, Mr. Magnusson was waiting inside. In his tuxedo, with his white hair and mustache, he looked like such a distinguished older gentleman. He nervously checked his pocket a few times.

Mr. Magnusson looked up and saw Kaya walking towards him. He was taken aback by her elegance and poise. He was living the day that he never had with his daughter.

As Kaya stood before him no words were said. Suddenly a breeze came out of nowhere and circled around the two of them.

Kaya heard a soft whisper, *"I will always be with you."*

Mr. Magnusson felt the breeze, and he heard the same voice. The breeze messed up his hair, he took his hand and brushed his hair back in place.

He heard a faint whisper, *"I love you, Daddy."*
A feeling of love and contentment surrounded them.

"I have a gift for you. This belonged to my beloved wife. I gave it to her on our wedding day. It would be an honor her for you to have it now."

He took a small diamond cross necklace out of his pocket and handed it to Kaya. As she touched the cross, her heart was filled with joy. Mr. Magnusson helped her put it on.

"Thank you Mr. Magnusson, I will treasure this forever."
As he replied, there was a tear in his eye.
"Kaya, you've brought so much happiness to my life. You mean everything to me."

It was two o'clock now, and it was time for Derrick and Kaya to take their wedding photos. Sven called out to Kaya to get her attention.

"It's time for your pictures, Kaya! They are ready for you in the courtyard."

The courtyard was lined with tall pillars, in the center there was a huge water fountain! They had beautiful flower arrangements everywhere. Kaya's beauty was captivating. When Derrick first saw her, he was in awe. Flash! Maryann got that one.

Derrick and Kaya slowly walked toward each other. When they were face to face he embraced her tightly. The photographer took wonderful photos of them together in front of the fountain. The bridesmaids, groomsmen, flower girls, and pagers all looked picture perfect.

Antoni was there along with the rest of his team. They all got a picture together after Kaya and Derrick finished their photos with the bridal party. In one of the photos Antoni gave Kaya a kiss on the cheek! Flash! Maryann got it.

"I'm so jealous, Corrine," Maryann pouted.
"Knock it off Maryann, remember we're just reporters."

After taking photos they all visited for a while in the courtyard. Kathleen listened in while Derrick and Antoni were talking.

"You are a very lucky man, Derrick. I think I've fallen in love with Kaya!"
Derrick laughed, "Everyone loves Kaya, but she's mine forever now!"

"Someday I hope that I find my one true love ..."

"You don't have to find her, Antoni, she is already with you every day! I see the love in Alessandra's face every time she talks to you. Somehow you fail to notice it, you just walk away. You just need to take the time to see what a beautiful lady she truly is."

Antoni looked amazed. "Really? I never knew she felt this way. Alessandra is so lovely, I would be completely lost without her!"

"You need to take a break from all the commotion! Alessandra would follow you to the end of the earth, and love you until the end of time. I wish you both the best of luck."

29. The Wedding Ceremony

Everyone was ready for the wedding, including the Gällivare Gazette ladies. Maryann and Kathleen were in the front of the sanctuary, and Carol was in the back. Outside of the church, Corrine had climbed up the ladder and into the tree! She was determined to get the best pictures of all the action. Even more people arrived than they expected. The whole town knows Mr. Magnusson, many of his friends and associates were in attendance.

Once the guests had entered the church and taken a seat, it was time for the ceremony to begin. The church became silent as the organist began to play. First the groomsmen took their place to the right of the altar.

Next the bridesmaids came down the isle in their elegant periwinkle floor length dresses: Leona, Cecilia, and Elsa. They were made of soft crepe satin, had a plunging sweetheart neckline, cap sleeves, and a slight train. The dresses were very flattering, side ruching, and figure hugging.

The flower girls and pagers entered the sanctuary next. First Eva and Lucas, then Tatijanna and Oliver. As they walked down the aisle they tossed flower petals high in the air, it looked like they were having so much fun!

Tatijanna picked up some of the petals to save them. Her mom started shaking her head, 'No, no!' Tatijanna smiled at her mom and kept walking, picking up a few more flower petals as she made her way. When they reached the front of the sanctuary, the girls went to the left and the boys to the right.

Derrick took his place next to Kaya at the entrance and they prepared to walk down the aisle. He handed her the bouquet, then they both looked up and saw Reverend Gabriel waiting for them at the altar. The moment had finally arrived for Kaya and Derrick to take their vows. Their hearts were racing; they smiled at each other so affectionately.

Kaya was a vision of beauty. Her dress had see through tulle sleeves, and a tulle illusion neckline with pearl beading over embroidered lace appliques. It had a fitted hip length bodice and a full ball gown skirt that flowed over her hips. It was white with a pale shade of periwinkle blue.

Derrick looked back to make sure that the pagers and flower girls were ready. As the music changed, their friends and family all stood to watch their entrance. Derrick and Kaya took their very first steps down the aisle together.

Everyone was in awe as they slowly walked toward the altar. They made such a beautiful couple. The flower girls and pagers followed behind them, Sara and Erick on one side, Lilly and Jethro on the other.

Kaya and Derrick walked up the steps of the altar and stood before Reverend Gabriel. After they turned to face each other Reverend Gabriel began the service.

"Welcome, dear friends and family. Thank you all for being here on this special day in the lives of Derrick and Kaya. Today they join in holy matrimony."

Derrick started to look pale and a little weak, Kaya tried to help to keep him calm. "Look at me, pretend there is no one here. It's just you and me, and Reverend Gabriel."

Kaya took Derrick's face in her hands, he smiled. "Just look at me, we can do this."

Reverend Gabriel looked concerned, Derrick took a deep breath and collected his thoughts. Little Tatijanna was swishing her skirt back and forth, Maryann took a picture! The Reverend began to read Derrick his vows.

"Before almighty God and this assembly in attendance, I ask Derrick Dean Norlander, will you take Kaya Susan Nilsson to be your wife? Will you love her in distress and pleasure?"

Derrick looked at Kaya, "Yes, I will."

Little Oliver ran behind the Reverend and clung to his robe. He was hiding and peeking out at all the people, some started to laugh. Flash! Kathleen got a picture. One of the bridesmaids took charge and got him back in place.

Next, Reverend Gabriel started reading the vows to Kaya.

"Before almighty God and this assembly in attendance, I ask Kaya Susan Nilsson, will you take Derrick Dean Norlander to be your husband? Will you love him in distress and pleasure?"

Derrick and Kaya held hands; she responded, "Yes, I will."

Oliver was getting tired, he yawned and swayed, then sat down on the stairs in front of the altar. Little Tatijanna went and sat down next to him. Reverend Gabriel continued with the vows. Oliver and Tatijanna listened and smiled, they kicked their feet back and forth once in a while.

Derrick repeated after Reverend Gabriel:
"I, Derrick Dean Norlander, take you, Kaya Susan Nilsson, to be my wife, to share in both joyful and sorrowful times, and to be faithful to you, until death do us part."

Oliver nodded his head yes!

Kaya repeated after Reverend Gabriel:
"I, Kaya Susan Nilsson, take you Derrick Dean Norlander, to be my husband. To share in both joyful and sorrowful times, and to be faithful to you, until death do us part."

Tatijanna nodded her head yes too!
Flash! Carol got a good picture of that one!

Reverend Gabriel announced: "As a commemoration of this blessed day, Kaya and Derrick would like to share a special song they wrote together, it's called '*Stars Of The Night.*' "

They began the song together and then took turns.

"A wonder of the universe lit up the evening sky."
"We saw a shooting star—a blessing for you and I."

"The aurora borealis waved like the tides of the ocean sea."
"In all their splendor it was such a solemn sight to see."

"We felt so blessed, we felt so very small."
"There we were in the center of it all."

"The stars sparkled like diamonds in the heavens above."
"In my heart I knew this is true love."

"I saw that twinkle in your eyes."
"I whispered 'I love you' for the very first time."

"In that heavenly moment God held us in his hands."
"Somehow we knew this was part of God's plan."

"We'll live hand in hand,
   with heart and soul in all that we go through."

"We're meant to be together.
   Forever I'll spend my life with you."

"We will always be together, no matter where we are."
"Whether near or far, we'll always be under the same stars."

Reverend Gabriel concluded with a blessing:

"May God bless your marriage as you travel through life together. May he guide and direct you, and bless you with many children. Derrick, you may now kiss the bride!"

The congregation all cheered as Derrick and Kaya kissed. For the very first time, Reverend Gabriel introduced them as husband and wife.

"Ladies and Gentlemen, it is my honor to formally introduce Mr. and Mrs. Norlander!"

Just then Oliver kissed Tatijanna on the cheek, and she gave him a big hug! She smiled, "I think we just got married!" Flash! Kathleen got it!

The music started playing and Derrick and Kaya began to walk back down the aisle. Everyone was smiling, cheering, and clapping their hands. Tatijanna, Oliver, and the rest of the bridal party all followed.

The church bells were ringing as they walked through the big church doors. Their parents met them outside and gave them a heartfelt congratulations. Some of the guests threw bird seed in celebration. The bridal party and the parents started the reception line.

Kaya saw Corrine was on the ground, she had fallen out of the big oak tree! Earlier Kaya had asked Svea why that ladder was by the tree. Kaya stopped to see if she was okay.

"Oh crap, someone stole the ladder," Corrine rubbed her head.
"Are you alright, Corrine? Do you need help?"
"I'm OK ... I got some great pictures, congratulations!"
Flash! "Got it!" Carol took a picture of them.

After everyone went through the greeting line, Kaya and Derrick prepared to leave for the reception. Everyone cheered as they walked over to the red helicopter. Val had painted *'Just Married'* on the side.

Derrick helped Kaya as she stepped into the helicopter, then he got in too. They both smiled and waved to everyone while Gary prepared for take off. Soon the helicopter rose up into the sky. Gary circled above the crowd before they flew away.

At the Magnifika Hotel everything was just perfect. There were flowers everywhere! The tables in the grand ballroom had white linen tablecloths, elegant candelabras, and arrangements of periwinkle flowers.

The wedding cake was so beautiful, it had bluebell flowers cascading down the sides over the white frosting. They had placed it upon a stand with tall pillars and a fountain in the middle. Four matching cakes were placed around it.

Gary took the scenic route on the way to the reception. He showed them some of his favorite places along the outskirts of Gällivare. Meanwhile, the guests all began to arrive at the hotel. They were so impressed, it looked like a scene right out of a classic romance.

When Derrick and Kaya walked through the door, their friends and family all let out a great cheer! Kaya put her arms around Derrick's shoulders and gave him a big kiss! Flash! Kathleen got a picture.

As Carol was checking out the cake, she started to look around to make sure no one was watching. When she was sure, she dipped her finger in the frosting and licked it! Flash! Maryann snapped a picture, she caught her!

Soon the ballroom became full and everyone started to take their seats. Derrick and Kaya were at the head table along with their parents and the bridal party. The pagers and the flower girls were at their own table. One of the bridesmaids placed a sign in front of

Tatijanna and Oliver that said *'Just Married'*, everyone who walked by saw the sign and laughed.

Sven gave a speech to start off the evening:

"Kaya and Derrick, congratulations to you both on this joyous occasion. We will always remember and cherish this day.

"It's been so much fun to watch as the two of you have grown up. Every day has been an adventure filled with happy times, and funny things you've done together. There's been plenty of healthy competition, and a few squabbles along the way!

"Derrick, you've been so close to us over the years. We are truly blessed to have you in our lives. I am proud to welcome you into our family.

"Kaya, Mom and I treasure every hug you gave us. We remember every song we sang together. We remember when you did a favor for Mr. Magnusson and tightened all his violin strings real tight! He was a little upset, but not for long, later that day you two were at the Storgatan Kafé having ice cream together.

"You have an honest and caring nature. You've captured the hearts of so many people. God has looked down on you with grace and cared for you in a special way. We are so happy to be here with you as you begin the next chapter of your life. God bless you both.

"A toast, to the bride and groom! Skål!"

Derrick's father Norv gave a speech, and Mr. Magnusson even said a few words too. After all of the speeches had been made, the staff lit the candles and dimmed the lights. An elaborate four-course meal was served, featuring some of their favorite Swedish specialties.

Svea heard about Corrine falling out of the tree while taking pictures at the church. She went to check on her to make sure she was okay. Other than bumping her head on the way down, Corrine wasn't hurt.

"Reverend Gabriel told her that climbing that tree was not a good idea!"

Svea asked the staff to bring her an ice pack. She helped to make sure that Corrine was doing okay. Flash! Kathleen got a picture of them together.

After dinner Sven got everyone's attention. He introduced the band and announced that the bride and groom were going to have their first dance. Oliver and Tatijanna were the first ones out on the floor, everyone laughed and cheered! Kaya and Derrick stepped onto the dance floor and did a twirl. Derrick held her close as they started to dance. Kaya's dress gracefully floated through the air as they danced across the floor. It was such a magical moment, from just a look them you could clearly see their love for each other. At the end of the dance Kaya curtsied and Derrick bowed.

Mr. Magnusson told Svea, "You've done such a great job raising this young lady. I'm so proud of the woman she has become."

As the night went on everyone danced together, even the pagers and the flower girls. Tatijanna was teaching Oliver a new dance step, Carol snapped a few photos of them dancing and having fun.

Later in the evening, people started asking Mr. Magnusson and Kaya to play their violins. They cheered 'Spela! Spela!' as they asked them to play. Kaya was a bit hesitant at first, she didn't plan to perform on her wedding day.

"I don't know … what do you think Derrick?"
"Follow your heart, it could make a wonderful memory."

The band brought two violins to Mr. Mag and Kaya. Silence filled the room as they faced each other. Kaya raised her violin and paused. She took a deep breath and sent great feelings of love and happiness into the violin. She began to play a lovely melody, so fine and pure. It swung from high pitched notes to a soft mellow sound filled with emotion. Her performance started to bring tears to the eyes of the audience.

Soon Mr. Magnusson began to play; a master of the violin, and such a great teacher. They played together in perfect harmony, Kaya kept right up with him. As they continued, they each took turns taking the spotlight. First Mr. Magnusson, then Kaya. The gradually building crescendo made for a very dramatic conclusion.

At the end of the song they placed their bows by their side, took a bow toward the crowd, then bowed once again to each other.

Victor approached Mr. Magnusson afterward, "Mr. Magnusson, you have given Kaya the wedding of her dreams!"

"She deserves the very best. She has brought me so much happiness in life. When I thought I had nothing left, she helped me find something to live for. Having her in my life has almost been like having my daughter back, they have so much in common."

"A toast," Victor lifted a glass of wine.

"To the bride and groom!" Mr. Magnusson replied.

As they clicked the glasses, Victor spilled some wine.

"Oops! Oh no! I spilled some wine on my best white shirt, and a red wine at that!"

Mr. Magnusson laughed, "Don't worry Victor, I can get you a clean shirt. I know where they keep extra shirts for the staff, just follow me."

Mr. Magnusson showed him to hallway behind the kitchen, where there was a huge closet.

"Here we are ... right here, an extra large tall."

As Victor changed his shirt, Mr. Magnusson noticed the mark on his shoulder.

"Hey Vic, what is that on your shoulder?"

"Oh, that is just my little butterfly. It's a birthmark, my mother had one just like it. It runs in our family."

"Mr. Magnusson, this might not be the right time to tell you ... Anaya and I were still living together before she left me for Johan. We were together right up to the day she left."

"I never knew for sure if Anaya's baby was mine or Johan's. The timing was right ... I saw her in town once with Anna ... she looked just like her mom, but she didn't look like me. It's strange how Kaya looks so much like Anaya."

318

Mag didn't know what to say, "I suppose they say we all have a look-alike out there somewhere. That shirt looks like a good fit, Vic. You're ready to get back to the reception. Let's go, I want to have a dance with the bride!"

After Mr. Magnusson and Kaya danced together, she had a dance with Victor. While watching the two of them, Mr. Magnusson recalled what Victor said. He couldn't help but imagine this is exactly what Victor and Anaya would have looked like.

The thought stayed in his mind the rest of the evening.

30. An Unforgettable Moment

The day after the wedding, Sven and Svea had a pleasant morning at home. They read the newspaper and tended to things around the house. Kaya and Derrick were on their honeymoon, and would be returning on Sunday.

As the morning went on, Dr. Leif called and said that he wanted to stop by for a visit. He didn't explain what he wanted to discuss. When he arrived, Sven and Svea invited him inside to join them for fika. Svea poured them each a cup of kaffe and brought them each a delicious pastry. She noticed that Dr. Leif seemed a bit unsettled, she knew something must be wrong.

"I have something very important to talk to you about. Please just hear me out; don't say a word until I finish. I've been considering what to do with Kaya's original birth certificate. I feel that we should give it to her. She deserves to know who she really is. Every child has a right to know.

"This guilt has been with me for many years now. I spoke with a friend of mine who is a child psychologist and explained the situation."

Sven and Svea both looked a little concerned, the subject caught them by surprise. They had always wondered if or when they should tell Kaya about the circumstances of her adoption. She had never asked about it and the time just passed by.

"Kaya has never recalled anything from her past, it seems she has post traumatic amnesia. Sometimes that can be a blessing. She must have witnessed some very sad, and painful things in her little life that she was not able to handle."

"The psychologist told me that I have done the right thing. As her Doctor, I've protected her best interests. Now that she has a loving family, and a loving husband, I know that we did the right thing. In the loving home that you gave her, she's grown into a truly wonderful young lady."

Dr. Leif explained, as he remembered what he was told.
"He told me that if I shared this with her, it could bring back traumatic memories from the past. However, he agreed that one day the time will come when she may want to know. It's possible that she may even begin to seek answers on her own."

"He gave me reassurance. He told me, *'As a doctor, you saved her life, that is what doctors do. You need to know, you did the right thing.'* "

"Speaking with him helped me to feel better, I needed to talk to someone. Sometimes I would wonder if I should just tear up that old certificate and leave this all in the past."

Sven and Svea didn't realize that Dr. Leif had carried these concerns with him for so many years. He had never spoken to them about it before. As such close friends, they were surprised that he never mentioned it.

"Dr. Leif, I'm so sorry that you've felt this way."
"We never knew how much all this has affected you."

"Well, it helped that I saw she was quickly getting better. Each day she was stronger and happier. I knew she was in a loving home, which is exactly where she needed to be. Nonetheless, I feel that someday she will want to know."

"You're right, Doctor. Svea and I have both thought about this and talked together many times. As the days and years went by, Kaya has never asked us any questions."

"Actually, we don't know very much about her past. I've often wondered to myself, how did she just show up on our doorstep? What was her life like before she arrived?"

"There are some things we may never know. Maybe it's best that we wait, and let it be up to her. The day will come when she begins to ask questions."

"When it does, we will all be here to support her."
"God bless you both. Thank you for hearing me out today."
Svea and Sven put their arms around him—
"God bless you, Dr. Leif."

On Monday, the Gällivare Ladies went in to see Mr. Karlsson at the Gazette. They had the photos developed over the weekend, and were very proud of their work. Today would be their last day as reporters. On the way there, they joked about putting in their resignations. Märta saw them coming, and went into Mr. Karlsson's office to let him know they had arrived.

"Mr. Karlsson, the Gällivare Ladies are here!"

Mr. Karlsson looked a little worried, he nervously shuffled through some papers on his desk.

"Thank you, Märta. Go ahead and send them in."

When they entered his office, Mr. Karlsson welcomed them with a forced smile.

"Welcome back ladies, I hope everything went well."

Maryann replied, "Yes, we've taken some wonderful pictures!"

The ladies stood together; having done their best to capture each moment, they looked so pleased with themselves. They had organized the photos in two separate groups.

"One is regular photos, and the others are behind the scenes. You know, sometimes unexpected things can happen at a wedding. We need at least half of the Gazette to do them justice!"

Mr. Karlsson took the folders and glanced at a few pictures.

"Not too bad of a job, ladies! Who is this?"

He held up a photo of Tatijanna and Oliver sitting in front of the altar.

"Oh, that's Tatijanna and Oliver. She was one of the flower girls, and he was a pager!"

"They thought they got married too!" Kathleen laughed.

"Make sure you put 'I think we just got married!' for the caption on that one!"

It turned out that Mr. Karlsson didn't have so much to worry about after all. He seemed to be very happy with their work. He came across one picture that caught his attention.

"What's going on here?"

He held up the photo of Corrine after she fell out of the tree!

Corrine began, "Well, the ladder—"

Maryann interrupted her, "Oh, nothing! Corrine just takes her work very seriously."

"Great work ladies! We'll feature the pictures in the Gazette on Wednesday. Leave your badges out front with Märta. I'll have my editor call you about the captions."

The Gällivare Ladies could hardly wait for the paper to come out. On Wednesday morning they met at the Storgatan Kafé for fika. They each had a copy of the gazette, the story was on the front page!

JP had stopped by to visit Mr. Magnusson, and mentioned that the Gazette was selling out all over town. They spent some time looking through the wedding photos together. Mr. Magnusson called Mr. Karlsson to congratulate him on a job well done.

"Congratulations! The whole town's talking about the wonderful photos from Kaya and Derrick's wedding. I think you need to hire those ladies!"

That weekend Sven and Svea spent time at home together, they took a break to rest and recharge after the wedding. On Saturday evening they had a wonderful dinner at the lodge. Everyone congratulated them on Kaya and Derrick's wedding. Upon returning home they saw that someone had left them a message.

Svea picked up the phone to check the message.

It was Mr. Magnusson, he asked them to meet him on Monday at two o'clock. He wants to meet at the old house on the hill, the one that burned down so many years ago.

Upon hearing this Svea became frozen with fear. Still holding the phone in her hand, she stood there with a blank look on her face. Sven walked over to her and asked what was wrong. She was silent; he hung up the phone.

"Svea, what is it? What's wrong?"

"Sven … Mr. Magnusson wants to meet us. He wants to meet at the old house on the hill, the house that burned down in the fire."

A wave of fear overcame them. They held each other tightly and began to wonder what was next to come. After a few moments they took a seat at the kitchen table.

Sven held Svea's hand and noticed that she was shaking. He looked deep into her eyes.

"Let's not make too much out of this. Kaya knows how much we love her, and Mr. Mag would never do anything to harm her. Even if he knows who she truly is, nothing is going to change."

"But Sven, she could have a total breakdown. Being in that horrible place could trigger bad memories. It could be too much for her to handle."

"We have to go, Svea … Mag called us."

"I hate to see the place where she endured so much anguish."

"Svea, let's say a prayer for Kaya."

"Dear God in Heaven,
> We know that Kaya is one of your chosen children. You've always watched over her and protected her from harm. We pray that you will stand beside her at this time. Please give her your strength. Please continue to bless her and comfort her as she begins her new life. Amen."

As the only living member of Anaya's family, Mr. Magnusson acquired the deed for the property where the old house used to stand. The day he waited for had finally arrived. Everyone would be coming to meet him today at two o'clock.

Mr. Magnusson was the first to arrive. Almost seventeen years had passed since he had returned to this place. Memories of his daughter came to mind. He recalled the stories that JP told him about how she had suffered in such an abusive marriage. She was trapped and had no one to help her. He vowed to turn this into a happy place.

One by one they arrived. JP still drove his old postbus. He couldn't hold back the tears as he drove down that old familiar road, which he had driven so many times before. He recalled the smoldering ashes that remained the day after the fire. After all these years he had never returned.

Thoughts of Anna flooded his memory: how she loved to read and play with Boulder, how excited she would be when he came to deliver the mail. She would always come running when she saw the postbus.

"Mommy! JP is here! JP is here!"

Her golden curls would bounce all around her happy face as she ran to give him a big hug. He loved that child like she was his own daughter.

He stopped and parked when he saw Mr. Magnusson. He sat in the postbus for a moment. He had to adjust to being back at the place where Anaya and Anna had suffered so much isolation and abuse.

Sven and Svea were next to arrive, followed by Dr. Leif. They stood together in front of the remnants of the old house. Over the years grass and weeds had grown around where the house used to stand. The ashes and soot were left behind from the fire.

As JP solemnly walked along he kicked at the ashes and soot. He could smell the smoke of the weathered wood. Old memories of the evil that happened in the house crept in. He stopped and told himself, "No—Kaya and Mag will turn this into a happy place."

In the front yard he found the bench that he made for Anna's rock friends. They were all right where she left them. You could hardly see the paint anymore, it had become so faded. He took the rock with 'JP' painted on it and slipped it into his pocket.

He noticed a flash, Carol had taken his picture!
Mr. Magnusson called out to the ladies, "Come on out girls!"
Corrine, Maryann, Kathleen, and Carol came walking out from behind the trees.
"Well, it looks like we've been caught!"

Just then Kaya and Derrick arrived, they parked next to the postbus. Kaya had on white jeans and a white blouse with butterfly sleeves. She was confused and surprised to see everyone.
"Why are you all here?" she asked.
"We heard you'd be here at 2 o'clock, so here we are!"
"That's right! We wanted to be here when you get your present from Mr. Mag!"
"Hush, Maryann! You're going to get us in trouble!"
"Present from Mr. Mag? What present?"

Mr. Magnusson chuckled, "It looks like the secret is out! I have a gift for you Kaya, one that will change the course of your future."

Mr. Magnusson handed Kaya an envelope, it had the deed to the property inside. She took the envelope and opened it up. Flash! Corrine took a photo. As she read the paper, she realized that he had given her the deed for the property. Kaya looked puzzled, she wrinkled her brow.

"Mr. Magnusson, why would you give me this old place? Why would you do such a thing?"

Mr. Magnusson began to share his vision for the future.

"Kaya, I think we can turn this rubble into a great treasure. We can start a school to teach violin. We can build a great amphitheater, we will have concerts under the stars and host the best musicians in all of Sweden! Just imagine what we can do! I will provide all of the finances. We can light up this hill so bright it will be seen all across Gällivare!"

"Well, I guess if you put your mind to it anything is possible."

She started to look through what remained of the old house. Her shoes got full of soot as she walked around. She caught a glimpse of a shiny object in the ashes.

"Hm, what is that?" She picked it up.

She tried to clean it off, then wiped her hands on her jeans.

"It is a locket, but it won't open."

Derrick walked over and tried to open it too.

"I can't get it, it seems to be stuck."

He scratched his forehead and got soot on his face.

Mr. Magnusson walked over to them. He recognized the locket as soon as he saw it. He had given this locket to his wife Ingrid many years ago.

"I remember this," he said with a somber look on his face. "It belonged to my wife. The fire was so hot, it sealed it shut." He looked at the back of the locket and read the inscription. *"I'll always be with you."*

Mr. Magnusson wiped his forehead, now he had soot on his face and clothes too. Somehow after so many years this locket had returned to him. He got a feeling that God's will was unfolding before them. This was all in God's plan.

"Mr. Magnusson, if anyone in the world can make this dream come true, it's you and I. With all of my heart, thank you for everything that you've done for me."

Mr. Magnusson put the locket into his shirt pocket. Kaya gave him a big hug! The Gällivare Ladies took photos, it was a very sentimental moment.

After they looked around for some time, JP made an announcement:

"Kaya, I have one more surprise for you!"

He led them back toward the postbus and got a leash from the front seat. He opened up the doors on the back and a shaggy black and white dog jumped out! Kaya was overcome with joy. She kneeled down and called him over to her.

"Come here! Come on little puppy!"
The puppy ran over to Kaya and jumped into her arms.

"Oh JP, he's perfect! I love him!"

The dog licked her face and got paw prints on her white pants!

"Maybe you can name him Rocky?" JP suggested.

"That sounds like a good name! I think he loves me already!"

"We will take good care of him," Derrick added.

Maryann took a few pictures with Rocky, Kaya, and Derrick all together.

Ever since the wedding, Dr. Leif had been wondering what to do with Kaya's original birth certificate. As she began this new chapter of her life he wanted her to choose what to do with it on her own. He had decided that giving the birth certificate to her was the right thing to do. Dr. Leif walked over to Kaya through the ashes of the old house.

"Kaya, for a long time I've wanted you to have this."

Dr. Leif handed Kaya a sealed envelope.

"This is a copy of your original birth certificate."

Kaya slowly reached out and took the envelope. She ran her fingers across the front of it. She remembered her trip to Uppsala with Sven and Svea. She remembered her welcoming party at the lodge. She paused and turned the envelope over. It looked like she was trying to make a decision.

Kaya thought to herself, "What should I do with this?"

Suddenly they heard the sound of Val and Gary's helicopter!

"I think we're in for one more surprise!"

They all looked up and saw the big red helicopter.

"Look, it's Val and Gary!"

Everyone started to wave.

As the helicopter hovered overhead they noticed something was falling down from the sky. Kaya held out her hand, a periwinkle blue flower petal floated down and landed in her palm.

"They're flower petals! Just like the ones at our wedding!"

There they were, with the soot and ashes of the old house on their clothes. A shower of flower petals rained down upon them! The petals floated from side to side as they slowly fell from the sky.

The Gällivare Ladies all started taking pictures, they had never seen such a beautiful sight! Kaya looked at Sven and Svea and she knew what to do. She tore the envelope with the birth certificate into small pieces and threw them in the air as high as she could!

Just then a strong breeze swirled all around them. The pieces of her birth certificate were lifted up into the air, higher and higher! For a moment time stood still.

As Kaya lifted her arms toward the sky, Mr. Magnusson noticed she had a birthmark on her shoulder in the shape of a small butterfly.

Kaya and Mr. Magnusson both heard the same soft voice—
"I will always be with you … I will always be with you."

Acknowledgments

Technical Support	Bobby Dean Hanson	Husband
Editor	Bobby Dean Hamilton	Grandson
Cover Design	Barbara L. Hanson Stepaniak	Daughter
Research	Susan L. Hanson	Daughter

The End

"If you follow the North Star you will always find your way home."

Made in the USA
Monee, IL
22 July 2022

10121070R00193